"A first-rate mystery story in the best British style."
—*The Springfield Republican*

"There's action . . . plenty of warmth and gentle humor."
—*San Francisco Chronicle*

AN INSPECTOR HENRY TIBBETT MYSTERY

DOWN AMONG THE DEAD MEN

PATRICIA MOYES

An Owl Book

HENRY HOLT AND COMPANY   NEW YORK

Copyright © 1961 by Patricia Moyes
All rights reserved, including the right to reproduce
this book or portions thereof in any form.
Published by Henry Holt and Company, Inc.,
521 Fifth Avenue, New York, New York 10175.

Library of Congress Cataloging-in-Publication Data
Moyes, Patricia.
Down among the dead men.
"An Owl book."
I. Title.
PR6063.09D6   1986   823'.914   86-9834
ISBN 0-8050-0117-4 (pbk.)

First published in hardcover by Holt, Rinehart and Winston in 1961.

First Owl Book Edition—1986

Printed in the United States of America
10 9 8 7 6 5 4 3 2 1

ISBN 0-8050-0117-4

DOWN
AMONG
THE
DEAD MEN

ONE

It is often interesting, in retrospect, to consider the trifling causes that lead to great events. A chance encounter, a thoughtless remark—and the tortuous chain reaction of coincidence is set in motion, leading with devious inevitability to some resounding climax.

For instance, it is virtually certain that if Emmy Tibbett had not broken her shoulder strap in a small, smoky restaurant just off King's Road, Chelsea, one spring evening, the Berrybridge murderer would have got clean away. For if Emmy had not snapped that slender pink ribbon, she would never have spoken to Rosemary Benson in the ladies' room, and accepted the loan of a safety pin; the friendship between the Bensons and the Tibbetts would never have sprung up; and Henry and Emmy Tibbett would never have found themselves, some months later, crammed first into new, tight, unyielding blue jeans and subsequently into an overloaded station wagon, en route for a fortnight's sailing holiday at Berrybridge Haven with the Bensons.

Henry felt miserably conspicuous in the teen-age uniform upon which Rosemary and Alastair had insisted. It was hardly fitting, he thought, as he regarded himself morosely in the mirror, for a Chief Inspector of the C.I.D. to inflict himself upon the world in such a rakish outfit. It was not as though he had the brawny, swashbuckling physique which he associated with the lordly ocean-racing characters whose pictures he had often secretly admired in glossy magazines: he could not pretend that his unremarkable, middle-aged figure lent itself to the casual heartiness of navy denim; while his pale face, with its mild blue eyes and sandy eyebrows, looked little short of ludicrous emerging from the white turtle neck of an enormous fisherman's sweater. However, these reflections did not trouble Henry for long, because he was one of those rare people who have no objection to making fools of themselves in a good cause.

Emmy, on the other hand, looked marvellously right in her sailing clothes. Admittedly, her plumpish, fortyish hips looked plumper still in jeans, but her short, curly black hair and strong, merry face gave her the air of one whose natural element is the sea, whose natural line of vision the horizon. Unlike Henry, she looked supremely comfortable.

This enviable state she shared with their hosts. When the slightly battered station wagon drew up in the narrow street outside the Tibbetts' Chelsea flat, Henry was amazed to observe from his window the transformation which had taken place in the Bensons. Rosemary—tall, blonde and willowy—had always displayed an exquisite flair for simple, elegant clothes. Henry had seen heads turn as she walked into a Mayfair restaurant in a straight black sheath of a dress, shimmering with an extravagance of pale blue and green beads at the neck, which echoed the magnificently artificial splendour of her eyelids. Now he saw a disarmingly gawky schoolgirl, her face free of make-up and scrubbed like an apple, in well-worn jeans faded to threadbare grey and a shapeless canvas over-blouse which had once been orange, but which seemed to be encrusted with salt. Alastair, dark and impeccable in the City, was tousle-headed and entirely happy. He gave the impression of a man who has lost his razor, and doesn't care.

Henry and Emmy settled themselves on the back seat, disposing round their feet two bulging picnic-baskets and a huge flask of Chianti. The space behind them was crammed with bright red blankets, two green sleeping bags ("You're lucky," Rosemary remarked, "they no longer smell. Just back from the cleaners"), an outboard motor and a reeking two-gallon tin of paraffin.

Conscientious office-workers who had stayed until seven

o'clock to finish up Friday's backlog of work glanced briefly and disinterestedly at the bizarre equipage as it sped through fast-emptying City streets. Soon London was left behind, as the white ribbon of Eastern Avenue unwound ahead of the car. The flat, fertile fields of Essex flashed past: the ancient garrison town of Colchester faded into the deepening dusk.

"We'll have a good hour in the Bush before closing time," said Alastair, with deep content.

Berrybridge Haven is, to its devotees, a closely guarded secret about which they cannot resist telling their friends. Inevitably, their eulogies have reached the ears of sharp-witted journalists, who descend on the place every so often, and come out a few days later with a lyrical piece devoted to "this unspoilt corner of the East Coast." Fortunately, in spite of their efforts, Berrybridge had contrived to remain just that. This happy fact is due in part to its distance from London—just far enough to discourage casual sight-seers—but mainly to the relentless attitude of the public transport authorities, who have contrived to make the place virtually inaccessible except by car. Anybody who has ever tried to reach Berrybridge Haven from Liverpool Street Station will endorse this. Connecting trains (you change three times) are carefully timed to miss each other by one minute. The bus that is advertised turns out to run on alternate Sundays only, and the whereabouts of the bus stop is a closely guarded secret. The intrepid traveller who manages to get farther than Ipswich in the course of a week-end does so only at the price of such anguish and frustration that he resolves never to go near the God-forsaken place again, which affords no little satisfaction to the local inhabitants.

It would be flattering to call Berrybridge a village. A huddle of cottages, a tiny grey church, a couple of shops selling everything from butter to rope, two boatyards and a pub are all it has to offer. Of these buildings, the pub is by far the largest. Nevertheless, Berrybridge has a spirit of civic pride which might be the envy of a great industrial city. It elects (unofficially) its own mayor every year, and his inauguration is an occasion of much merriment, solemnity and ritual consumption of beer at The Berry Bush. *You are now entering the Borough of Berrybridge Haven* proclaims a notice, shakily inscribed in white paint on an ancient, black-tarred board, as you drive down the twisting lane from the main Ipswich road: and another sign, affixed to two planks placed haphazardly across a stream, informs the visitor that *This Bridge was erected for the convenience of the citizens of Berrybridge Haven and formally opened by the Mayor, His Honourable Ephraim Sykes. This,* adds the notice, darkly, *is OUR bridge.* The visitor may be tempted to wonder why the builders of this particular bridge should be so sensitive to the threat of competition. There is no other bridge.

There is, however, the River Berry. It is no longer an important river. It begins nowhere in particular, and meanders through mud flats and sandbanks to the inhospitable vastness of the North Sea. At Berrybridge, four miles from the river mouth, it is half a mile wide at high tide, and less than a quarter when the tide is low. On either bank, pale green fields and massed, deeper green trees sweep down to the water. The river gives the landscape a constantly changing fascination.

To those who love it best, Berrybridge Haven is probably at its most beautiful as Henry and Emmy first saw it, at half past nine on a summer night, when the last red-gold blaze of sunset is just disappearing behind the hills, and the moon is already up, touching the mud flats with a cold, silver gleam. On the black water, barely broken by the glittering ripples of the evening breeze, the boats ride in slender silhouette, their spindle masts scraping the sky. Nothing breaks the cold, damp stillness except the distant barking of a dog, or the sudden wave of warm, conversing voices as the bar door of The Berry Bush swings momentarily open, splashing orange lamplight onto the grey foreshore. This is the peace which justifies the clamour of a working week. The peace for which many Englishmen have been content to die.

"I hope," said Alastair, "that Bob has tapped a new barrel of bitter. The last one was lousy."

They all clambered stiffly out of the car, and walked over to the pub.

The Berry Bush is an ancient inn, frequented by mariners since the days when Berrybridge Haven was an important shipbuilding centre, and wooden-walled men-o'-war and merchant vessels stood on the slipways. Generations of shipwrights, bargees and fishermen have polished its black wooden benches with the seats of their trousers, and blackened its heavy beams with their pungent tobacco fumes. Today, only a handful of fishermen remain, and the big bar is monopolized by yachtsmen. The Berry Bush welcomes these newcomers kindly, and is glad of their custom: but always it dreams of a past which was more commercial, more real, rougher and more honest. Still, beer must be sold, and these Londoners aren't bad chaps, taken by and large. Let them in. They pay, don't they?

Henry and Emmy pushed their way into the crowded bar in the wake of Alastair and Rosemary, who seemed to know everybody, which made progress slow. Suddenly Henry felt vastly relieved to be wearing the uniform. Down here, anything other than jeans and a sweater would have seemed eccentric in the extreme. They installed themselves at a table in an inglenook, and Alastair took their orders for four pints of bitter. To ask for anything else would have smacked of heresy.

Almost at once, a very old man dressed entirely in nondescript navy blue made his way over to the table. His white hair made a brief appearance from beneath a venerable and oily yachting cap, which he touched perfunctorily as he approached. He came very close to Rosemary, drew himself up as if to deliver an important message, and said, "Ar."

Rosemary beamed. "How are you, Herbert?" she said.

"Heard about your boat?" asked the newcomer in a thick Suffolk accent.

"No. What about it?"

"Sunk. Six foot under." Herbert cackled thinly.

"I don't believe you," said Rosemary calmly.

"Hay?" said Herbert, putting a hand to his ear. Rosemary repeated her remark louder. Herbert chuckled.

"No more do I, but if she was, I'd know 'oo to blame."

"There are our friends, Henry and Emmy Tibbett," said Rosemary. "This is Herbert Hole. A very great friend of ours. He's the Harbour Master."

"Pleased to meet you," said Herbert, with a touch of gloom.

"What," added Rosemary quietly, "are you drinking, Herbert?"

Herbert brightened visibly. "I'll take a small gin, since you ask," he said graciously.

"And a large gin for Herbert, darling," said Rosemary to Alastair's retreating back. Herbert sat down.

"I got the new mooring you was after," he said confidentially. He dug Rosemary in the ribs with a skinny elbow. "Nice and snug she is now, just off the hard. Had to bale her out, of course."

"Had she made a lot of water?" Rosemary asked solicitously.

"Not more 'un you'd expect. 'Bout enough to sink the Harwich ferry." Herbert laughed again, with macabre glee.

"How's Mrs. Hole?" said Rosemary.

Herbert became plunged in melancholy again. "Poorly," he said. "Proper poorly. It's her feet." He nodded several times. "Still," he added, more buoyantly, "mustn't grumble, I suppose." There was a short pause. "Sir Simon's in again," Herbert went on. He jerked his head significantly towards the bar. Henry saw an athletic, florid-faced man in his sixties talking to Alastair. "Took a glass of wine with him earlier on. There's a gentleman for you," said Herbert. After a moment he added cryptically, "I could tell you a thing or two."

At that moment, Alastair arrived with the drinks, accompanied by an enormous young man in regulation sailing kit.

"Hamish," said Alastair, "meet Henry and Emmy. Hamish Rawnsley," he added, in explanation. "Friend of ours. Lives here, lucky sod. Has a four-tonner, name of *Tideway*."

"All present an' correct, Cap'n Benson," said Herbert, raising his large gin and winking prodigiously.

"And the same to you, you old rogue," said Alastair. "What have you been doing to *Ariadne*? Stopped that leak in the port-hand garboard yet?"

As the beer flowed freely, Rosemary, Alastair and Herbert became engrossed in a technical discussion in which the terms caulking, tingles and hanging knees were bandied shamelessly. Hamish lowered his well-distributed thirteen stone onto the bench beside Henry and said, "Got a boat down here?"

"No," said Henry. "We're sailing with Rosemary and Alastair on *Ariadne*. It's our first time."

Hamish looked at him with something like disbelief. Then he said, "I envy you."

"I'm longing to see *Ariadne*," said Emmy.

"I meant," said Hamish solemnly, "I envy you because it's your first sail. That's something nobody can do twice."

"We've had grave doubts about doing it once," said Henry.

"Then you're fools," said Hamish shortly. "The only sport in the world," he went on. "Sorts people out. Either they like it, or they don't. If they don't . . ." He broke off, and then added, "D'you enjoy this pub?"

"Enormously," said Emmy with enthusiasm.

"Then you'll enjoy sailing. *Not*," said Hamish, "yachting. Don't ever use that word with us. It's dirty. Sailing. Boating. That's what we do. Uncle Pete always used to say—did you know Uncle Pete?"

"No," said Henry.

"Pity," said Hamish. "One of the best. Terrible thing he should have died like that. Still, it was the way he would have wanted to go. With his boat."

"Was he lost in a storm?" Henry asked tentatively.

Hamish looked surprised. "Good God, no," he said. "Didn't Alastair tell you? Oh, well, he will."

Across the table, the technical talk had languished, and Herbert said to Hamish, "Got a buyer for the *Blue Gull* yet, then, Mr. Rawnsley?" There was a touch of malice in his voice.

"No," said Hamish briefly.

"Ah, well, no point in rushing into a sale," remarked Herbert. "Thank you, Cap'n Benson. Same again. No, as I was sayin', best wait for the right buyer. After all, you've no lack of money now Mr. Pete's gone, have you?" As an afterthought he added, "Sir."

Hamish stood up abruptly, with a clatter of glasses. "I'm off now," he said to Henry and Emmy. "Good night. Good sailing." And he strode out of the bar, banging the door behind him.

Herbert watched him go, reflectively, his head cocked to one side like a shrewd sea bird. "I wouldn't feel too happy about *Blue Gull* for all that, if I were Mr. Rawnsley," he said provocatively.

Alastair winked at Rosemary.

"Unlucky boat," Herbert went on, in a voice vibrating with rustic wisdom. "Drowned her owner. Unlucky. And unlucky in more ways than one, if you ask me."

"I understand Bill Hawkes is looking after her, and acting as agent for selling her," said Alastair, in a voice of exaggerated innocence. Rosemary gave him a reproachful look, and suppressed a giggle. Herbert's face darkened.

"Looking after her—that's what some people might call it," he said, with a sardonic snort. "Others might call it wrecking her, if they'd a mind to. I'm not making accusations, mind, but I know. No use pretending I don't."

"Now, look here, Herbert——"

"Remember *Dulcibella*?" Herbert asked darkly. "Sunk at her moorings for want of a bit of caulking. Remember *Miranda*? Mast snapped. Remember——"

"Hey, Herbert! Come and have a drink!" The big, florid man who had been talking to Alastair at the bar bellowed resoundingly across the room. Herbert, with a mumbled apology, got up and went to join him.

"Who's that?" Emmy asked.

"Sir Simon Trigg-Willoughby," said Alastair. "Local squire. Lives in Berry Hall, the big house on the point. Bit of an old bore, actually."

"But the house is beautiful," Rosemary put in. "We'll try to take you over there one day this week."

"The person who fascinates me is this Bill Hawkes," said Henry. "Which is he? Does he really go round sinking boats deliberately?"

Alastair and Rosemary both grinned broadly, and Rosemary said, "That's Bill over there by the door. The stout chap in sea boots."

"He looks inoffensive enough," said Emmy.

"So he is," said Rosemary, "but he's Herbert's deadly enemy. The two of them are in a permanent state of feud."

"Good heavens," said Henry. "What about?"

"Boats," said Alastair. "You see, they each run a boatyard, and everyone down here employs one or other of them to do repairs, keep the boat baled out in the summer, lay her up in the winter, and so on. Bill only opened up a couple of years ago, and before that Herbert had everything his own way. But Bill's a young man, and a very efficient boatman. So more and more of Herbert's clients are going over to the other camp. Of course, Herbert has one enormous advantage."

"What's that?" Henry asked.

"He's the Harbour Master," said Alastair, "and the Harbour Master controls most of the moorings in the river, which are Council property. So if you entrust your boat to Herbert, you've a much better chance of getting a decent position. Poor old Herbert—if he ever lost that job, he'd be done for."

"I shouldn't think there's any fear of that," said Rosemary. "Old Harbour Masters go on till they drop dead. He'd have to do something really frightful before Trinity House fired him."

The bar door swung open, and a tall, lanky man with fair hair and a weather-beaten face came in. Alastair and Rosemary jumped up.

"David! So you've made it! Why are you so late?"

"Beastly car broke down outside Chelmsford. Petrol pump. Had to mend it."

"Have a beer, David," said Alastair. "Oh, by the way,

meet our crew—Henry and Emmy Tibbett. This is David Crowther."

"Sorry I can't shake hands," said David, with an attractive smile. He held out a pair of grimy paws. "Covered in oil from the car. Thanks, Alastair. I'll come and help you."

The two men pushed their way to the bar, and Rosemary said, "You'll adore David. He's one of the Fleet."

"What does that mean?" Emmy asked.

"Oh, it's just what we call ourselves," said Rosemary. "There are five boats"—she checked herself, and amended —"there were five, I mean. Only four now. *Ariadne, Tideway, Pocahontas*—that's David's boat—and *Mary Jane.* We're all friends, and we tend to sail in company and meet up for drinks in the evening. Then we all get together for a Laying–Up Dinner in London at the end of the season and make speeches and pretend to be a proper club. It all sounds very silly, I suppose," she ended, lamely, "but we enjoy ourselves."

David came back with three brimming pint mugs.

"Signal from *Mary Jane*," he said. "Anne has to work in the morning, so she and Colin won't be down till the afternoon. They wanted us to go on to Walton without them, but I said we'd just have a day sail tomorrow and meet them here in the evening. Hope that's O.K. with you."

"Fine," said Rosemary.

"Actually," David added, "I probabiy won't go out tomorrow. Lots of odd jobs to do on board."

"Lazy devil," remarked Alastair, coming up behind him with the remaining beers. "Oh, well, we'll just have to stooge around and show Henry and Emmy the finer points of sailing. When's the tide?"

David gave him a severe look. "What have you been doing all the week—working?" he asked scornfully. "Too busy to look up your tide tables? High water 6.41 A.M. And I trust you'll be up to catch it."

David stayed for only one drink. "I'm dead tired and filthy," he remarked, "and the tide's going out fast. You may enjoy lugging your dinghy half a mile over the mud, but I don't. See you tomorrow."

It was some time and several beers later when the barman broke into one of Herbert's lengthier reminiscences with his pessimistic chant of "Time, Gentlemen—*if* you please!" Herbert departed with alacrity, consulting a massive watch on a gold chain, and announcing that he never stayed until closing time because he had some consideration for Mrs. Hole, the poor soul, and her with her feet. Henry and Emmy finished their beer, and walked out into the cold, fresh night, feeling that life as they knew it was a million miles away, and that they were now and for ever involved in the small, slow, beautiful events of Berrybridge Haven. The beer lent a warming, sentimental glow, and the stars were shining in a black velvet sky.

"Now for getting aboard," said Alastair briskly. "You drive the car down the hard, Rosemary love, while Henry and I get the dinghy."

The tide was very low now, and Rosemary was able to drive the station wagon down the hard almost to the water's edge, where she and Emmy unloaded it. Henry, his lyrical mood rapidly evaporating, found himself padding about on the damp mud with Alastair, searching for *Ariadne*'s dinghy by the light of the moon, augmented by a small torch. It was very cold. They found the dinghy eventually—a small, varnished rowing boat lying forlornly on the shore.

"Right," said Alastair. "I'll take the bows if you take the stern."

"Where to?" Henry asked.

"Down to the water, of course," said Alastair. He nodded towards the ink-black river, a quarter of a mile away across the silvery mud. "I should take your shoes off, if I were you," he added, "and roll your trousers up. You'll only get them soaked."

Henry found it difficult to believe that a small boat could weigh so much. As he staggered through the chilly, oozing, ankle-deep mud, his alcoholic-sentimental mood suffered an abrupt sea change, and his thoughts turned longingly to hotwater bottles and centrally heated London flats. Soon, however, the satisfaction of manual labour asserted itself, and with it the realization of the true beauty of his surroundings. Panting from exertion, he stood with Alastair on the end of the hard, straining his eyes to follow the fast-vanishing shape of the dinghy on the dark water as Rosemary and Emmy rowed out with the first load of gear, and savouring the salty, nostalgic smell of the river and the quiet glory of the stars. Then Rosemary returned, the two men and the remaining picnic-baskets were loaded into the dinghy.

Soon a dark hull loomed above them, with lamplight glowing reassuringly from her open hatch. They scrambled on board into the snug warmth of the cabin, where coffee was already brewing on a hissing Primus stove. Tired and content, Henry and Emmy drank coffee and brandy, and were nodding drowsily even before the two green sleeping bags had been stretched out for them on the hard floor of the fo'c'sle. As their heads touched the rolled-up sweaters which served as pillows, they were both engulfed in a dreamless, utterly satisfying sleep.

TWO

Henry woke next morning to the sound of sausages sizzling in the pan, and a delicious smell of newly fried bacon. Through the dispersing mists of sleep he became aware of a steaming white mug of tea beside his face, and then of Rosemary, grinning at him through the curtains that separated the fo'c'sle from the main cabin.

"Come on, lazybones," she said cheerfully. "It's a gorgeous morning. We've been up for hours. Breakfast's nearly ready."

She withdrew into the cabin again, like a retreating snail, and reappeared a moment later with a blue enamel bowl.

"Hot water for washing," she said. "You'll have to share it. Can't spare any more. No need to shave unless you feel like it. And if you want to spend a penny, use the bucket."

With that, she disappeared. Henry struggled stiffly out of his sleeping bag into a sitting position, took a gulp of tea, and looked around him. Last night he had been too exhausted to take in the details of *Ariadne's* living accommodation. Now he saw that he and Emmy were ensconced in a narrow, triangular section in the bows of the boat, where there was just room for two sleeping bags to be laid side by side. The frames and timbers of the boat, which formed the walls, were painted gleaming white, and hung with coils of rope: beyond Henry's feet, in the tapering bows, bulging canvas sailbags were stacked: between Emmy and himself, a stout anchor chain ran down from a hole in the decking to disappear through another opening in the floor boards. Overhead, sunshine slanted in through the square forehatch, which had been propped slightly open for ventilation. There was just enough room to sit up in comfort.

Henry woke Emmy, and when they had washed and dressed, they pulled back the curtains and crawled through into the main cabin.

Here it was possible to stand nearly upright, thanks to the fact that the level of the floor was lower, and the roof built up. Sunshine flooded in, through the skylight in the ceiling and through the open hatch which led to the cockpit. The cabin was about ten feet long by eight feet wide, and its layout followed the traditional pattern which contrives to cram an amazing amount of comfort and storage space into such limited dimensions. Two bunks— now made up for the daytime into settees, with bright red covers and blue cushions—ran down the sides, while in the centre a folding table was set up for breakfast. Between the bunks and the cockpit, there were, on one side, a small galley containing a doubleburner Primus stove, with a plate rack above it and a cupboard below, and on the other, a large locker for storing food, saucepans and crockery. On the wall above one bunk was a neat rack for books, in which Henry noticed *Reid's Nautical Almanack*, a well-thumbed copy of *East Coast Rivers, The Yachtsman's Weekend Book, The Venturesome Voyages of Captain Voss*, Joshua Slocum's *Sailing Alone Round the World,* Peter Heaton's *Sailing* and *Cruising,* and a battered and outdated copy of *Lloyd's Register of Shipping.* A similar rack above the other bunk held a selection of charts, rolled up neatly and secured with elastic bands. Another rack held a small fire extinguisher, and a fourth, a portable wireless set.

On the varnished bulkhead, a shining brass oil lamp swung in gimbals, and this was flanked on one side by a white-faced, brassbound clock, and on the other by a matching barometer. As in the fo'c'sle, white paint alternated with bronzed varnish: the effect was spruce, comfortable and exceedingly attractive.

Rosemary was sitting on the step that led up to the cockpit, breaking eggs into a frying pan.

"Won't be a moment," she said. "The coffee's just perco-
lating. Why don't you go out and have a look at the
morning?"

"What time is it?" Emmy asked.

"Late," said Rosemary. "Eight o'clock. We woke early
to catch the tide, and then thought better of it. After
all, we're not trying to get anywhere special today, so we
thought we'd have another couple of hours in bed."

She moved aside to let them pass, and they clambered
into the open cockpit.

Berrybridge Haven was putting on a fine show for its
weekend visitors. The sun blazed from a sky the colour of
a robin's egg, and danced merrily over the deeper blue
water, which—since it was little more than an hour after
high tide—stretched dazzlingly from the whitewashed walls
of The Berry Bush on one bank to the distant greensward
of the other. The dinghies, which had been mud-stranded
the night before, now bobbed and curtsied like coloured
shells on either side of the grey concrete hard. The main
channel in the centre of the river was marked not only
by two rows of buoys (pillar-box red and cylindrical on
one side, black and conical on the other), but also by two
parallel lines of moored boats. The sun, glancing off the
rippling water, threw up shifting gleams of light on to
their gaudy hulls—white, red, green, blue, black or gold-
shimmering varnish. In the channel, several boats were
already under sail.

On shore and on the boats, things were stirring. Henry
could see besweatered figures in yachting caps carrying
cans of water and sailbags down the hard: canvas began
to flutter whitely from moored boats, as their crews hoisted
sail and prepared to put to sea. Alastair, who was sitting
cross-legged on the foredeck of *Ariadne* splicing a rope,
waved cheerfully as a decrepit grey motor launch hic-
coughed past—and Henry recognized its occupant as Herbert Hole, going about his official business of collecting
mooring fees and cups of tea from visiting boats.

On the next mooring to *Ariadne*, slightly upriver,
there was a small, black-hulled boat with a short mast
and an excessively long bowsprit.

Emmy said, "Look, that's *Pocahontas*. David's boat. I can see her name on the back."

"On the stern, if you please," said Alastair. "Good-morning. Sleep well?"

"Like logs," said Henry. "What a wonderful morning."

"Not bad," said Alastair. "Not enough wind, really. Still, can't have everything." Suddenly he opened the fore-hatch and bellowed down it, "Rosemary! Where's the whipping?"

Rosemary's head emerged into the cockpit. "In the after locker, of course," she said. "At least, it should be. I'll look." She scrambled into the cockpit and pulled open a locker door under the tiller. "Oh, blast," she added, "I remember now. We used the last bit on the main halyard. I meant to buy more."

"Have I time to row over and borrow some from David?"

"No," said Rosemary firmly. "For one thing, break-fast's ready. For another, David won't be up yet, if I know him. And for a third, he won't have any. He never does. He'll be over to borrow some from us soon—he told me he wanted to renew his jib sheets and topping lift today."

"This," said Henry, "is exactly like talking a foreign language. Are you going to translate for us?"

"You'll learn," said Rosemary. "It's not as difficult as it sounds. Come and eat."

They did—hugely. Even Emmy, whose usual idea of breakfast was a cup of coffee and a roll, worked her way through cornflakes, eggs, sausages, bacon, fried bread and tomatoes, and then accepted toast and marmalade. Henry began to see the reason for the two massive picnic-baskets.

Afterwards, when everything had been carefully washed up and stowed away, Alastair said, "Right. Now for the first sailing lesson. And let's hope we don't make a mess of it. One generally does, trying to impress people."

"Tell us about *Ariadne* first," said Emmy, "so that we don't look too foolish when people ask us. What sort of a boat is she, for a start? I mean, what's the technical term?"

"She's a six-ton Bermudian sloop," said Alastair. "That means that she carries two sails. One little one—the jib—forward of the mast, and the mainsail. That's the big one," he added kindly.

"What does Bermudian mean?" Henry asked. "Was she built there or something?"

"No. It simply means that the mainsail is triangular."

"I thought they all were," said Emmy.

"Goodness, no. It's quite a recent innovation. All the old boats were gaff-rigged—like that fishing smack over there. *Ariadne* used to be gaff before she was converted. She's pretty ancient, poor old lady."

Henry and Emmy followed Alastair's pointing finger, to see a large, dignified old boat ploughing her way slowly downriver. "You see? Her mainsail's almost rectangular—wider at the bottom, of course, but with four distinct corners, and a second boom running along the top of it."

"So she's a gaff sloop," said Emmy proudly.

"No," said Alastair, "a gaff cutter."

"Oh, heavens. Why?"

"Because she carried two foresails—a jib and a staysail."

"This is much too complicated," said Henry. "Let's get back to *Ariadne*. A Bermudian sloop. Six tons, you said. You mean, that's what she weighs?"

"No," said Alastair. "Sorry to be difficult. That's a measurement called Thames Tonnage, and it hasn't anything to do with weight. You work it out from a formula involving length and beam—width, to you. So the exact dimensions of six-tonners can vary, but they're all about the same size of boat. We're thirty-two feet long over-all, with an eight-foot beam and a five-foot draught, which is about average. *Pocahontas* is smaller—a three-tonner. You soon get to judge the tonnage of a boat fairly accurately by just looking at her."

"I don't," said Emmy firmly.

Alastair grinned. "It doesn't matter a hoot anyway," he said. "The only thing you need remember is that there's five solid feet of *Ariadne* under the water, so if you sail her into water that's less than five foot deep—wham. You're on the putty."

"That at least sounds logical," remarked Henry, with some relief.

"Now," said Alastair, "we'll set the sails. It's very simple. Each sail has two ropes attached to it. The halyard and the sheet. The halyard, as you might guess, is the one you haul it up with. The sheet is the one that pulls the sail in or lets it out, according to the direction of the wind. O.K.?"

"O.K.," said Emmy, a little dubiously.

"Right, then we'll set the jib." Alastair reached down through the forehatch into Henry and Emmy's erstwhile bedroom, and fished up a canvas sailbag. "Now," he went on. "See this—this is the jib halyard." He unwound two ropes from the mass of rigging secured to the mast. "It's a single rope running through a pulley up aloft—except that a pulley is always called a block. You see? Very simple." He demonstrated. The rope jammed in the block.

"I see it is," said Henry.

Swearing softly, Alastair proceeded to get involved in a sort of cat's cradle of rigging, from which the jib halyard eventually emerged, running freely. He shackled it to the peak of the jib.

"Now," said Alastair, "we attach the jib to the forestay." Tucking the sail under his arm, he crawled out to the end of the bowsprit, missed his footing, and very nearly fell into the river.

"Very simple," said Emmy.

"I want no back answers from the crew," replied Alastair with dignity, hauling himself back to safety with one arm, while the other held the precious bundle of canvas out of the water. When he had fastened one corner of the sail to the end of the bowsprit, and strung the curtain-ring clips on the length of its forward edge to the forestay, he scrambled inboard again.

"Can we hoist the jib now?" Henry asked.

"Not yet. Not till the sheets are attached."

"Wait a minute," said Henry. "I thought you said there was only one sheet per sail."

Alastair looked at him pityingly. "If the jib didn't have a port and a starboard sheet, how could you come about?" he asked. Henry said he had no idea, and watched humbly as Alastair picked up another rope from the deck. This was, in fact, two ropes, one of which ran down either side of the deck and back into the cockpit. The forward ends were shackled together, and these Alastair proceeded to attach to the third corner of the jib.

"Now," he said. "Haul her up."

"Alastair darling," said a sweet voice from the cockpit, "haven't you forgotten the burgee?"

"Oh, blast," said Alastair. "Didn't I tell you one always messes things up trying to demonstrate? I should have done that first."

He took the small, triangular, blue and white flag from Rosemary, and quickly ran it up to the masthead, where it fluttered encouragingly. Henry looked round at the other boats, and said, "Every boat seems to have a different burgee."

"That's because they belong to different clubs," said Alastair. "Ours is the Little Ship Club. That red and blue one is the Berrybridge Yacht Club, and the one over there is the Royal Harwich."

"This one is just plain white," said Emmy, indicating a small, swift boat which was skidding past.

"That's because she's racing," said Alastair. "When you see that, you keep out of her way. Now, up with the jib."

Henry, feeling very seamanlike, tugged on the jib halyard, and was immensely gratified to see the shapeless mass of white cotton on the foredeck rear up, and assume the shape of a sail.

"Tighter than that," said Alastair.

Henry pulled again, wincing as the rope bit into his soft, townsman's hands. The leading edge of the jib remained undulating.

"Sweat it up," said Alastair.

"I am," said Henry, panting slightly.

Alastair grinned. "I don't mean like that," he said. "Look. Take a turn round this cleat"—he passed the end of the halyard round a wooden peg which protruded from the mast—"now . . ."

He leant his full weight on the halyard, pulling it out from the mast with one hand, while with the other he snatched up the slack of the rope round the cleat. The sail stretched bar-taut up the forestay. "Now we make it fast—and there she is."

Henry and Emmy looked up admiringly at the big sail flapping gently in the breeze. Then Emmy said, "Why doesn't the boat try to sail away, now we've got the sail up?"

"Because the sheets are free, and we're facing directly into the wind. When a boat's moored, she always puts her nose into the wind or the tide, whichever is the stronger. This morning they're both in the same direction. So long as we don't tighten the sheets, the jib'll flap away there quite happily forever. Now for the main."

The mainsail was already in position along the boom, protected by a canvas sail cover, which Alastair unlaced and threw down into the fo'c'sle. "All you have to do with the main is haul her up, and then you'll have them both flapping and ready to go."

"But the mainsail can't flap," Henry objected. "The boom is fixed in that thing."

"That thing," said Alastair, "is the boom gallows."

"What an unfortunate name," said Emmy. "Why is it called that?"

"I've no idea," said Alastair, "but that's what it is."

The thing in question was, in fact, no more than two pieces of wood bolted together to form an X, which stood on deck behind the cockpit and supported the end of the boom.

"Don't worry about the gallows," said Alastair. "When the sail goes up, she lifts the boom right out of them. They're only there to keep the thing out of the way when we're anchored."

Sure enough, as Henry hauled on the halyard and the great white sail ran up the mast, the end of the boom lifted suddenly, and the gallows fell with a thud onto the deck. The two sails flapped noisily, and Rosemary went up to the foredeck and untied the rope that held *Ariadne* to her mooring, letting it go until only a single turn round the oaken Samson post in the deck secured the boat. At the tiller, Alastair tightened in the mainsheet, and then hauled on the starboard-hand jib sheet. To Henry's surprise, the jib filled with wind, and the nose of the boat swung to port, towards the centre of the river. Immediately the mainsail, too, caught the wind, and Alastair said, "O.K. Let her go."

Rosemary threw the mooring buoy overboard into the water, where it bobbed like a seagull on the wavelets. Alastair quickly released the starboard jib sheet and tightened the port one. And silently, smoothly, *Ariadne* moved across the river, leaning gently to port, her bows cutting sharply through the shining water.

"Ease sheets," said Alastair. He pulled the tiller over, and the boat swung round in a left-handed circle. Simultaneously, Alastair let the mainsheet run out until the boom hung out over the water, and Rosemary released the jib sheet until the big foresail, nearly masked by the main, was barely filling with wind. *Ariadne* steadied herself onto an even keel, and moved downriver towards the sea.

"The wind's dropped," said Emmy.

"No, it hasn't," said Rosemary. "You always get that impression when it's dead behind you."

"But we're hardly moving now," Henry put in.

"Rubbish. We're steaming along. Just look at the rate we're passing that buoy. You get a tremendous illusion of speed when you're beating into the wind, but when you start to run, it always feels as though you're standing still."

Sure enough, the moored boats and marker buoys were slipping rapidly past.

"And that," said Alastair, "is all there is to sailing. In theory. When you're going against the wind, haul in the sheets. When it's behind you, let them right out. And here we are, on an ebbing tide, with the wind astern and headed for Holland." And he began stuffing tobacco into a very old pipe, keeping one hand on the tiller and one eye on the burgee.

From Berrybridge, the river runs southward for several miles, and then widens dramatically as it approaches the North Sea. For an hour, *Ariadne* ran smoothly downriver, with the north wind behind her. Apart from a moment of activity when Alastair shouted "Gybe-oh," and the boom swung noisily over from starboard to port, the crew relaxed lazily in the sunshine. Now they could see the ocean ahead of them, and the horizon beckoned with its siren song.

"Let's go to Ostend," said Rosemary. "Why not?"

"Because we're meeting Colin and Anne in The Berry Bush tonight, for one thing," said Alastair.

"Oh, to hell with Colin and Anne."

"Be sensible, darling. We haven't even got our passports with us. No, we'll turn north and go up to the Deben."

They were near the mouth of the river by now. On their right, the southern shore stretched sandily away towards the playgrounds of Clacton and Frinton. On their left, a wooded promontory ran out into the sea, surrounded on three sides by water—for the coastline to the north swept sharply back, almost parallel to the river, making an isthmus of the last few miles of riverbank.

On this isthmus, Henry caught a glimpse through an avenue of elms of a magnificent Palladian façade. "Berry Hall," said Alastair. "Home of our friend Sir Simon Trigg-Willoughby, the lucky devil. One of the architectural gems of southern Suffolk."

"Can we go in a bit closer and have a look at it?" Emmy asked.

"No," said Alastair firmly.

"Why not?"

"Because there's no water."

"What do you mean?" Emmy asked indignantly. "The water goes right up to the trees."

"I told you," said Alastair patiently, "that *Ariadne* draws five feet. In another hour or so, when the tide has gone out a bit, there'll be nothing but sand between us and Berry

Hall. At the moment, there's probably less than three feet. We're as near inshore as we dare go."

By this time, *Ariadne* was approaching the actual river mouth, and Henry could see how the great, beautiful house dominated the landscape, sited proudly as it was on a green hill that sloped to the water on three sides. The front of the house looked straight out over the wide North Sea, and at the edge of the lawns that swept down to the water there was a small boathouse and a jetty.

"How does Sir Simon get his boats out, if it's all sand?" said Emmy. "Can he only go out at high tide?"

"There's a tiny channel," Rosemary said. "It runs from the boathouse as far as Steep Hill Sands—that's the big bank we've got to go around—and then it sort of meanders round Steep Hill and into the sea. But it's very shallow at low water. Sir Simon can use it, because he's got a motor boat and a dinghy, and they don't draw much."

"Sir Simon Trigg-Willoughby," said Henry slowly. "The name rings a bell. Wasn't there a case, about two years ago—a robbery or something?"

"That's right," said Alastair. "Cat burglar got the family jewels."

"I remember," said Henry. "They were never found, were they?"

"I don't see why Sir Simon and Priscilla go on making such a fuss about it even now," said Rosemary. "After all, the insurance paid up—which was jolly decent of them, considering that the whole thing was Priscilla's own fault. But then, of course, she's slightly bats."

"Who's Priscilla?" Emmy asked.

"Sir Simon's sister—curious old girl, spinster and more than half-way round the bend. She insisted on wearing the entire family loot to a hunt ball, and then forgot to lock it up afterwards. Personally, if I'd been Sir Simon, I'd have much preferred the insurance money to a lot of badly set diamonds that would have gone to some distant cousin in the end—because the two old dears are the last of the Trigg-Willoughbys. But to hear them go on, you'd think it was the end of the world. Of course," Rosemary added, "they're a tremendously family family, if you know what I

mean. Berry Hall, the jewels, the Trigg-Willoughby tradition . . . it's all very well, but——"

"Sir Simon's not married then?" Henry asked.

"Poor chap never had a chance," said Alastair. "Nor
did Priscilla. They were brought up by a Victorian martinet
of a father who considered that nothing short of royalty
was good enough for a Trigg-Willoughby. The old boy only
died a few years ago, and by that time Simon and Priscilla
were both a bit past it."

By now, Berry Hall had been left behind, and *Ariadne*
was heading out into the North Sea, cutting the gently
crinkling waves with her sharp bows. Henry said, "I thought
we were going northward up the coast."

"We are," said Alastair.

"But we're heading straight out to sea."

"And shall do, for quite a bit. Steep Hill Sands run out
about a mile from the point. You should see it at low water,
then you'd understand."

Half an hour later, when it seemed to Henry and Emmy
that they must be well on the way to Holland, Alastair said,
"All right. Harden sheets. I'm turning up now."

He hauled in the mainsheet until the big sail was hugged
closely in to the boat, while Rosemary did the same for the
jib. At the same time, Alastair pushed the tiller to starboard, and the nose of the boat swung round to the north,
and almost into the teeth of the wind. Immediately, *Ariadne*
leant gently over to starboard, and the bow wave creamed
frothingly as she headed to windward, setting a north-east-
erly course.

"We're beating now," said Alastair. "We can't go directly
up the coast, because that would be straight into the wind.
So we have to tack. We can go as far as we like on this
course, because we're heading out to sea, but when we come
about we'll have to make sure we don't go too far inshore
and hit the sandbank. It is buoyed, but . . ."

"We're getting awfully far away from the land," said
Emmy, "and I do want another look at that house. Can't
we keep closer in?"

"All right," said Alastair. "Ready about. Keep your heads
down, you two. Lee-oh."

The next few seconds seemed to Henry and Emmy like a pandemonium of flapping sails and the sound of ropes running through blocks. They raised their dutifully lowered heads as the noise ceased, and saw that the boom and sails were now on the other side of the boat, and that *Ariadne* was setting a course almost straight towards the shore. A black, conical buoy bobbed innocently in the water ahead of them.

"That buoy marks the edge of Steep Hill Sands," said Alastair. "It's as far as I dare go on this tack."

"You're an old fuss-pot," Rosemary remarked. "It's still half-tide. We can go quite a bit closer in."

"I don't like taking risks," said Alastair.

"Then give me the helm," Rosemary replied with spirit. "I'll show you how close we can go. I've often done it."

"Women," remarked Alastair gloomily, "should never be allowed on boats. All right, take the helm. And don't blame me if we go on the mud."

Rosemary and Alastair changed places, and the black buoy approached at speed, until they could see the words STEEP HILL painted on it in big white letters. Soon they were inshore of it, and getting a fine view of the eastern elevation of Berry Hall.

"Come about now," said Alastair.

"Rubbish," said Rosemary. "I've got another fifty yards."

"You're a bloody fool," said Alastair, with some heat.

"Who's sailing this boat anyway, you or me?"

"You are, but——"

"Very well then." Rosemary's pretty mouth was set in a stubborn line. "I say we can go closer."

"And I say we can't."

"My dear Alastair, it may interest you to know that—oh, hell . . ."

There was an ominous, crunching sound.

"What's the matter?" said Henry.

Rosemary was swearing, quietly but with a fine command of Anglo-Saxon. She pulled the tiller towards her, and shouted, "Free sheets. I'll try to blow her off."

"What's happened?" said Emmy. "We don't seem to be moving."

"Dear Emmy," said Alastair grimly, "we are not moving. My adorable wife has put us on the putty. On a falling tide. It's no good, darling. Get the sails off her, and I'll try the kedge."

Working with desperate speed, Rosemary set up the boom gallows and lowered the mainsail and the jib, while Alastair took the anchor into the dinghy and rowed out with it into deep water, where he dropped it. Then he came back, and hauled with all his might on the anchor chain, hoping to pull *Ariadne* off the sandbank by brute force. But, with the tide running out fast, her keel was by now firmly embedded, and nothing would shift her. Already they could see little white wavelets beginning to break on the topmost point of the sandbank, as the retreating tide left only a few inches of water covering it.

Rosemary was near tears, and Henry and Emmy, embarrassed, waited for the expected recriminations. But none came. At sea, as they soon learnt, mistakes are forgiven and forgotten more quickly than ashore. Alastair put his arm round his wife's shoulders, and said, "Cheer up, old love. Could happen to anyone."

"Oh, darling, I'm so terribly sorry," moaned Rosemary. "I really thought there was enough water."

"Never mind," said Alastair cheerfully. "I'm sure Henry and Emmy will forgive you. And it's a lovely day for a sunbathe on Steep Hill."

"I like it here," said Emmy truthfully. "There's a wonderful view of the house."

Alastair grinned, and consulted his watch. "You may get a bit sick of this particular view by the time we get off," he said. "We've got a good five hours before the tide comes up enough to float us. Still, at least we're on sand and not on mud, so we can get out and walk around. I imagine lunch will be a more comfortable meal on the sand than on board."

As Alastair spoke, they could see that where before had been breaking waves, there was now an island of golden sand. And, as *Ariadne* heeled over unhappily to landward, this island spread rapidly in circumference until the water had retreated all round them, leaving them and the boat stranded, high and dry, in the sunshine. Inshore, it was now possible to see the narrow, winding channel which ran from Sir Simon's boathouse to the sandbank: to seaward, a smart, green-hulled sailing boat was coming down the main channel, with a cheerfully waving figure at the tiller.

"Oh, lord," said Rosemary in dismay, "that's Hamish in *Tideway*. What *will* he think?"

"I've seen him on Steep Hill before now," said Alastair, returning the salutation. "Let him have a good laugh. He can do with it."

"Poor Hamish," said Rosemary. "He certainly hasn't been his old self since——" She stopped, suddenly.

"You know, darling," said Alastair, "we must be in just about the same place now—where we found Pete, I mean."

"Tell us about this man Pete," said Henry. "We keep hearing about him. What's the story?"

"Well," said Alastair, "it happened just about here, on Steep Hill."

"Darling," said Rosemary, "I'm sure Henry and Emmy don't want to——"

"We've got plenty of time," said Alastair. "If you'd like to hear about it."

"Yes, please," said Emmy.

"Let's have lunch," said Rosemary. There was a curious urgency in her voice.

But when they had all finished their plates of cold chicken and salad—extracted with some difficulty from the galley, which was now listing at forty-five degrees—Alastair leant back on the sand, lit his pipe, and said, "Well . . . if you're interested . . . it was like this. . . ."

THREE

"Pete Rawnsley," said Alastair, "was a wonderful chap. At least, we thought so. I think everybody did. A great big bear of a man, with one of those weather-beaten faces and bright blue eyes. I suppose he was about fifty—he was Hamish's uncle—but that sort of chap could be anything from forty to sixty. He was as tough as nails, and what he didn't know about boats could be written on a sixpence— I tell you, he was the finest sailor I ever knew. That's why it seemed so terrible when . . . oh, well, I'll come to that later.

"Anyway, a couple years ago he came into some money and retired down here and bought a beautiful Dragon-class boat called *Blue Gull*—Hamish is trying to sell her now. Except when he was racing, he nearly always sailed single-handed. Said he knew where he was that way. I must say I see what he meant," he added, with a glance at Rosemary, who put her tongue out at him.

"Well," Alastair went on, "we met him down here, and became great friends. He was one of the original group that we call the Fleet."

"We know about that," said Emmy. "Rosemary told us."

"One day a few months ago—in May, it was—Pete was taking *Blue Gull* up to the Deben for regatta week, picking his crew up there, and we decided to make a Fleet Outing of it and all sail there in company. It was a glorious morning—I remember we had to set sail at seven to catch the tide. We were the first away, then Pete, then the others— they were late getting up, and were some way behind us. *Blue Gull* is a much faster boat than *Ariadne,* of course, so we fully expected Pete to overtake us, but somehow we were lucky and caught a bit of breeze that he didn't, and we managed to keep ahead until we got right down here, near the river mouth. We were pretty pleased about it, as you can imagine, and Pete was determined to pass us. So he thought he'd be a bit clever and cut a corner over the sandbank. He overtook us all right, but the next thing we saw— wham, he was on the putty. Just about here.

"I'm afraid we laughed like a row of buckets. Poor old Pete, flying his racing burgee and all set to cover himself with glory, stuck for the day on Steep Hill. We shouted some fairly derisory remarks about explaining to his racing friends in the Deben just exactly where *Blue Gull* was. Old Pete was quite imperturbable, though. When we last saw him, he'd snugged the boat down, got the sails off her, and was sitting on the edge of the cockpit, puffing away at his pipe, as serene as you please. I dare say he was thinking up suitable replies to shout at *Tideway* and *Mary Jane* and *Pocahontas* when they came along and saw what had happened.

"Actually, though, none of us got to the Deben that day. We hadn't been sailing for more than an hour after that when a fog suddenly came down. I don't know if you've ever experienced fog at sea, but it's horrifying. It comes up from nowhere, all in half an hour, and suddenly you're in a blanket of white cotton wool, with no wind and no visibility. Frankly, I was scared. There's a fair amount of big shipping round this coast, not to mention sandbanks. I reckoned the safest thing to do was to go as close inshore as I dared and anchor, and then sit on deck blowing the foghorn and beating the bottom of the bucket with the starting handle of the engine. Not a pleasant way of passing a day, believe me. We could hear other boats blowing their horns —it's the most mournful, eerie sound I know—and the occasional throb of an engine, which we felt certain was going to materialize into a dirty great steamer looming through the mist and crashing into us.

"It seemed like a thousand years before the fog lifted. As a matter of fact, it was about six hours. Round about three o'clock in the afternoon a smart little northerly breeze blew up, the fog dispersed, and all was well again. However, the tide had turned by then, and we decided it was too late to go on to the Deben, so we turned round and headed back to Berrybridge. We reckoned Pete would have the laugh on us after all; he should have floated by about half past three, and been back and moored and having a pint in The Berry Bush by the time we arrived. But when we rounded the point at nearly half past four, there was *Blue Gull,* well afloat, riding quietly to her anchor and with nobody aboard. At first, we thought Pete must be in the cabin, but we couldn't understand what he was playing at, staying there. We kept the glasses on her, and when there was still no sign of life, we got worried and decided to investigate.

"We anchored as near the bank as we dared, and rowed over in the dinghy. I'll never forget it—the empty boat with her big boom swinging from side to side with a faint creaking noise, and not a soul to be seen. When we got there, we beached the dinghy—the top of the sandbank was still dried out—and then we saw Pete. The incoming tide was gradually washing him up onto the dried-out sand. He'd drowned in a few inches of water."

"Drowned?" Henry repeated. "How on earth did that happen?"

"The boom," said Alastair. "There was an inquest, of course, and they worked out what must have happened. Pete evidently got out when the boat was high and dry, and walked around on the sand. And somehow the boom caught him a whack over the head and knocked him out. It may even have knocked him right out of the boat. So there he was, lying unconscious on the sand, and when the tide came in——"

"There's no doubt that that's what happened?"

"None at all. They found traces of blood and hair on the boom, and a cracking great bruise on the side of Pete's head. Of course, at the time, we didn't realize straight away that he was dead: we hoped we'd be able to revive him with artificial respiration. We got the poor chap into our dinghy and rowed him up the creek to Sir Simon's boathouse. Rosemary went for help, and I tried to do what I could for him. I laid him down on the pontoon and—it's silly, isn't it, the things one does at moments like that? I remember being obsessed with the importance of getting dry cushions under him and wrapping him up with rugs, to make him comfortable. I found some rugs in Sir Simon's motorboat, but there weren't any dry cushions—everything was soaked from the fog. I remember I was ridiculously worried about it—not that it could have mattered less. The poor man was already dead, as it turned out. Anyway, I did what little I could. I tried artificial respiration, and then old Herbert Hole turned up to help—he'd been chugging round in his motor launch and seen us. Unfortunately, Sir Simon was in Ipswich for the day, so Rosemary had to tell Priscilla, who promptly got hysterics. If it hadn't been for Riddle—that's Sir Simon's man—I don't know what would have happened. But he was very efficient and called the doctor and—well, that's all. It was a very nasty experience, I can tell you."

Alastair's voice trailed off into silence. Henry said slowly, "Did *Blue Gull* have a boom gallows?"

"Of course," said Rosemary quickly. "And now for heaven's sake let's talk about something cheerful for a change."

"Please don't think I'm being officious," said Henry apologetically, "but I'm a policeman by profession, and it seems to me that there are some very odd things in the story you've just told us."

"Odd?" said Alastair. "Oh, for Christ's sake, Henry, don't try to make a mystery out of poor old Pete's death. It's perfectly clear what happened."

"I don't think it is," said Henry, with a sort of sad stubbornness. "You told me that when you last saw him, he had taken the sails off the boat and was smoking a pipe."

"That's right."

"Then surely the boom must have been in the gallows."

"Of course it was," said Alastair at once.

"Then," said Henry, "how did it get out again?"

There was a silence. Rosemary said brusquely, "It must have been the wind." She got up and began to clear up the picnic things.

"The boom was swinging freely when you saw it?" Henry persisted, addressing himself to Alastair.

"Yes. And the gallows were lying flat on deck. I remember. But there was quite a brisk breeze, as I told you."

"Yes," said Henry, "but at the time when Pete died—when the water was still low enough for him to be walking about on the sandbank—there was still fog, wasn't there?"

Alastair began to look worried. "I see what you mean," he said. "Fog, and no wind. So even if Pete had for some reason taken the boom out of the gallows—which he wouldn't have——"

"I wish you'd stop this nonsense," said Rosemary. "Remember that *Blue Gull* was well heeled over. The boom could have slipped out."

"Look at *Ariadne* now," said Henry. "She's leaning at a considerable angle, but the boom's firmly in position. I suppose in a gale it might come loose—but there was no wind."

"And in any case," said Alastair, "now I come to think of it, why was the mainsheet free? Because it was—otherwise the boom couldn't have been swinging the way it was. Pete would never have left his mainsheet loose—he was much too careful a sailor."

"So," said Henry, "the boom lifted itself out of the gallows, the mainsheet untied itself, and your friend Pete got hit on the head—hard enough to knock him unconscious—all in a fog, without a breath of wind."

There was a long silence. "I'm sorry," Henry went on, "but it seems to me that something very strange happened on Steel Hill Sands that day. Without wishing to be melodramatic, I'd say that——" He stopped abruptly.

Emmy shivered. "What a horrible thought," she said. "You mean, someone might have seen him hit the sandbank, and then waited until the fog came down and——"

"Oh, for God's sake——" said Rosemary. She had gone very pale, and sounded near tears.

"Do shut up, darling," said Alastair, very seriously. "I think Henry's got something."

"Presumably," said Henry, "anybody with a dinghy or a flat-bottomed motorboat could get to the sandbank easily enough, either from the main channel of the river or from Sir Simon's boathouse."

"From the river, certainly," said Alastair. "I doubt if it would be possible to get up that creek from the boat-house in fog. At least——"

Surprisingly, Rosemary said, "Oh, yes, it would. I mean, I've heard Riddle say . . ." Again she stopped in mid-sentence.

Alastair scratched his dark head meditatively. "You've got me really worried, Henry," he said. "It was bad enough when . . . when all this happened, but it never occurred to any of us that it wasn't just an accident. If someone really did kill Pete, I'd . . . Well, look here. Why don't you look into it a bit further while you're down here? That is, if you don't mind. It couldn't do any harm, could it, if it was unofficial?"

"Oh, Henry—not again," Emmy protested. "Can't we have a single holiday in peace?"

"I'm only going to meet people and talk to them a bit," said Henry mildly. "I promise you it won't spoil our holi-day, darling." He looked at his watch, and then went on, "We still seem to have quite a while to wait here. Tell me more about Pete Rawnsley. Was there any reason why anyone should want to kill him?"

"None," said Alastair promptly. "Everybody liked him."

"Except Colin," said Rosemary.

"Oh, that." Alastair looked at his wife with displeasure. "That was just silly."

"What was?"

Alastair said quickly, "Oh, it was just that Anne—Colin's fiancée—was having a bit of a thing with Pete. He was very attractive to women—the strong, silent type with a wife in every port and really wedded to his boat."

"Had he?" asked Henry.

"Had he what?"

"A wife in every port."

Alastair considered. "Pete was a solitary type by nature," he said at length. "He certainly ran through an impressive list of girl friends, but he used to take fright and be off as soon as any of them looked like getting serious. That's what made Colin mad—the fact that he knew Pete was bound to let Anne down in the end. Personally, I don't think Anne ever did take Pete at more than his face value. After all, she knew his reputation well enough. But when Colin found out that Anne had been down here to the cottage on her own to see Pete, there was a hell of a row. It was the night before Pete died. We were all in The Berry Bush, and Herbert let the cat out of the bag. I don't know whether he did it deliberately or not. It was just as well for Pete that he wasn't there, because Colin might have——" Alastair stopped, and then said, "I don't mean that it was really serious. Just one of Colin and Anne's usual tiffs, and ending in the usual way with Anne refusing to sleep in *Mary Jane* and spending the night with us, and then sailing with good old reliable David in *Pocahontas* next day."

"So Colin was alone in his boat," said Henry. "What did he do when the fog came down?"

"Anchored, just as we did."

"Whereabouts?"

There was a pause, and then Alastair said, "Look here, I can see what you're driving at, and I'm not going to have you getting ideas about Colin. He's a friend of mine."

"Meaning," said Henry, "that *Mary Jane* was just off the sandbank when the fog came down."

"Fool," said Rosemary quietly.

"What if she was?" Alastair retorted, with some heat. "For that matter, so were *Pocahontas* and *Tideway*. They all set off at the same time, and they were still in company when the fog came down. Of course, they all saw Pete on the sands, and waved and so on. When the fog lifted, there was no sign of Pete, but as *Blue Gull* was still aground, they naturally thought he was below in the cabin, so they just upped anchor and sailed back."

"No sign of him?" said Henry. "Where was he, then? He must have been——"

"That's one of the most tragic things," said Alastair. "Pete must have been lying on the landward side of his boat, so that he was hidden by her hull. I know Hamish can't get over the thought that he might have saved his uncle if only he'd gone ashore to investigate. But nobody could possibly blame him. The coroner said that."

"If somebody from one of the anchored boats had put off in a dinghy and rowed over during the fog," said Henry, "do you think the others would have heard anything?"

Alastair thought for a moment. "Possibly," he said. "It's very difficult to say. Fog does the most extraordinary things to sound, you know. You can't tell where a noise is coming from, or how far away it is. But surely, Henry, you can't seriously think that any of the Fleet would——"

"I don't think anything yet," said Henry. "I'm just feeling my way a little. I suppose Hamish got his uncle's money."

"Yes," said Alastair, rather grudgingly.

"Where did the money come from?"

"Inherited, I think," said Alastair. "I don't know. Never asked. But I'm damned sure it was honestly come by. If Pete had a fault, it was an exaggerated respect for law and order. He used to be in some police force—Kenya, I think—he spent a lot of his life abroad—and the one thing he wouldn't tolerate at any price was dishonesty or double-dealing."

"How long has Hamish lived down here?" Henry asked. "Only since Pete died?"

"No, no. They shared the cottage in Berrybridge. Hamish is an architect, works in Ipswich. He and Peter were extremely popular round here, right from the word go, even though they were outsiders. They just seemed to settle in right away." Alastair took a puff at his pipe, and then added, "You know, the more I think of it, the sillier it is to imagine Pete could have been murdered. It's just stupid."

"Most murders are," said Henry sombrely. "Stupid and basically simple. In fact, I think it's true to say that every murderer kills for love or money. I'm talking about the sane ones now—if anyone can be said to be entirely sane at such a moment. Often you find that the murderer has built up a great pyramid of specious reasoning in his own mind, to convince himself why his victim should die: but under it, you'll always find one thing or the other. Love or money."

Rosemary said, "Please don't talk about murder, Henry. Pete is dead, and there's nothing we can do to bring him back. Can't you forget it and leave him in peace?"

For a moment, Henry studied Rosemary's beautiful, clear-cut profile. He was both puzzled and distressed by the agony that he saw there. He lay back on the sun-warmed sand and closed his eyes.

"I'm sorry, Rosemary," he said. "I'll try. I really will try."

At one o'clock, the tide turned. The marooned sailors, perched on the edge of *Ariadne*'s sharply tilted deck like sparrows on a telephone wire, watched the water creeping back to them inch by inch, at what seemed a snail's pace by comparison with the indecent haste of its retreat earlier in the day. Soon after three, however, the first wavelets were lapping at the hull: the water grew deeper, climbed the deck rail that lay on the sand, covered it, and swilled along the sloping deck itself.

Henry said, in a voice from which he had not quite succeeded in erasing all traces of alarm. "We don't appear to be floating, Alastair."

Alastair grinned broadly. "I know just how you feel," he said. "I've been aground umpteen times, and every time, at this particular moment, I get a twinge of panic that she won't come up—that she's somehow stuck to the sand and will just lie there until the water covers her completely. But don't worry—you'll see."

Henry glanced down at the deck rail again. "She's not moving at all yet," he said.

"Watch the mast," said Alastair.

Obediently, Henry transferred his gaze to the mast, which lay over at a drunken angle, its blue and white burgee fluttering not far off the sand.

"Watch it against the trees. Can't you see it moving?"

Henry watched and, with a lightening of heart, saw that the mast was indeed moving—very slowly but steadily it was swinging more and more upright. In a surprisingly short time *Ariadne* was on her feet again, even though her keel was still held fast. Then came the moment of glory that every yachtsman knows. The boat, with a graceful, dipping gesture, shook herself clear of the paralysing grip of the sand and curvetted joyfully to the wind—for all the world like a living creature, ecstatic to be in the freedom of her own element again.

Up went the white, trembling sails. Up came the mud-caked anchor. *Ariadne* took off like a bird, skimming silently out to sea.

" 'As I was a-walking down Paradise Street,' " chanted Alastair Benson, stockbroker of the City of London, as he snugged down the anchor and wiped his muddy hands on the seat of his jeans, " 'Way-hay, blow the man down . . .' "

And " 'Give us some time to blow the man down,' " sang Henry Tibbett, Chief Inspector of the C.I.D., bracing one bare foot against a varnished thwart to get a better purchase on the jib sheet.

Rosemary, at the tiller, looked at Henry and smiled.

"Thanks for trying, Henry," she said.

"It's not tight enough yet, blast it," said Henry. " 'Way-hay'—I'll get it in if it kills me—'blow the man down' . . ."

"I didn't mean the jib sheet," said Rosemary, "I meant——"

"I know you did," said Henry. Then, lifting his voice, he added ringingly, " 'O-o-oh, give us some time to blow the man down. . . .' "

At five o'clock they turned round and ran before the wind southward down the coast, and back to Steep Hill Point. A small speck which had materialized far out to sea revealed itself on closer inspection to be the green hull and snowy sails of *Tideway*, and the two boats reached the river mouth almost simultaneously.

Both started to beat upriver against the wind, their zig-zag courses crossing and recrossing.

"Enjoy your day on Steep Hill?" called Hamish, without too much malice, as *Ariadne* passed within ten feet of *Tideway*'s bows.

"Wasn't it *awful?*" Rosemary yelled back. "All my fault."

"Get that jib sheet in tighter," said Alastair. "We can make a better course than this."

"I think we're doing beautifully as we are," said Emmy.

"No, we're not. Hamish is catching us," said Alastair shortly. And Henry and Emmy learnt another truth about the people who sail—that it only takes two boats of comparable size and speed, on the same stretch of water and heading in the same direction, to start a race. They could see that Hamish, too, was tending his sheets with extra care, and glancing anxiously up at the burgee to look for the minutest variation in wind direction.

Henry also noticed, with some amusement, that although the two boats were clearly and seriously competing with each other, this fact was never acknowledged in the conversational exchanges that took place whenever they drew close enough together.

"So David didn't come out today—didn't think he would," Alastair called to Hamish, as he edged *Ariadne* up in an effort to take *Tideway*'s wind.

"No—trust old David. When I left, he looked as though he was counting his screws again. Probably spent all day sorting them out into little boxes." Hamish moved his tiller, bearing away for a moment to get out of *Ariadne*'s lee, and then put his nose up and skimmed off across the river.

At the next encounter—by which time *Tideway* had gained a yard or so, to Alastair's chagrin—Hamish said, "See you all in the Bush later on, I dare say." To which Alastair replied, "Yes, but come on board for a snort first."

"Thanks, I will."

Hamish put *Tideway* about, and sped off towards the far bank of the river.

The two boats battled their way up the broad, quiet stream in a light, summer-evening breeze that threatened every moment to grow lighter still and die on their hands, so that the last yards to the moorings were a matter of drifting rather than of sailing.

To a spectator on the quayside, Henry reflected, the scene must present an appearance of utter tranquillity—the idyllic evening of pink and gold in the sky and on the water, the two swanlike sailing boats drifting dreamily back to harbour. In fact, the atmosphere on board *Ariadne* was anything but tranquil. Alastair and Hamish, both accomplished helmsmen, were trying every trick they knew with sails, sheets and tiller—each working desperately to turn the drifting match to his own advantage. At last, slowly as a falling leaf, *Ariadne* nosed her way past the red buoy which marked the start of the line of moorings—some six feet ahead of *Tideway.* Alastair and Rosemary looked at each other and smiled happily, and Rosemary said, "Well done, darling." On *Tideway,* Hamish removed his yachting cap with a flourish and bowed in acknowledgment of defeat.

"Goodness, that was exciting," said Emmy. "I'm so glad we won. Do you race a lot?"

Alastair looked at her in surprise. "Race?" he said. "Good heavens, no. Never. We don't enjoy it."

FOUR

Ten minutes after *Ariadne* had tied up at her mooring, when the crew were sitting down gratefully to mugs of tea and hunks of bread and honey, there was the unmistakable bumping of a dinghy alongside, and David's voice called, "Anybody at home?"

"Come aboard," said Alastair, peering out through the hatchway.

A moment later, David Crowther came into the cabin. "I just wondered," he said diffidently, "if you could lend me some whipping. I seem to have run out."

Rosemary looked at Alastair and grinned. "What did I say?" she remarked. "Sorry, David, dear—you're out of luck. We haven't any. But have a cuppa while you're here."

"Thanks."

David lowered his six feet of lanky body onto a bunk and said, "Had a good day?"

"No, dreadful," said Rosemary quickly. "I put *Ariadne* on the mud. Please don't let's talk about it. What have you been up to?"

"Oh, nothing much. This and that. Sorting things out below and reeving some new rigging. Didn't think there was enough of a breeze for a decent sail." David took a gulp of tea and glanced at his watch. "Colin and Anne should be here soon. Perhaps they'll have some whipping."

"Have you tried Hamish?" Alastair asked. "He's in—we came up the river together."

"No," said David, shortly. He contemplated the interior of his tea mug in silence.

Henry watched him with interest. Last night, in the smoky, badly lit bar of The Berry Bush, he had put David Crowther down as an engaging, carefree young man—the sort of character whom one associates with old motor cars and decrepit boats and cheerful, badly channelled enthusiasms. Now he saw that the thin, attractive face was finely lined, that the sun-bleached hair had traces of grey in it—and he decided that David was nearer forty than thirty. He also remarked that the long, sensitive hands were restless and nervy, and trembled slightly as David lit a cigarette. The tiny cabin seemed alive with vibrant and unstable energy.

David looked up, met Emmy's clear, direct gaze, and looked away again quickly, as he said, "Not a very pleasant introduction to sailing for you people, a day on the mud."

"I enjoyed it," Emmy said stoutly.

"The perfect crew," remarked Alastair. "Six hours on Steep Hill, and not a word of complaint from either of them. In fact——"

"Steep Hill," said David. "Yes. Well, I think I'll be off now. I thought I heard . . . Thanks for the tea, Rosemary. See you later." And, abruptly, he was gone.

"Dear David," said Rosemary. "I don't know why he keeps a boat. There's always either too much wind or too little. It's the hardest thing in the world to induce him to leave his moorings."

"He's perfectly happy," said Alastair. "He loves just sitting there by himself sorting out his little boxes. You should see *Pocahontas*," he added to Henry. "David's a bit of an old woman in some ways. One box for inch screws. Another for shackles. Another for bits of string. All neatly labelled. The funny thing is that he never seems to have what he needs when it comes to doing a job."

"Don't be catty, Alastair," said Rosemary.

"What does David do for a living?" Henry asked.

"He's an artist, believe it or not," Alastair replied. "Has a studio in Islington. Commercial stuff, mainly, but he does serious painting on the side. I believe he even sells some of his things."

"He seems rather a restless sort of character," said Emmy. "Not tranquil, like you two."

"David was a fighter pilot in the war," said Rosemary. "He got badly shot up. It's left him a bit . . . well, a bit untranquil, as you said."

"Earlier on," said Henry, "Alastair referred to him as 'good old reliable David.' I was expecting something rather different from that description."

"Were you?" Rosemary opened her blue eyes wide. "I wonder why. David's a tower of strength."

"But not tranquil."

"Goodness, no. But the two things don't necessarily go together, do they? David's kind and straightforward and tremendously loyal. The sort of person you could turn to at any time for help or moral support or just a shoulder to cry on. He'd do anything for a friend—and no questions asked."

"That's a remarkable tribute," said Henry. "You must be very fond of him."

To his surprise, Rosemary blushed very slightly. "I am," she said.

The tea mugs had only just been washed up when Hamish arrived. Alastair produced a bottle of whisky from under one of the bunks.

"I like the way *Ariadne* behaves with that new jib," Hamish remarked, as he tried vainly to find room for his long legs. The cabin seemed very full with Hamish in it.

"Yes, we're delighted with it," said Alastair.

"When I get my new boat," said Hamish, "I want a proper complement of sails. Storm jib, beating jib, a Genoa for reaching and a spinnaker. I'm fed up with this one-main-two-jib setup on *Tideway*." There was a strong undercurrent of excitement in his voice.

"Why ever do you want a new boat?" Emmy asked. "*Tideway* looks lovely to me."

"Not big enough," said Hamish. "I want to do some real cruising—Holland, France, Spain, the Med. Perhaps even the Canaries and the West Indies. I've been coast-hopping long enough."

Rosemary smiled indulgently. "Don't listen to him," she

said. "Hamish has been talking about this mythical new boat ever since we've known him. Personally, I'm prepared to take a small bet that he'll still be sailing *Tideway* in and out of the Berry in ten years' time."

"Then you'll lose your money," said Hamish. The excitement had reached boiling point. "Look at these."

He pulled a large envelope out of his pocket, and spread its contents out on the table.

"What on earth have you got there?" demanded Alastair.

"Plans," said Hamish.

Alastair and Rosemary craned to look, immensely interested. Over their shoulders, Henry glimpsed the graceful skeleton of a yacht design. Alastair drew his breath in sharply.

"By Giles," he said. "I say, you are going it. What is she? Doesn't look like one of his regular designs."

"She's not," said Hamish. "He's done her specially for me. A ten-ton ketch for extensive off-shore cruising."

There was a small, awkward silence, and then Rosemary said bluntly, "Hamish, you must be mad. Have you any idea how much this is going to cost?"

Hamish lit his pipe with a certain bravado. "Yes," he said. "I suppose I am mad. But this is something I've wanted all my life. The only thing I've ever really wanted. If I choose to behave like a lunatic with my own money, surely that's my business."

"Yes, but—" Rosemary began, and then stopped, embarrassed.

As if reading her thoughts, Hamish said, "Pete would have approved. He knew how much I'd set my heart on it. In fact, he as good as promised me the money before——"

"Of course Pete would have loved her." Alastair's voice was just a fraction too loud and too cheerful. "She's a beauty, Hamish. Let's see. You don't think the turn of the bilges is a bit too steep? I know she'll draw six-foot-six, but . . ."

In a moment, Hamish and Alastair were deeply involved in a technical discussion of the proposed boat. A

long time later, when Alastair had practically redesigned
the hull and sail-plan, using the stub of a pencil and the
back of an old envelope, Rosemary interrupted them to
say, "Look here, you two. It's after seven. Colin and Anne
will have been in the Bush for hours. Put it away, like good
boys, and let's go ashore."

Reluctantly, the precious drawings were returned to their
envelope, and the two dinghies skidded their way over
the quiet water to the shore.

The tide was at its highest. Indeed, the water was
lapping right up against the wall of The Berry Bush, and
Alastair remarked, unoriginally, that this was one of the
few places where one really could tie up snug to a pub.

The bar was almost empty. The locals were at home,
having supper. Most of the yachtsmen who based their
boats on Berrybridge had taken advantage of the good
weather to make a cruise to some other harbour.

Colin and Anne were at the bar, talking to David. In
the mêlée of greetings and introductions, Henry took a
good look at Anne Petrie—and understood at once why
Colin Street wanted to marry her, and why Pete Rawnsley
had attempted to add her to his list of conquests. She
was a tiny slip of a girl: indeed, with her cropped dark
hair and faded blue jeans, she might almost have been
taken for a schoolboy, were it not for a certain very definite
femininity of contour that even a sweater several sizes too
large could not hide. She was as brown as honey, and
her green eyes—which slanted upwards as delicately as a
cat's—sparkled with high spirits and a zest for life which
was immensely attractive. She had, Henry decided, the
miniature perfection of a Japanese girl, without the latter's
doll-like fragility. In fact, even as he admired, the thought
crossed his mind, This girl's like a nut—smooth and brown
and sweet and hard.

"And so I said to Colin"—Anne was chattering away
as merrily as a chipmunk, in a delicious, slightly husky
voice—"'It's monstrous,' I said, 'and if you won't tell
Herbert what you think of him, I jolly well will.' You
know how hopeless Colin is. So anyway, the moment we
arrived this evening, I collared Herbert and I told him

just what I thought of him. I mean, I ask you—water over the floor boards. I swear he hasn't been near her all the week. 'If you're not very careful, Herbert,' I said, 'we'll hand the boat over to Bill Hawkes, and see how you like that.' "

"What did Herbert say?" Rosemary asked.

"He said 'Hay?' " Anne cupped a hand to her ear, in a wickedly accurate imitation of the Harbour Master of Berrybridge Haven. "So I said, 'It's no good pretending you can't hear, Herbert, you old rogue. You're no more deaf than I am—especially when somebody's offering you a drink.' And do you know what he did then?" Anne paused, to give the denouement its full effect. "He slapped my bottom!"

"He didn't!" Alastair gave a great roar of laughter, in which everybody joined, with the exception of Colin.

"Herbert adores Anne," Rosemary said to Emmy. "She's the only person who stands up to him and says exactly what she thinks. I wouldn't dare."

"So if the boat's not pumped dry next weekend—just watch out. There'll be trouble," said Anne darkly. But her eyes were laughing over the rim of the pint mug.

In contrast to Anne's vivacity, Colin was silent and grave. He looked the picture of a young intellectual, with his pale face and untidy brown hair. His features were pleasant enough, and there was a lively intelligence in his dark eyes. Only in his hands and his jawline—both of which were strong and square—was there a hint of stubbornness and power. He seemed torn between pride in Anne's animation and a certain disapproval of those very qualities which he obviously found so attractive.

"Get on with your drink," he said, not unkindly. "You're talking too much."

"I always do. I can't help it." Anne turned her kitten eyes to Henry. "I hear you had a dreadful day on the mud. Steep Hill, of all places. I'm sure it's haunted."

"Don't talk nonsense, Anne!" Colin's voice was brusque and angry.

"No, but really," Anne went on, quite unperturbed, "when we were coming into the river in the dark last Sunday night, we passed the very spot where—where it happened—and I swear I heard something. I swear it."

"What did you hear?" Henry asked, intrigued.

"I don't know." Anne wrinkled her nose. "Just a sort of something. And I said——"

"Shut up, Anne," said Hamish suddenly. To Henry's surprise, Anne shut up. She buried her nose in her tankard and looked abashed. David glared at Hamish, but the latter had already started talking to Alastair about the new boat, and apparently did not notice.

A few minutes later, Anne said gravely to Henry, "You never knew Pete, did you?"

"No," said Henry.

"I loved him," said Anne. Colin's face darkened with sudden anger, and he slammed his glass just too forcibly onto the table. Anne added quickly, "Now don't start bristling like an old bear, darling. You know what I mean. I just loved him in a friendly way, as darling David loves me."

David said nothing, but turned away to the bar and ordered another drink. When David picked up his beer tankard, Henry saw that his hands were trembling again.

The hands of the big white-faced clock on the wall crept towards eight o'clock, and The Berry Bush began to fill up. Herbert arrived in garrulous mood.

"Fine tickin' off I had from your young lady," he remarked to Colin, winking incessantly. "Proper little spitfire. I wouldn't be in your shoes, I can tell you."

"I must say, we were both very upset to find *Mary Jane* in such a state, Herbert," said Colin pompously. "I know you have a lot to do, but——"

"Leaks like a bloody sieve," said Herbert, promptly and defiantly. "Pumped 'er every day. I can't help it if she's rotten. You want your garboards recaulking, that's what you want." He managed to make it sound like an unmentionable insult.

Colin flushed angrily. "I don't need any advice from you on how to look after my boat," he said.

"Some people . . ." remarked Herbert ominously, to the bar in general. He turned his back rudely on Colin, and went over to inflict himself on Hamish and Alastair. Anne, Colin and David drifted over to the bar and began a lively conversation with a venerable, grey-bearded fisherman whom Henry had heard alluded to as Old Ephraim.

"Poor Colin," said Rosemary. "He's so nice really, but he does put people's backs up. Anne can tear a strip six feet wide off Herbert, and he just adores her all the more. But Colin only has to remonstrate mildly, and——"

"I know," said Henry. "Anne has the very rare gift of being able to speak her mind without offending anybody."

"I don't know either of them, of course," said Emmy, "but—well, they seem rather an oddly assorted couple to me. Do you think they'll be happy?"

Henry glanced crossly at Emmy. It always annoyed him deeply when his wife made what he considered to be a typically female, platitudinous and prying remark such as this. In his masculine estimation, she was letting herself down by conforming to the conventions of her own sex. Rosemary, however, pondered the question gravely.

"I wish I knew," she said. "We've often wondered ourselves. But of course, it's entirely their business. They keep on having the most monumental fights, and every time we expect to hear that the whole thing is off. But a couple of days later they're together again. I suspect that it's always Colin who climbs down and apologizes."

"What does Colin do?" Henry asked.

"He's a barrister," said Rosemary, "and absolutely brilliant, by all accounts. Of course, he's young yet, but everybody is convinced he's going right to the top. Sir Colin Street, Q.C., without a doubt. I sometimes wonder if that's why Anne—" She stopped. "I'm sorry. I'm being bitchy. I don't really mean that at all."

The bar door swung open, and the burly figure of Sir Simon Trigg-Willoughby came in. He greeted Rosemary warmly.

"Nice to see you, Mrs. Benson," he boomed. "Pity you don't spend more time down here. Priscilla was saying only the other day that we never see you up at the Hall."

Rosemary introduced Henry and Emmy, and then said, "It's so difficult when we're only here for weekends, Sir

Simon. But this time we're on holiday—two whole weeks. So we'd love to come and see you while we're here."

"You do that, Mrs. Benson. Priscilla will be delighted. She doesn't get out much, y'know. Does her good to see some young faces about the place. Come whenever you like, and bring these good people with you. Any time. Any time at all."

"It's very kind of you," said Rosemary.

"Nonsense. A great pleasure. Of course," added Sir Simon, with a smile, "I know you sailing folk. Never waste a good day ashore. We'll expect you the first time it rains. You'll have to come when the sun's shining, though, if you want to see the way the west terrace has been repaired. A beautiful job. And the Adam room is completely restored now. Only got rid of the workmen last week."

"Oh, yes—I'm longing to see that." Rosemary turned to Henry and Emmy. "The Adam room is marvellous—one of the finest in England. Sir Simon's just had a lot of work done on it."

"Well, Mrs. Benson, the invitation's open. Come soon."

Sir Simon made his way over to the bar, obviously not ill-pleased by the gratifying number of raised caps and tugged forelocks that accompanied his progress. Emmy and Rosemary became engrossed in a discussion on eighteenth-century architecture. Anne was talking to Herbert and Old Ephraim—a process which evoked much cackling and thumping of mugs on the table from the two old men. Colin had joined Hamish and Alastair, and the plans were out of their envelope again. Henry spotted David Crowther sitting by himself on one of the high-backed wooden settles, and made his way over.

"This new boat of Hamish's seems to be causing quite a stir," he remarked as he sat down. "Alastair seems very critical of it."

David looked up and said, "It's Hamish's business what he does with his own money."

"Of course it is," said Henry, embarrassed at being misunderstood. "And I'm sure that his uncle——"

"What does it matter now what Pete would have said?" said David. "He's dead, isn't he?"

"He must have been a remarkable character, by all accounts," said Henry. "I wish I'd known him."

"Pete was a strange mixture," said David. He spoke quietly, as if to himself. "So bloody high-minded in some ways and absolutely unprincipled in others. It's all very well to talk about responsibility to the community, but——" He looked straight at Henry. "Which do you think is the worse sin?" he demanded. "To run a harmless racket just a shade outside the law, or to play fast and loose with the life of another human being?"

Henry considered. "It depends how harmless the racket is," he said at length.

"Absolutely harmless," said David without hesitation. "Just making a few bob on the side. That was a deadly sin to Pete. The authorities must be informed. No chance of an appeal. And yet, when it came to his private life . . ." There was a pause, and then he added, "I'm afraid I didn't have much time for Pete Rawnsley. I think there's such a thing as loyalty."

Feeling his way carefully, Henry said, "He must have been very fond of Hamish."

"Hamish." David brooded for a moment. "Yes, I suppose he was, in his own way. Tried to drum a sense of proportion into him. If Pete had been alive, Hamish wouldn't have had this new boat, I can tell you."

"Well, I suppose he's only able to afford it now that he's inherited——"

"Even if he'd had the money." David lit a cigarette. "You know what he plans to do, don't you? Throw up his job—everything. Take his boat round the world, picking up a bit here and there by chartering and odd jobs. He wouldn't have dared to do that if Pete had been alive. Pete was the only person Hamish was afraid of." He paused, and then went on, "I'm not saying I approve of what Hamish is doing. I think he's a bloody fool. But I'll defend to my last breath his right to do it if he wants to."

"I didn't realize," said Henry, "that sailing could get such a hold on people."

David smiled, a secret smile. "It's a disease," he said. "Usually fatal. I haven't caught it myself. I love my boat—

she's an escape, a safety valve. And there's so much beauty. . . . I don't do very much sailing, actually. I suppose they told you that. I'm quite content to sit in harbour, and potter about the boat and be alone. Hamish and Alastair are only really happy if they're soaked to the skin in the middle of the North Sea with a gale blowing and the lee rail awash. That's not my idea of fun."

"You said today," said Henry, gently, "that there wasn't enough wind for your liking."

David looked at him, and smiled ruefully. "One plays the game according to the rules," he said. "I suppose they all see through me. I don't much care."

"David, darling, are you going to buy me a beer?" Anne's husky voice broke the silence that had fallen, and David jumped up.

"Of course," he said. "Of course. Sit down. Bitter?"

"Please." Anne sat down astride the bench on the other side of the table, and smiled ravishingly. "A pint, David. None of your mingy halves."

"I don't know where you put it," said David. "A pint for you, Henry?"

"Half will do me, thanks."

David departed to the bar, and Anne said, "Coward." Her green eyes glistened across the table at Henry. "You can't come into our pub and drink halves."

"I drink what I like," said Henry, good-humouredly. "I'm quite old enough to make up my own mind on such matters, worse luck."

Anne eyed him appraisingly. "Yes, you are older than most of us," she said. "Almost as old as Pete."

"How old was he?"

"Fifty-one," said Anne promptly.

"And you loved him?" asked Henry gravely.

Anne wrinkled her nose. "Yes, I did. In a funny way. I've never met anyone else quite like him. He was such an exciting man. And so wise."

"Just as a matter of interest," said Henry, "how old are you?"

"I'm twenty-three."

"So Pete was more than old enough to be your father."

Anne sat up very straight, her small mouth hardened into an angry line. "For heaven's sake, don't you start," she said. "I'm sick and tired of hearing people say that— especially Colin. Well, he's had his revenge. Pete's dead. I hope he's happy."

"You don't mean that Colin . . . ?"

All the anger had gone out of Anne's face, and she looked like a small, bewildered child. "I don't know what I mean," she said quietly. "It's just something I feel. Like the feeling that Steep Hill is haunted." She was silent for a moment, her dark head bent. Then she looked up and smiled at Henry. "Don't pay any attention to me," she said. "I've had too much beer. It always makes me talk nonsense."

"Anne," said Henry very seriously, "forgive me for asking you this—but it interests me very much. Besides yourself, who else really liked Pete Rawnsley? It's obvious that Colin hated him, and David doesn't seem——"

Before Henry could finish, Anne burst out, "Nobody! Nobody at all! Except Hamish, of course. But all the others—they pretended to like him, but they loathed him!"

"Why?"

For a moment Anne didn't answer. When she did, it was in an entirely different voice—a voice of deliberate seduction. "They were jealous," she said.

"Jealous of what?"

Anne gave him a slow look from her slanting green eyes.

"Guess," she said.

Then David came back with the beer, and Anne began to recount the gist of her recent conversation with Herbert, which seemed to centre round the latter's chances of being elected Mayor of Berrybridge Haven when the unofficial voting took place the following week.

"Herbert's a three to one chance," Anne confided, "according to Sam Riddle, who's making the book. Bill Hawkes is fancied in some quarters, but the more conservative element say he's too young and hasn't lived in the borough long enough. He's four to one. Old Ephraim, the sitting mayor, is odds-on favourite for re-election, but Herbert says to his face that he's too old to know a chain from a cocked hat. I mean a mayoral chain, of course," she added demurely. "Herbert's also accusing Bill Hawkes of bribing the electorate and providing an illicit bicycle to convey voters to the polls. But that's only to be expected. And talking of illegal transport—the gossip is that if Mrs. Hole's feet are too bad, Herbert intends to trundle her down to the booths in a wheelbarrow. He can't afford to lose a vote—not with four candidates and a voting population of forty-seven."

"Who's the fourth candidate?" Henry asked.

"Sam Riddle," said Anne. "The big fisherman over there. Father of George Riddle, who works at the hall. He's not much fancied. He's giving six to one against himself."

"What a pity we can't vote," said Henry.

"I'm just as glad," David remarked. "I couldn't stand Herbert's canvassing. Anyway, we're all invited to the inauguration ceremony next weekend, so we get the best of both worlds."

"What happens?" Henry asked.

"Beer is drunk," said David, "in unbelievable quantities, both before and after a rather splendid cold collation donated by Bob, the landlord. The newly elected mayor is robed and invested by Sir Simon, and they both make speeches. Then we all sing the Berrybridge anthem. Then more beer is drunk. By about ten o'clock, the mayor is generally unrobed again, and most of the aldermen are under the table. Those who can still stand are all making speeches. It's all very foolish and great fun. There's seldom any fighting, and not more than three or four civic dignitaries are sick. A charming piece of old English forklore."

"How long has this tradition been going on?" Henry asked.

"Its origins," Anne replied solemnly, "are lost in the mists of time. About six years, actually, but don't tell anybody. The landlord who had The Berry Bush before Bob heard about the election of the Mayor of Pin Mill,

and decided to imitate it. Of course, Pin Mill is quite
different. Much more dignified and ancient. Anyhow,
Bob has kept it on here to boost the sale of bitter."

"Which is Bob?" Henry asked, surveying the three or
four figures who scurried busily on the far side of the bar.

"He's away for the weekend," said David. "You'll meet
him when he comes back tomorrow. He's quite a character."

"You seem to go in for characters in this part of the
world."

"All part of the show," said Anne pertly. "Give the customers what they want. It's amazing how a few local
eccentrics can stimulate trade in the public bar."

"You're a horrible little cynic," said David, fondly. Anne
rewarded him with a sidelong grin. "I don't hold much
brief for Herbert," David went on, "but I do believe he's
genuine."

"Oh, Herbert's a genuine character all right," said Anne.
"But not quite in the way that people think."

David looked at her sharply, but said nothing.

"If you knew what I know about Herbert," added
Anne, "you'd be amazed." She gave Henry a provocative
look.

"Go on, then," said Henry obediently. "Tell us. What
do you know?"

"It's a secret," Anne said virtuously. "I can't possibly
tell you."

"You're dying to tell me," said Henry. "You may as
well get it over."

Anne grinned, like a street urchin. "O.K.," she said.
"Well, the fact is that Herbert——"

"Anne," said David suddenly, "you've got a smut on
your nose."

"I haven't."

"Yes, you have. Take a look."

Anne pulled a tiny powder compact out of her pocket,
and studied her face with loving care.

"You liar," she said, at length. "I haven't." All the
same, she began to dab at her nose energetically with a
small pink puff.

David turned to Henry and demanded a full account of the day's misfortunes on Steep Hill Sands. The secret life of Herbert Hole was forgotten. Henry made a mental note to return to the subject at a more propitious moment. Meanwhile he gave himself up to the undeniable pleasure of relating his experiences to an enthralled audience, and to the stimulus of Anne's company.

At nine o'clock, Rosemary announced that whatever the rest of the party might want to do, she personally was going back to the boat for supper. So they all went.

In a ridiculously short time, a delicious meal emerged, steaming, from the galley. While Emmy and Rosemary washed up, Alastair and Henry smoked a last cigarette in the cockpit under the clear night sky.

Henry said, "Anne's a fascinating girl."

Alastair did not take his eyes off the particular star which he was studying. "Do you think so?" he said.

"Don't you?"

There was a silence, and then, softly, Alastair quoted,

> "Dorinda's sparkling wit and eyes
> United cast too fierce a light,
> Which blazes high, but quickly dies,
> Pains not the heart, but burns the sight.
>
> Love is a calmer, gentler joy,
> Smooth are his looks, and soft his pace.
> Her Cupid is a blackguard boy,
> That runs his link full in your face."

There was a moment of absolute silence under the stars. Then Alastair smiled shyly. "Learned it at school," he said, almost apologetically. "I've always remembered it. It reminds me of Anne."

Henry looked steadily at Alastair's thin, handsome profile. He heard Rosemary's soft laughter from the cabin, and vividly, he remembered the expression in Anne's slanting green eyes as she said the one word—"Guess."

I wonder, thought Henry. I wonder very much.

FIVE

The next day it rained. Unaccountably, from nowhere, black clouds had massed over the horizon in the small hours of the morning, and *Ariadne*'s crew woke to the dismal sound of rain pattering on the cabin-top, interspersed by spasmodic swearing from Alastair, who had found out—by the only known method of discovering such things—that there was a small leak in the deck immediately above his left ear. Otherwise, however, the boat was warm and dry, and breakfast a cheerful enough meal.

When it was over, Alastair put his head out into the dripping cockpit, and said, "Hamish is going out. He's getting his sails on."

"Well, don't let it give you ideas," said Rosemary, "because we're staying exactly where we are."

"It's going to be pretty dreary, sitting in here all day," said Alastair wistfully. "After all, we've got oilskins. And there's a nice breeze."

"I can hear it," said Rosemary, with a shudder. Then she added, "If you want to go, darling, why don't you join Hamish? I'm sure he'd be glad of company."

"Are you sure you don't mind?" Alastair was like a boy out of school. "It really is a marvellous day."

"I don't mind anything so long as I don't have to come with you," said Rosemary. "Come on, I'll row you over. And for heaven's sake take care of yourselves."

She and Alastair embarked in the dinghy, arrayed in copious yellow oilskins and sou'wester hats, while Henry and Emmy washed up. As she washed the mugs, Emmy said, tentatively, "Henry, do you really think that man was murdered?"

"Yes," said Henry, "I'm pretty sure of it." And then he said, "I wish I didn't."

"Can't you forget it, darling?" Emmy's voice was really worried. "I mean—these people are friends. It would be so terrible if . . ." She trailed off into unhappy silence.

Henry looked at her seriously. "I have to know," he said. "I'm sorry, but I have to. Trust me to be as tactful as I can."

"Oh dear," said Emmy. Then she smiled at him.

Henry kissed her across the washing-up bowl. "I don't like it any more than you do," he said. "You know that, don't you?"

"Yes, darling," said Emmy.

When Rosemary came back, she looked upset, and there was a thin edge of bitterness in her voice as she said, "Well, I hope the three of them enjoy themselves."

"The three of them?" Emmy said. "I thought——"

"That little fool Anne has gone with them," said Rosemary, shortly. "She'll only be in the way."

"What about Colin?" Henry asked.

"He and David are spending the day on *Mary Jane,* doing odd jobs," said Rosemary. "They've got a bit more sense."

There was a short pause, and then Emmy said, "I don't suppose we could take Sir Simon at his word, could we? I mean, about going over to Berry Hall. I'm just longing to see that house."

Rosemary brightened at once. "What a splendid idea," she said. "We'll go ashore, and ring him from The Berry Bush. I'm sure he'll be delighted."

The trip to the quayside was damply unpleasant. The dinghy butted and rolled dangerously as the driving wind whipped up the grey river into sizable waves. It was with a distinct sensation of relief that they felt their feet on dry land—if such a term can be used to describe the wet, slippery hard.

Rosemary went off to telephone, and came back a few minutes later with the news that Sir Simon would be only too pleased to see them, and insisted that they should lunch at Berry Hall.

Driving through the sodden, dripping lanes, Rosemary said, "I'd better warn you about Priscilla."

"What about her?" asked Henry.

"Well, she's very sweet really, but a bit bats. They both are, in a way, but it's more obvious in her case."

"Sir Simon struck me as being very much all there," said Emmy.

"Oh, I don't mean they're actually crazy," Rosemary amended, hastily. "It's just this fetish they've got about the family. It takes them in different ways. With Sir Simon, it's the house. With Priscilla, it's the family jewels. That's what's really the matter with her. I believe she went almost out of her mind after the robbery and she's still distinctly odd. It's better to keep off the subject if you can, but it's not easy."

"They were insured, weren't they?" said Henry.

"Oh, yes, but it's not jewellery as such that she cares about. Just The Jewels. I don't believe she's attempted to replace them. She's convinced the originals will turn up sooner or later. Some hope. . . . I suppose they're all broken up and sold by now, aren't they?"

"You never can tell," said Henry. "Professional thieves are sometimes prepared to hide the stuff for years until the hue and cry dies down. What were the jewels worth, do you know?"

"Oh, thousands," said Rosemary vaguely. "There were some famous pieces amongst them—the tiara in particular. They should have been kept in the bank, but Priscilla . . . ah, here we are."

The station wagon turned right, and passed between a magnificent pair of wrought-iron gates flanked by stone lions. Ahead, a gravelled drive wound upwards between green fields and dripping trees.

"I'm sorry you're seeing it on such a bad day," said Rosemary. "The view of the house from here is rather spectacular."

The car swung round a right-handed corner, and they saw Berry Hall—through a fine mist of rain, but still in undeniable glory. Slender, pale grey columns paced out a stately, motionless pavane across the terrace, from which a flight of shallow steps led down to a sweep of lawns. Above, a Palladian pediment reared in geometric perfection. For a great country house, Berry Hall was not large: but it had a perfectly proportioned quality of elegance and lightness that gave it the air of a filigree crown set on the head of the green hill.

"It's beautiful," murmured Emmy, reverently.

Sir Simon greeted them warmly, and insisted on taking them for an immediate tour of the house, with special emphasis on the newly restored portions. They saw the famous Adam Room, with its two magnificent fireplaces and delicately intricate ceiling: they admired the colonnade, the orangery and the mirrored ballroom. Sir Simon, delighted to find that Emmy shared his passion for neo-classical architecture, was an enthusiastic and enthralling guide.

The tour ended in the Blue Drawing Room—a large and exquisitely proportioned room whose long windows looked out over a vista of grass and trees to the open water of the North Sea. As they came in, a small, stout woman jumped up from one of the big armchairs by the fire, as disconcertingly as a jack-in-the-box. Her grey hair was grotesquely crimped into a mass of tight curls on her forehead, and an untidy snowdrift of very white powder gave a clownlike quality to her soft, plump face. She wore a shapeless brown tweed skirt, and a mauve jumper knitted out of a limp, silky thread. At her throat, a crumpled yellow silk scarf was held in place by a superb diamond brooch, shaped like a rose.

"My sister Priscilla," said Sir Simon, without enthusiasm. "Mr. and Mrs. Tibbett. Mrs. Benson you know."

"Oh, *yes*." Priscilla's stubby hands fluttered in greeting. "Dear Mrs. Benson. So kind of you to come. Nobody ever comes to see us these days, you know. Nobody. I keep telling Simon——"

"A glass of sherry, Mrs. Tibbett?" said Sir Simon loudly. Henry and Emmy expressed their willingness to take a drink.

"Of course," Priscilla went on, mournfully, "I suppose

we are very dull. Very dull indeed, for young people like you. In the old days, we used to have so many visitors. People used to come quite a long way, just to see my beautiful jewels. But since . . . since . . ."

"Prissy," said Sir Simon sharply. Priscilla's inane, tragic face seemed to be on the verge of breaking up into a clumsy pattern of weeping, but she pulled herself together, and said, "I'm sorry. I brood too much, that's what it is. That's what Simon tells me. One has a duty to be happy, don't you think?" She added, inconsequentially, to Emmy, "A duty. One owes it to other people."

Sir Simon, who had been busying himself with decanter and glasses, saved Emmy from the embarrassment of replying by handing round drinks. The sherry was sweet and not very good. Henry noticed that Sir Simon did not offer a glass to his sister. While the others drank, she sat, quiet and watchful, in her big armchair, nervously clasping and unclasping her hands, and glancing from face to face as though trying to follow a conversation in a foreign language.

"You must take a good look at this view," Sir Simon was saying. "Best in the house, to my way of thinking. Pity about the rain."

He shepherded Emmy and Rosemary over to the window. Henry rose to follow them, but Priscilla stopped him. With a glance at her brother's retreating back, she laid a hand on Henry's arm, and said, with curious urgency, "It's so kind of you to come here, Mr. Babbitt."

"It's a very great pleasure," said Henry staunchly.

"Tide's on the way out now." Sir Simon's voice was fruity and authoritative. "You can see the creek, and Steep Hill Sands, just down there."

"Do you ever," Priscilla asked, earnestly, "*imagine* things, Mr. Hackett?"

"Frequently," said Henry, hoping that his desire to join the group at the window was not too obvious. "It's one of my principal amusements."

"Amusements?" Priscilla sounded bewildered. "Oh, I wouldn't ever call it an amusement. It's just that things hap-

pen and you know they've happened and then they haven't."
She paused, and then added, "It's a wonderful thing, imagination, isn't it?"

"Fascinating," Henry agreed. He could hear that Sir
Simon had broached the subject of Pete Rawnsley, and it
was agonizing not to be able to catch all that was said. Dis-
jointed phrases drifted across the room. "Terrible tragedy
. . . my greatest friend . . . if only I'd been here . . ."

"I see you're admiring my brooch, Mr. Hibbert." Priscilla
simpered at Henry with a sort of monstrous coyness. Reluctantly, he wrenched his attention from Sir Simon's conversation.

"All that remains of my lovely, lovely jewellery. The
only piece. It was away being repaired that night. That
terrible night. I lock it up in the safe every evening, you
know."

"Very wise of you."

". . . had to go into Ipswich to see my solicitor . . .
there all morning . . . and then of course the fog . . . but
Riddle tells me that Herbert . . ."

"I always lock my jewelry up," said Priscilla, virtuously.
"Always. Papa insisted upon it. And he was right. Dear
Papa was always right. And so thoughtful."

"I'm sure he was."

"That's why it's so unfair, what people say." There was
a distinct tremble of tears in Priscilla's voice. "So terribly
unfair. But what can you do, if it's imagination? Nobody
knows the things I imagine. It's so hard to talk to people.
Of course, dear Simon was wonderfully helpful. He said
everything was all right, and I wasn't to worry. But it
wasn't all right, you see. He was just trying to comfort me.
Now Mr. Rawnsley——"

The name caught Henry's wandering attention. "Pete
Rawnsley was a friend of yours, was he?" he asked with
interest.

Priscilla gave him a reproachful look. "Oh, dear me, no,"
she said. "Mr. Hamish Rawnsley. Such a charming young
man. He comes here sometimes, and talks to me . . . that is,
he used to, before . . . a really delightful young man. So

unlike many of the modern generation. Full of enterprise. Dear Papa always said a man should have enterprise."

". . . and my great-grandfather himself designed the Folly . . . you can just see it, over there in the trees . . ." Sir Simon boomed cheerfully on, and Henry realized dismally that the subject of Pete Rawnsley had come and gone, and he wondered if he would ever find a suitable opportunity of introducing it again later on. Simultaneously with his exasperation, Henry was aware of a distinct feeling of guilt. Alastair, Rosemary, even Emmy—they had all begged him to forget the whole affair. The coroner's verdict had been perfectly straightforward. And yet . . . there were inconsistencies. Pick up a loose thread of circumstance, follow it through the labyrinth of events—and where would it lead? Perhaps to havoc and misery in the lives of a pleasant group of people. Better to leave it alone. If you can. If you can . . .

"Luncheon," announced a pontifical voice, "is served."

Henry jerked himself back to reality, and turned, expecting to see a vast and ponderous butler in the old tradition. Instead, the owner of the voice turned out to be an excessively thin and lugubrious young man in a white jacket, who went on to add, in a marked Suffolk accent, "And the 'ot plate's fused again."

"Oh, *dear*, Riddle—not again. It's not fair," Priscilla said, in a tremulous voice. "Every time we have guests, it happens. And then they don't come again. Of course they don't. Why should they?"

Sir Simon walked over to his sister, and put an arm round her shoulders. "Now, now, Prissy," he said, kindly, "it's not as bad as all that. Smile and sing under all difficulties, eh?"

"I do try, Simon," said Priscilla, with the suspicion of a quaver, "but it's very hard. Ever since——"

"That's enough of that, now. Come along and have some food."

After an ample but indifferent lunch, served by the mournful Riddle, Priscilla announced her intention of lying down, and disappeared upstairs. Ensconced comfortably in the Blue Drawing Room once more, Sir Simon said, "You must forgive my sister. It's this wretched robbery, I'm afraid. She took it very badly. Blames herself, that's the trouble. And the hard fact is that it was her fault. No getting away from it."

"What actually happened?" Henry asked.

Sir Simon took a long pull on his pipe. "It was the night of the local Hunt Ball," he said. "Over at Rooting Manor. Priscilla insisted on getting all her jewellery out of the safe, and wearing most of it. Ridiculous, of course, but it gave her great pleasure to do so. When we got home, Priscilla was . . . was very tired and overexcited, and she forgot to put the stuff back in the safe. Left it in her dressing room, with a window open at that. Everybody in the district knew she'd been wearing the beastly things—tiara, necklace, bracelets, the lot. Next morning, what do we find? Ladder pinched from the potting-shed and left in the shrubbery. Marks of it in the flower-bed under the dressing-room window. And the jewellery gone. Very sad, but there it is. The only thing left is the rose brooch—you may have noticed my sister wearing it today. It was away having the clasp mended."

"You think this was the work of somebody local, then?" Henry asked.

"Who knows?" replied Sir Simon heavily. "She'd been chattering to everybody about wearing the full regalia to the Hunt Ball. Somebody local might have had a contact . . . I don't know. . . ."

"These big robberies are generally the work of a professional gang," said Henry. "Apart from anything else, it would be difficult for an amateur to dispose of the stuff afterwards."

"That's true," Sir Simon agreed. "That's why we haven't altogether given up hope that the jewels may still turn up. But it's over a year now, and no sign of them."

At three o'clock the rain stopped, and a few shafts of watery sunshine began to filter through the dispersing clouds. Henry led the conversation round to the subject of boats, and expressed such interest in Sir Simon's motor launch that he was very soon being pressed to go down to the boathouse and have a look at it. Emmy and Rosemary decided against trampling through wet grass, so the two men left them by the fire.

Henry was depressed. When he had first seen the Blue Drawing Room, and the magnificent view of Steep Hill Sands from its window, he had had high hopes that Sir Simon might have seen *Blue Gull* going aground, and watched the subsequent actions of her owner: but from the snatches of conversation which he had overheard before lunch, it seemed that, as luck would have it, this perfect observation post had been unmanned during the vital hours. It was just possible, of course, that Priscilla had seen something, but Henry did not feel very sanguine about the reliability of her memory.

The boathouse was dark and damp. It was a long, low shed made of black-tarred wood, and built right across the little creek that ran from Sir Simon's grounds through banks of sedge and sand to join the main stream of the Berry at Steep Hill. Coming into the shed from the landward side, Henry followed Sir Simon through a small door, and found himself standing on a wooden landing stage. The seaward end of the shed was open, like the mouth of a tunnel, and through it, framed in darkness, was a vista of sand and sea. The floor of the shed was the water itself.

Two boats were tied up to the landing stage—a small, dilapidated racing dinghy which had once been white, and a very smart, varnished motor launch, which was carefully protected from the ravages of the weather by a waterproof canvas cover. This completely shrouded the cockpit and decking, giving the boat the appearance of being under a dust sheet. Both craft were bobbing gently on the dark water.

"I know," said Sir Simon, suddenly, "that fellows like Benson and Rawnsley don't agree with me, but to my way of thinking, *Priscilla*'s the great beauty in Berrybridge. Not as young as she was, perhaps, but I'd back her against these jazzy modern types any day. Do you agree?"

For one hysterical moment, Henry thought that Sir Simon was talking about his sister. Then, in the nick of time, he saw that the motor launch had the name *Priscilla* picked out in brass letters on her stern.

"She's lovely," he said sincerely.

"I used to be a sailing man myself," said Sir Simon. "Dinghy racing, mostly. Magnificent sport. Too old for it now. There's a lot to be said for a reliable engine when you get to my age." He gave *Priscilla* a wistful look. "Don't suppose you'd care for a spin?" he said, almost shyly. "It's not raining, and in any case there are plenty of oilskins aboard."

In fact, Henry did not relish the prospect of a cold, damp ride: but he was eager to see for himself the possibilities of reaching Steep Hill Sands from the boathouse, so he accepted.

Instantly, Sir Simon became brisk and businesslike. He unclipped the waterproof cover and folded it away, revealing a snug cockpit upholstered with blue cushions, and, ahead of it, a doghouse which gave shelter to the helmsman as he stood at the wheel. Through the open fo'c'sle door, under the foredeck, Henry could see the usual gear of a small cruising boat—blankets, ropes, fenders, flags, and anchor, oilskins and a Primus stove.

Henry, with one day's experience on *Ariadne* behind him, volunteered to help with the business of getting under way, but Sir Simon would have none of it. He insisted that Henry should sit passively in the comfortable, dry cockpit, while he himself bustled about efficiently with boathook, ropes and chain. Since the boat had been moored stern first, casting-off presented no difficulties. As soon as the motor was ticking over, it was only necessary to release the stern mooring warps, haul up the light anchor which held the bows of the boat, and slap her into gear. The engine purred contentedly, and *Priscilla* moved slowly out of the shelter of the boathouse and down the creek.

The tide was running out fast, and already the creek had assumed its own identity, as more and more patches of sand and sedge were uncovered, leaving the narrow, twisting channel clearly defined.

"Want to take her?" asked Sir Simon.

"I'd be terrified," said Henry. "I'd hate to run you aground on a falling tide."

"Nonsense. Just like driving a car. All you do is follow the stream."

Gingerly, Henry took the wheel, and steered an erratic course down the creek. Every so often, Sir Simon would put out a hand and gently correct Henry's wildly fluctuating steering. After five minutes, Henry had developed a crick in his neck from the strain of concentrating on the convolutions of the channel. He had also discovered that he tended to move the wheel much too violently, whereas in fact the merest touch was enough to swing the boat onto a new course.

"You'd better take over again now," he said. "It's only by the grace of God that I've got this far without disaster. I don't believe in tempting fate."

"Just as you like." Sir Simon took the wheel again, and Henry marvelled to see that he hardly bothered to glance at the stream ahead. The boat seemed to steer herself.

"I don't know how you do it," Henry said admiringly.

Sir Simon smiled. "Local knowledge, that's all," he said. "If you'd done this run as often as I have, you'd be just the same. I reckon I know every blade of sedge and every grain of sand by now. Ought to, after all these years. The only other person who knows this creek as well as I do is Herbert. But young Riddle is getting pretty good at it, I admit."

Ten minutes later, they were rounding the pale, inhospitable expanse of Steep Hill Sands, and the open water of the River Berry stretched out in front of them. Outside the sheltering banks of the creek, the boat began to pitch and buck, as she felt the choppy seas under her hull. Every so often, a larger-than-usual wave would break over the bows in a scatter of spray, and in spite of the shelter of the doghouse, Henry was glad of the warmth and dryness of his thick black oilskin coat.

Looking back over his shoulder at Steep Hill Sands, Henry said, "We went aground there yesterday—at just about the same spot as poor Pete Rawnsley."

Sir Simon, his hand on the wheel and his eyes on the horizon, said, "That was a great tragedy. Did you know him?"

"No," said Henry.

"A remarkable man. A great friend of mine. One of the few people round here one could really trust. A gentleman."

"A very good sailor, too, I understand," said Henry.

"First class. Nobody to touch him in this river."

"It seems extraordinary," said Henry, carefully, "that such an experienced yachtsman should be killed like that, by his own boom."

Sir Simon took his eyes off the horizon for a moment, to give Henry a sharp look. "Not at all," he said. "I can tell you're not a man of the sea, or you wouldn't say such things. Could happen to anybody. Look at Slocum."

"Nobody knows what happened to him," Henry pointed out. "He just disappeared, didn't he, with his boat?"

"Exactly." Sir Simon spoke with dogmatic emphasis. "Could have been run down by a steamer, certainly. Or it could have been an accident just like Pete's—knocked out by his own boom."

There was a pause, noisy with the throb of the engine and the pounding of the waves on the hull. Then Henry said, "I suppose you're right. But it interests me, just the same. It's a pity you weren't on the spot—you might have been able to do something."

"I doubt it," said Sir Simon. "The whole thing happened in fog, you know. Quite impossible to see Steep Hill from the house, and only a fool would have taken a boat out in weather like that. Anyhow, as it happened, I was in Ipswich all day—didn't get back till evening, when it was all over. I'd intended to come home for lunch, but when the fog came down, I decided it was a mug's game to try driving in it. So I had lunch in Ipswich and went to the cinema." He steered in silence for a moment, and then said, "Ah, well—no sense in brooding on it. Nothing we can do now."

"I understand that your man Riddle was very helpful," said Henry.

"Yes, he's a good lad. A bit slapdash about the house sometimes, but I suppose that's not to be wondered at, when you think of his background. He's the son of old Sam Riddle, you know—the fisherman. The boy wanted to better himself—and, give him credit, he's succeeded. . . ."

Yes—Riddle and Herbert and Benson among them did all that could be done for poor old Pete, but it wasn't much. The poor chap was dead by the time they found him."

"I wonder," said Henry, "what Herbert was doing there?"

Sir Simon looked strangely grim. "I have asked myself that question," he said. And then, "Better set course for home. The ladies will be waiting tea for us."

Henry was glad to get back into the warm cheerfulness of the Blue Drawing Room. Priscilla had reappeared. Her rest had apparently refreshed her, for her eyes were bright, and she was chattering away merrily to Rosemary and Emmy.

"Here we are, then." Sir Simon rubbed his big, red hands together before the crackling fire. "Took the boat out for a spin. Wonderful afternoon. Ring for tea, will you, Prissy?"

"What? Oh, yes. Tea. Of course." Priscilla seemed flustered. She jumped up and ran clumsily over towards the bell. Then, suddenly, she stumbled, put out a hand to steady herself, and grasped the edge of a small table. It rocked, stood poised for an eternal instant on one leg, and crashed to the ground, taking with it a very beautiful small urn in Wedgwood black jasper. Simultaneously with the crash of wood on wood came the sound of splintering porcelain.

Sir Simon let out a roar of anguished fury. "Priscilla!" he shouted.

Priscilla looked stupidly at the debris at her feet, and began to giggle. Two bright spots of colour had appeared in her cheeks.

"Oh, dear," she said, helpless with incoherent laughter. "What have I done? Oh dear."

In two strides, Sir Simon was beside her and down on his knees, gathering up the precious fragments.

"I suppose you realize what you've broken," he said in a voice of cold fury. "Papa's favourite piece. The antique Wedgwood."

Priscilla laughed again, a high-pitched, unnatural laugh. "Poor Papa," she said. "Naughty Priscilla."

Sir Simon looked up sharply, then got to his feet and

took his sister's arm. "You'd better go and lie down," he said. He turned to the others. "Please forgive us." With that, he led Priscilla out of the room.

There was an embarrassed silence. Then Rosemary said, "Oh, dear. The cat's out of the bag now, isn't it? I was hoping you wouldn't need to find out."

"She's drunk, isn't she?" said Henry.

Rosemary nodded. "I was afraid there might be trouble when she said she was going to rest after lunch," she said. "That's always a bad sign. Poor Sir Simon."

"I suppose that means," said Henry, "that on the night of the robbery——"

"Pickled as a newt," said Rosemary succinctly. "The Hunt Ball was altogether too much for her, and she fairly let rip when Sir Simon wasn't looking. She practically had to be carried out. It was rather awful—to happen in front of everybody like that. They'd kept it very well hushed-up, before. And as luck would have it, Herbert was there, helping behind the bar. He adores functions. So of course it was all round Berrybridge in no time. But most people think it was just a solitary lapse. They don't realize that——"

The door opened, and Sir Simon came in. "I must apologize," he said, red-faced. "My sister hasn't been at all well lately. It's her nerves." He went over to the fallen table, set it upright, and began to pick up the pieces of broken pottery. "I suppose they may be able to mend this," he said, "but of course it will never be the same. My father's favourite piece." He straightened, and gave his guests a somewhat grim smile. "And now," he said, "perhaps we can have our tea in peace."

After tea, Rosemary and the Tibbetts drove back to Berrybridge Haven. The sky was clearing fast, and the declining sun was touching the clouds with pink—the prelude to a hearteningly red sunset, with its promise of fine weather to come.

They reached the hard just in time to see *Tideway* coming upriver to her moorings. Two tall, oil-skinned figures moved about on her deck, while Anne sat at the helm: but as the boat approached the bobbing red and white mooring buoy, Henry noticed that Hamish went aft and took the tiller himself. Alastair grabbed the buoy and made the chain fast. Anne clambered up on deck and waved energetically.

Rosemary glanced at her watch. "Half past six," she said. "Another half hour to opening time, it being Sunday. But I'm sure Bob won't mind us going in and waiting. The others are bound to be ashore in a minute."

They walked back up the hard to The Berry Bush. Outside the pub, in the yard, stood a sleek red Aston-Martin.

"Bob's back," Rosemary remarked, when she saw the car.

"That's a very handsome vehicle for a country publican," said Emmy.

Rosemary smiled. "It's Bob's pride and joy," she said. "Heaven knows how he affords to run it."

They went into the bar, where a fire was already blazing. A small man with a sharp-featured face and very bright blue eyes was busying himself behind the bar.

"Hello, Bob," said Rosemary. "D'you mind if we sit by the fire till opening time?"

" 'Course not, Mrs. Benson, make yerself at 'ome," said the landlord kindly, in a marked Cockney accent. "Just got in meself, and glad to be in the warm, I can tell you, out of——" He suddenly stopped, and looked at Henry. There was a moment of dead silence.

"How are you, Bob?" said Henry. "Fancy meeting you here."

Bob came out from behind the bar, hand outstretched. "Well, well, well," he said. "It's a small world, I always say. And 'ow are you, Inspector?"

"Very fit, thank you."

"What brings you 'ere, then?" There was the faintest note of anxiety in Bob's voice. "Expectin' a crime wave in Berrybridge?"

Henry smiled. "No, no, this isn't a business trip," he said. "We're sailing with Mr. and Mrs. Benson."

"Sailin', eh? Been out today?"

"No," said Henry. "We've been over at Berry Hall."

For a moment, a wary look crept into Bob's blue eyes.

Then he said, "Well, well, well. 'Ave a seat by the fire, then. Lucky I didn't suggest servin' you with a drink before hours, eh? I'd 'ave bin in trouble, and no mistake."

Henry grinned. "I know how honest you are, Bob," he said.

Bob shot him a suspicious glance, but all he said was, "Well, if you'll excuse me, ladies and gents, I've got work to do." He disappeared through the door behind the bar.

"You know Bob, Henry?" Rosemary asked, surprised.

"Yes," said Henry. "He's an old friend. Used to keep a pub in Soho."

"What's his surname?" Emmy asked.

"Calloway," said Rosemary.

"Bob Calloway?" Emmy turned to Henry, and frowned slightly in an effort at recollection. "Wasn't that the man who——"

Henry gave her a reproving look. "He's the man who used to keep the Duck and Doorknob in Bear Street," he said. "An old haunt of mine."

"I see," said Emmy. But she looked thoughtful.

SIX

A little later, Henry said to Rosemary, "I believe there's a telephone here, isn't there?"

"Yes," said Rosemary. "Out of that door and down the passage. Next to the gents."

"I've just remembered some loose ends at the office," Henry explained apologetically, "and I don't want to hold up the sailing programme by coming ashore to phone to-morrow. Thank goodness the law never sleeps. There should be somebody reasonably intelligent to take a message even on Sunday evening."

He armed himself with the requisite small change for a call to London, and stepped out into the corridor. The telephone was at the far end of the gloomy, unlit passage, and somebody was already using it. As the shaft of light from the bar doorway fell across the red-tiled passage, there was a tinkle as the receiver was replaced, and a small, nimble shadow disappeared through a door near the telephone. This door remained slightly ajar, but no light came from behind it.

Henry walked down the corridor and into the cloak-room. When he came out, the door was still not closed. He sighed, and went back up the passage to the outside door, and out of The Berry Bush into the crisp evening air. It was ten minutes' brisk walk, uphill all the way, to the main road: but Henry could remember having seen a public telephone box on the corner. It was half an hour later when he rejoined the others at the bar.

Promptly at seven, as the bar opened, the intrepid mariners from *Tideway* came in. Hamish and Alastair were both unusually silent, exchanging a few, sparse remarks on the day's sail, but for the most part brooding with apparent contentment on remembered exhilaration. Anne, however, was garrulous and excited.

"We went all the way up to the Deben and back," she said, a trifle breathlessly, "and the seas were huge. Honestly, Rosemary, *huge*. And it was raining and spray was breaking all over the boat and we got soaked and it was wonderful."

"It sounds horrid," said Rosemary drily.

Anne looked at her reproachfully. "Oh, *no*—it was just marvellous. But we were all absolutely wet through. We've just been up to Hamish's house and had a gorgeous whisky to warm us up."

"Mean brutes," said Rosemary. "You might have called in here for us on the way."

There was a tiny, awkward silence, and then Anne went on quickly, "The deck was so slippery, Hamish made me wear a lifeline when I went forward to help change the jib. We rolled down two reefs and set the storm trysail off Berry Head, so that'll show you how rough it was."

"You shouldn't have been on deck at all," said Hamish. "You weren't strong enough to be useful. You were just in the way."

"What a vile thing to say."

"She wasn't in the way," said Alastair. "She was a great help. I think it was very plucky of her to come out at all."

Anne rewarded him with a brilliant smile. "Darling Alastair," she said. "I do love being appreciated." She turned to Henry. "And what have you been doing all day? Cooped up in a stuffy cabin drinking gin, I suppose."

"On the contrary," said Henry, "I've been out on the river."

"In a boat?"

"Of course. What else?"

"I don't believe you. Which boat?"

Henry told her about his trip with Sir Simon. Anne was scornful. "Oh, *motoring*," she said, wrinkling her minute nose. "That's quite different. Still, you can bear me out about how bad the weather was."

"I think the wind must have moderated by the time we

went out," said Henry. "It didn't seem too terrible to me."

"It wasn't at all terrible," said Hamish. "Anne always exaggerates."

Anne grinned. "It's all very well to take that attitude now that you're snug in a pub," she said. "You know very well you had some nasty moments out there."

"Rubbish," said Hamish, and relapsed into a moody silence.

It was not long before Sir Simon arrived in the rapidly filling bar. He came straight over to Henry and Emmy, and began to talk in a friendly way. He did not mention his sister.

After a polite but somewhat aimless speculation as to the possibilities of improved weather, Sir Simon said, "I've been thinking over what you said about Pete Rawnsley, Mr. Tibbett."

Henry said nothing, but waited hopefully. After a moment, Sir Simon went on, "It's perfectly clear what happened. I saw him go aground, you know, before I left the house. About nine o'clock, it must have been."

"Did you?" Henry was deeply interested.

"Yes. I remember it distinctly. I saw the boat go ashore, and I couldn't believe it was Pete. There are several Dragonclass boats in the river, so I took a look through the glasses to make sure which one it was. But it was Pete all right—I could even make out the Royal Harwich burgee. I could hardly believe my eyes."

"Did you watch him to see what he did?"

"What should he do? Just the ordinary things. Got the sails off her, and so on. I didn't watch him for long—I had to get to Ipswich. It did occur to me, though, that he might be feeling a bit under the weather. I mean, it was so unlike the man . . . broad daylight, and he knew the river like the back of his hand."

"I suppose it's inconceivable," said Henry, "that he should have run aground on purpose?"

To his surprise, Sir Simon did not immediately refute this idea. He looked thoughtful. "Funny you should say that," he said. "I almost wondered myself. . . . But it's a preposterous idea. Why ever should he do such a thing?"

"I don't know." Henry rubbed the back of his neck abstractedly. "By the way, did *Priscilla* go out that day?"

Sir Simon looked surprised. "Go out?" he repeated. "I think it's highly unlikely. We don't lead much of a social life these days, you know, and my sister isn't——"

Henry grinned. "I meant the boat," he said.

"Oh, you mean *Priscilla*. Good heavens, no." Sir Simon was emphatic. "In the fog? It would have been madness."

"You're sure of that?"

"Of course I'm sure. The only other person who handles her besides myself is Riddle, and he's not a lunatic. He'd never have managed the channel in bad visibility."

"I suppose, though, that some unauthorized person could have——"

"My dear Tibbett, what on earth are you suggesting?" Sir Simon was at once amused and slightly nettled. "In any case, what does it matter whether she went out or not?"

"It probably doesn't," said Henry. "I'm sorry."

David and Colin came ashore at half past seven, and Henry found himself standing next to David at the bar, waiting for Bob to replenish the beer mugs. The landlord was as sprightly as a sparrow, darting about his business among the big, dark barrels. When he saw Henry, he came over at once.

"What can I get you then, Inspector?" he asked pertly. "Always see the law gets served first, that's my motto. Never know when you'll need a p'liceman."

"Two pints of bitter, please, Bob," said Henry.

David had turned to look at Henry. "Are you a policeman?" he asked.

"Yes. When I'm on duty."

David said nothing, but his face had grown grave.

"What's that you say, Tibbett? A policeman?" Sir Simon's voice came resoundingly from behind Henry's left ear. "A great sleuth from Scotland Yard, eh? Who'd have thought it. We'd all better mind our Ps and Qs, what?"

"I'm trying to forget my job at the moment," said Henry. "I'm on holiday."

"Had a lot of your chaps nosing round after the burglary," Sir Simon went on. "Not that they did any good. Waste of the taxpayer's money. Fellow got clean away."

"Still, I wouldn't give up all hope of getting your property back," said Henry. "The case isn't by any means closed, you know."

Sir Simon snorted. "After nearly two years——"

"All the same," said Henry, "you never know. Excuse me—my wife is waiting for her drink."

He made his way back to the inglenook where he had left Emmy, and found her in conversation with Herbert. To be more accurate, Herbert was carrying on a monologue, which—through the mists and mazes of his rolling Suffolk accent, aided and abetted by several missing teeth—was virtually incomprehensible. The gist of it seemed to be a dark tale of the disasters which had overtaken various boats unlucky enough to fall into the hands of Bill Hawkes, but the details were far from clear. Fortunately, however, Emmy's encouraging nods and appreciative monosyllables seemed to satisfy the Harbour Master. Only once did he show disapproval: he had reached an exquisitely comic highlight in an anecdote, and broke suddenly into a delighted cackle of laughter, in which Emmy, who had been taken by surprise, failed to join. Herbert gave her a cryptic look.

"There's them as 'as a sense o' 'umour and them as don't," he remarked, severely. "Take Mrs. 'Ole."

Quickly, Emmy diverted the conversation to the ever-absorbing topic of Mrs. Hole's feet: but she felt considerably relieved to see Henry making his way back to the table with his cargo of glasses.

Herbert greeted Henry affably. "Comin' to the ceremony?" he enquired, graciously.

"You mean the inauguration of the new mayor?"

"Hay?"

"The new mayor," Henry shouted raucously.

"Ar. Next Sat'day. Proper booze-up," said Herbert succinctly.

"Yes, we'll be there," Henry bellowed. "I understand you're running for office."

Herbert looked suspicious. "I don't do nothing what's not legal," he said defensively. Then, after a pause, he added, "Never 'ad the perlice in, up to now."

"Of course not," said Emmy, slightly baffled.

"Will 'ave this time, though, eh?" Herbert gave Henry a sly dig in the ribs with his skinny elbow. Henry looked surprised. "You," explained Herbert.

"How did you know I was a policeman?"

"Size of yer boots, o' course," retorted Herbert impishly. But a significant jerk of his head indicated the landlord of The Berry Bush. "All round the borough, it is," he said. "You'll 'ear some pretty tales, I wouldn't wonder, now they know 'oo y'are. Not so fancy as what you might 'ave 'eard a while back, though."

"What do you mean?" Henry asked. But Herbert contented himself with dark rumblings about people who minded their own business, and least said soonest mended, and eventually took himself off to cadge a drink from Alastair.

Emmy glanced quickly round to make sure that she could not be overheard, and then said softly, "Wasn't Bob Calloway a fence?"

Henry nodded. "We always thought so," he said. "Couldn't ever prove anything. It's extremely interesting to find him here."

"Perhaps," said Emmy, "Priscilla is right, and her precious jewellery will turn up after all."

"If it's still intact," said Henry, "it's almost certainly in the neighbourhood. But it's a hell of a place to search."

"Do you think," Emmy ventured, "that the robbery could be connected with . . . with the other . . . ?"

"I don't know," said Henry. "And the fact that everybody now knows who I am isn't going to help."

David Crowther came over to the table and sat down. "Nothing but boring talk about today's sailing over there," he said. "Colin and I are regarded as spineless outcasts because we didn't go out. I simply cannot understand the passion that some people have for making themselves thoroughly uncomfortable and then boasting about it afterwards."

Henry grinned sympathetically. "I'm on your side," he said.

David finished his drink in one gulp. "Well," he said, "I'll be off now. It's a long drive to London in my old bus. Will you be here next weekend?"

"If we're not drowned," said Emmy cheerfully.

Surprisingly, David said, "Yes. Do be careful, won't you? Well . . . goodbye. Till next Friday."

He collected his oilskin jacket and went over to say goodbye to the other members of the Fleet. Henry heard Anne saying, "But *what* are you doing on Wednesday, David? You always say you never go out, and it's the first party for ages that Colin and I——"

"I'm busy," said David briefly. "Good night."

He made his way over to the door, and went out. A couple of minutes later he was back. He came straight over to Henry.

"I say," he said, diffidently, "I'm terribly sorry to have to ask you, but I wonder if you'd give me a hand with the car. I can't start her."

"Of course," said Henry, "but I'm afraid I'm not much of a mechanic."

"That's O.K. I know what has to be done."

Henry followed David out of The Berry Bush. The moon was up, throwing a pathway of cold light across the river. The two men walked over to the ancient black Riley which stood on the hard.

"Get in," said David.

Henry obeyed. To his surprise, David climbed in beside him.

"Sorry to drag you out," said David. His voice was serrated with nervousness. "There's nothing wrong with the car. I wanted to talk to you."

"Oh," said Henry. "What about?"

David lit a cigarette. His face, illuminated momentarily by the flame, looked haggard and old. "It's fairly obvious why you're here," he said.

"Is it?"

"About Pete."

"Why should you think that?"

"It was too much to expect that nobody would tumble to it," said David. "I've been expecting you—or somebody like you."

Henry said nothing. David took a long pull at his cigarette. "I suppose you think it was Colin," he said.

"I don't think anything," said Henry. "I'm here on holiday."

David did not appear to have heard him. He went on in a low voice. "It's so damned hard to know what's the right thing to do. I think I told you, I didn't like Pete myself. But disliking a man is one thing, and killing him——"

"It's the first time I've heard anybody suggest that he was killed," said Henry quietly.

"Oh, God," said David. "Now I suppose I've said too much. All right. Forget it. It was an accident."

"I'm not at all sure that it was," said Henry, "but I do assure you that this isn't an official investigation—yet. I really am on holiday. It was only when I heard the whole story of what happened . . ."

David was staring fixedly straight ahead. "It wasn't Colin," he said.

"From the way you say that," Henry said, "you make me think that you know who it was."

There was a long silence. "I've been nearly mad, wondering what to do," he said.

Henry said gently, "Anything you tell me now is absolutely unofficial. And whatever standards of loyalty you may have, nothing can justify you in shielding a murderer, you know."

After another endless pause, David swung round in his seat to look at Henry. "All right," he said. "I'm not accusing anybody of anything. I just think you ought to know that Hamish rowed ashore to Steep Hill Sands that day in the fog."

Henry considered this information. "How do you know?" he said.

"Because," said David, "I was there myself."

"I think," said Henry, "that you had better elaborate that a bit."

David began to speak rapidly, as though the relief of

speech were immense. "Anne was sailing with me that day. We saw Pete go aground. When the fog came down, we anchored, just off the sandbank, a couple of hundred yards behind *Tideway*. Anne and I talked for a long time. Anne was infatuated with Pete. I suppose you knew that. He was a swine. He'd deliberately led her on, made trouble between her and Colin—and then dropped her. Wouldn't even talk to her. The poor child was nearly frantic. So when she knew he was there on Steep Hill, she got this crazy idea of going ashore to speak to him. I told her she was a fool— that she'd only lose herself in the fog, and that it was a stupid and dangerous thing to do. But when Anne really sets her mind on something . . ." David broke off, and grinned ruefully. "She talked me round in the end. The tide was out, and the channel was only a few yards wide by then, so I strung all my available warps together, and we rowed ashore, with the dinghy still attached to the boat, so that we could haul ourselves back. I beached the dinghy, and left Anne sitting in it, while I went off on the end of another rope to look for Pete. Frankly, I didn't think I'd find him. I told Anne that if I found *Blue Gull*, I'd give two tugs on the rope, and she could follow it up."

David stopped again, and lit another cigarette. His hands were shaking badly.

"Well," said Henry, "did you find him?"

"I walked about on that bloody sandbank for what felt like hours," said David. In his nervousness he had developed a slight stutter. "The f-fog was white and damp, and I felt lost and m-miserable. I kept on thinking that Anne might have done something d-damn silly like letting go of the other end of the rope, and then I'd have been in the soup, all right, when the tide came up. And then, suddenly, I heard v-voices. Close to me. I couldn't see a thing, but the voices were quite clear."

"Whose voices?" Henry asked.

"Pete and H-Hamish. They were fighting."

"Fighting?"

"Arguing, I m-mean. I didn't stay long to listen. But I heard Pete say, 'I've t-told you before that it's out of the question. Now for God's sake get back to your boat and don't be a b-bloody fool.' And then Hamish said, 'The money's just as much m-mine as yours,' and Pete said, 'That's not true.' Th-then Hamish said, 'I've got as much damned right to it as you have.' He sounded furious and s-sort of desperate. I didn't wait to hear any more. I f-followed the rope back to the dinghy."

"And what did you tell Anne?"

"I told her I hadn't been able to locate Pete," said David. He seemed more self-possessed now, and the stutter had almost disappeared. "I didn't see any point in telling her about Hamish. Of course, she wanted to go and look for herself, but she was pretty cold and wet by then, and I imagine she realized she was making a c-considerable fool of herself. So we hauled the dinghy back to *Pocahontas* and went below and brewed coffee."

"What time was this?" Henry asked.

David considered. "The fog came down about half past nine," he said. "I suppose it was about a quarter past ten."

"And when the fog lifted, in the afternoon—what did you see then?"

"We saw *Blue Gull*, of course," said David. "She was surrounded by water, but still hard aground. No sign of Pete. We assumed he was below. Actually, the poor sod must have b-been on the sand, on the far side of the hull. If only we'd seen him . . ."

"You haven't told anybody else about this? About going ashore, I mean."

There was the faintest hesitation before David said, "Of course not. I didn't see any point." He paused for a moment, and then added, "You said something about shielding a m-murderer. That's rot. It wasn't murder."

"Wasn't it?"

"Of course not. Hamish must have lost his temper and hit Pete. I'm certain he never meant to kill him."

"Isn't it rather strange," Henry remarked, "to knock somebody senseless and then leave him on a sandbank, knowing that the tide would be coming up?"

David considered. "Perhaps he didn't know he knocked him out," he said. "Don't these things have a delayed reaction sometimes? I mean, suppose Hamish hit Pete, and then p-panicked and made off to his boat, leaving Pete still on his feet, and then Pete c-collapsed and——"

"The boom," said Henry, "was out of the gallows. Swinging free. And traces of blood and hair were found on it. How do you account for that?"

David was silent. Henry went on. "That was what you meant when you said that somebody was sure to tumble to it. Wasn't it?" There was another long pause. Then Henry said, "You can't go back on it now. You've accused Hamish Rawnsley of murder."

"For Christ's sake," said David. "I d-didn't mean——"

"Unless, of course," Henry added, "you've told me a pack of lies." He opened the door of the car and got out. "You'd better get back to London now," he said. "Thank you for an extremely interesting talk."

David said nothing, but started the engine and slammed the car into gear. It shot forward and disappeared up the twisting lane. Henry watched it go, thoughtfully. Then he walked back into the bar.

He found Rosemary and Alastair just preparing to leave.

"We're going out to dinner," said Alastair.

"Good heavens," said Henry, glancing down at his muddy jeans. "Where?"

"On *Mary Jane*. Colin and Anne have invited us."

"Don't you have to get back to town?" Henry asked Colin.

Colin, who had been gazing at Anne with a darkly adoring intensity, wrenched his attention away, and said, "What? Oh, no, not tonight. Anne's got tomorrow off as a compensation for working on Saturday, and I'm able to take the odd free day here and there."

"Well," said Rosemary, "I absolutely insist that we bring the wine."

"That's very sweet of you," said Anne. "If you can spare . . ."

"You go back to *Mary Jane* with Colin and Anne in their dinghy," said Alastair to Henry and Emmy, "and Rosemary and I will come along via *Ariadne* and pick up the booze. O.K.?"

Mary Jane was a beautiful boat. Until then, Henry and

Emmy had considered *Ariadne* the peak of perfection, but now they saw the difference between an elderly converted fishing smack and a modern, made-to-measure yacht. For, no getting away from it, *Mary Jane* was a yacht. Her saloon—considerably larger than *Ariadne's*—had a fitted carpet of royal blue whipcord, which matched the tailored settee-covers and was echoed in the handles of the battery of aluminum saucepans hanging up in the galley. While Rosemary washed up in a tin bowl and cooked on an ancient Primus, Anne had the use of a stainless steel sink with a tap which worked, and a handsome stove, fed from a big bottle of liquid gas. A door led into the fo'c'sle, which was equipped with two comfortable bunks, and was unencumbered by the gear and tackle which cluttered the visitors' sleeping quarters aboard *Ariadne*. Most impressive of all, there was even a miniature lavatory enclosed in a small compartment opposite the galley.

"All mod. con.," remarked Emmy, admiringly.

Colin's sombre face broke into a gratified smile. "Do you like her?" he asked, almost diffidently.

"She's marvellous."

"Next season," said Colin, "I'm going to fit a diesel engine and run electric light off the batteries. And we need a fridge badly."

"A fridge?" Emmy was almost speechless.

"Oh, yes," said Anne. "We must have one. Everybody does, nowadays."

"And do you mean to say," said Henry to Colin, "that you can handle a big boat like this on your own?"

"Good lord, yes. For a short trip. She's only eight tons."

"The menu," said Anne, "is watercress soup, followed by roast chicken, new potatoes and beans. O.K. for everyone?"

Henry and Emmy murmured reverently that it was most certainly O.K., and Emmy volunteered to help with the potatoes. The two girls disappeared into the galley, and Colin poured Henry a stiff whisky. Henry noticed that, as on *Ariadne*, the wine cellar was located under one of the bunks.

When the two men were comfortably settled with their

drinks, Colin said, "Alastair never told us that you were a
detective. Puts us more or less in the same line of country."

"I'd hardly say that," said Henry. "My work is done
before yours starts. And if you're acting for the defence,
you spend your time trying to undo everything that I've
done."

"That's true." Colin considered for a moment. "Now
that I come to think of it, haven't I read about you somewhere? Wasn't there a case in Italy—something to do with
skiing?"

"Yes," said Henry. "That was a messy business. It interrupted my holiday."

"I wonder," said Colin thoughtfully, "if you'll find this
holiday similarly interrupted?"

Henry looked at him with interest. Colin's intelligent
face was puckered into what looked like secret amusement.

"It's rather fun to speculate, don't you think?" Colin
went on. "The only unnatural death that occurred round
here recently was poor old Pete Rawnsley. You must have
heard all about it. Perfectly straightforward, on the face of
it. And yet I wonder. As a matter of fact, I've been amusing myself by trying to work up a murder mystery over it."

"Have you succeeded?" Henry asked.

Colin frowned. "Motive. Plenty of that, when you look
a bit. Hamish passionately keen to get a new boat, and unable to lay hands on the money while Pete was alive.
Sounds a bit thin as a motive for murder unless you know
Hamish. Me—better still. Pete had been running around
with Anne—she told you so herself. I don't pretend I
liked him. Unfortunately, when you get to know my fiancée better, you'll realize that if I was going to commit murder for that reason, I'd have several deaths on my hands
already." Colin spoke with a bitter lightness. "Still, better
put me down on the list. Then there's Anne herself, of
course—a woman scorned. That's nonsense, too, but I
could make a great deal of it in court if I were leading for
the prosecution. And of course we mustn't forget Herbert."

"Herbert?" Henry was taken aback. "Good heavens,
what did Herbert have against the man?"

Colin smiled. "What I meant was . . ." He stopped. "I'd

better not say any more. After all, you are a policeman."

"Don't tantalize me," said Henry. "I can't imagine that any misdemeanour of Herbert's could possibly excite Scotland Yard's interest."

"No," said Colin. "It wouldn't be fair. All I'll say is this. Pete had it in his power to lose Herbert his job. In fact, he had threatened to do just that. I heard him. The day before he . . . died."

"Pete sounds rather a vindictive character," said Henry.

"Not really," said Colin reasonably. "He was quick-tempered, certainly, and Herbert can be maddening. I don't think Pete'd ever have done anything about it, in fact."

"I see," said Henry. "Any more suspects?"

"That's all I can think of, off-hand," said Colin. "Isn't it enough?"

"Not for a really ingenious detective story," said Henry, grinning. "What about David?"

Colin shook his head. "No motive and no opportunity," he said. "David was sailing with Anne that day, and Rosemary and Alastair were together. That lets them all out, I suppose, unless it was a conspiracy."

"Who did have the opportunity, then?"

"Hamish and I are the obvious suspects," said Colin promptly. "We were both single-handed. We both saw Pete go aground, and we both anchored just off Steep Hill in the fog."

"Could you have rowed ashore and found your way back to your boat?" Henry asked.

"I wouldn't have enjoyed it much," said Colin, "but if I'd been desperate to kill Pete, I'd certainly have had a go. With the dinghy on the end of a long line. After all," he added, warming to his theme, "it was a perfect situation for murder, wasn't it? What with the fog, and——"

Anne suddenly came out of the galley, and it occurred to Henry that she must have overheard the whole conversation. She looked angry and a little frightened.

"I've never heard such childish rubbish," she said. "You know very well that none of us could have rowed ashore. We were all much too far off the bank."

"I wasn't," said Colin. "I was only about thirty yards

from the bank at low water, and I've got a light nylon line sixty yards long. The one I use for——"

"Oh, shut up," said Anne. "I don't think it's funny. In fact, I think it's beastly, and in very bad taste. I wonder where Rosemary and Alastair have got to?"

Like a stage effect that comes promptly on its cue, there was a bumping sound as a dinghy drew up alongside. Rosemary and Alastair climbed aboard, Emmy came out of the galley, and the conversation became general.

After an excellent dinner, the crew of *Ariadne* took to the water again, having arranged a rendezvous with *Mary Jane* for the following day. As they settled themselves into their green sleeping bags, Emmy said to Henry, "That was a curious conversation you had with Colin."

"I don't like it," said Henry. "I don't like it one little bit."

"Oh, dear," said Emmy. "You mean it's getting serious."

"Too damn serious," said Henry. "And the worst of it is that I'm not the only person who thinks so."

"What do you mean?"

"I mean," said Henry, "that someone has been expecting me. Or at least has considered the possibility of someone like me turning up. And, if I'm not mistaken, a pre-arranged plan of action is coming into operation."

Emmy shivered. "You don't mean . . . ?"

"I don't know exactly what I mean," said Henry. "It's just something I feel, supported by a few odd facts. Oh, God, why do these things always have to happen to me? I don't want trouble."

"You never do," said Emmy, "but you always seem to walk into it." She smiled in the darkness. "Can't you see, darling, that you go out of your way to look for it?"

"I don't. I'm a quiet-living man."

"I seem," said Emmy, "to have heard that somewhere before."

She leant over and kissed him, and then snuggled down into her sleeping bag. Lying in the dark, listening to the soft lapping of the water against *Ariadne*'s hull, Henry reflected bitterly on the policeman's lot, decided that he would not be able to sleep, and almost at once drifted into a wave-rocked slumber.

SEVEN

At ten o'clock the next morning, *Ariadne* and *Mary Jane* set sail on an ebbing tide, headed for Walton Backwaters.

"It's a stupid place to go today," Rosemary remarked at breakfast. "The tides are all wrong. We'll be against the ebb going down and against the flood coming home. What's the matter with going to the Deben?"

"Anne's set her heart on Walton," said Alastair.

"She would have," said Rosemary, with more than a touch of asperity.

The sun shone, fitfully, through a thin tracery of very white clouds, and a light easterly breeze ruffled the blue-gray surface of the river. With the wind abeam, both boats skimmed merrily downstream, with *Mary Jane* drawing inexorably ahead, until her sail was only a white speck in the distance.

"I just can't compete," said Alastair. "She's bigger and faster than we are, and that's all there is to it."

"Perhaps she'll go aground," said Emmy, with amiable malice.

"Not a hope. Not with a beam wind and Colin at the helm. He knows what he's doing."

By the time they reached the river mouth, the clouds had been swept neatly away onto the horizon. Henry, pulling off his heavy white sweater in the warm sunshine, was not surprised to see *Priscilla*'s bright, varnished hull throwing up a creamy arrow of spray as she roared out towards them from the Berry Hall boathouse.

"Sir Simon's out," he remarked. "Don't blame him. Gorgeous day."

"He's got somebody with him," said Rosemary. "Riddle, probably. They often go fishing together."

"Can't see from here." Alastair screwed up his eyes into the sun. "Might be anybody."

"We'll see in a moment, when they get closer," said Rosemary.

At that moment, however, *Priscilla* quite suddenly turned to starboard in a tight arc, and headed noisily upriver.

"Unsociable types," said Alastair. Henry gazed thoughtfully after *Priscilla*'s retreating stern. Two blue-jerseyed back views were visible in the cockpit, but they were too far away for identification.

Ahead of *Ariadne,* the North Sea stretched dazzlingly to the horizon, the foreground dotted with the dark shapes of the buoys that marked the entrance to the River Berry. In the distance, a low-slung, black, oil tanker ploughed solemnly down the coast towards the Thames Estuary, while to starboard the Harwich-Hook steamer made her way out of harbour. The salty breeze was fresh and invigorating. Emmy sat in the cockpit, pouring over a chart, and deriving a ridiculous amount of pleasure from identifying the various buoys as they slipped astern in measured, silent procession. At the helm, Alastair puffed at his pipe and kept a wary eye on the sails. Nobody spoke. After half an hour, Alastair said to Henry, "I do hope you're not bored."

"Bored? Good heavens, no."

"Good. Some people get bored in fine weather."

Emmy looked up from the chart. "Then they must be mad," she said. "Is that Harwich down there on the right?"

"No," said Alastair. "What you can see on the starboard beam—which is I presume what you mean by 'down there on the right'—is Felixstowe. Harwich is on the opposite side of the river mouth. We'll see it soon when we turn down the coast."

A mile out to sea, *Ariadne* rounded the last of the cylindrical red buoys, and Alastair freed the sheets and put the helm to port. The big white mainsail, now nearly at right angles to the boom, filled with the following wind, masking the jib, which flapped idly on the forestay. Once again, Henry and Emmy noticed the strange effect of turning down-wind. The boat, riding on an even keel, seemed becalmed: only the rapid retreat of the red buoy astern showed that she was, in fact, making progress.

"I wish to God we had a spinnaker," said Alastair. "We've got another two and a half hours of ebb to plug."

"Told you so," said Rosemary, sleepily.

"I don't care how long we take to get there," said Emmy. "This is my idea of heaven." She leant back luxuriously and closed her eyes. Silence reigned once more.

Slowly, *Ariadne* forged her way down the coast. The estuary of the River Orwell opened up to starboard, marked by the thin steeple of Harwich church and the distant, angular shapes of the cranes and derricks on Parkstone Quay. At half past twelve, Rosemary roused herself and went below with Emmy to open the bar, while Alastair scanned the water ahead with more than usual concentration.

From Dovercourt, the coastline swings southward in an arc which terminates in the Naze. As far as Henry could see, *Ariadne* was now sailing straight into the centre of this bay, and could only end up on the beach. He said as much.

Alastair smiled. "Don't worry. The entrance is there, all right, but it's almost impossible to see it until you're right on top of it. What I'm looking for now is a small black buoy that marks the centre of the channel."

Rosemary and Emmy had just distributed mugs of beer all round when the black buoy bobbed into sight, ahead and to starboard. It was followed by a red buoy, inscribed "Pye Hill," which lay stranded on a bank of sand to port. From then on, the channel was clearly marked, and Henry could see that a wide-mouthed inlet was opening up ahead of them. In the centre of it were two more buoys, red and black respectively, apparently only a few feet from each other.

"What are those two doing so close together?" he asked.

"That's the entrance," said Alastair. "We go between them."

Emmy surveyed the wide expanse of water and grimaced. "You mean," she said, "that all that lovely water——"

"Is less than a foot deep at low tide," said Rosemary. "The channel widens once you're inside, but the entrance is murderously narrow. That's why Walton is so nice and quiet."

"It's easy enough with a following wind," said Alastair, "but beating in and out can be amusing, to say the least of it."

Ariadne slipped smoothly between the entrance buoys, and Alastair said, "Stand by to gybe. Mind your head, Henry. Gybe-oh."

The boom came across with very little fuss: Alastair quickly paid out the sheet and put the helm to port. As *Ariadne* turned her nose obediently to starboard, Henry realized for the first time that there were two separate channels ahead of them, converging just inside the entrance.

"The port-hand channel goes up to the club and to Walton itself," Alastair explained. "Not that you can get right up there at low water except in a dinghy. The starboard one, which we're taking, is called Hamford Water, and it goes nowhere. Just meanders about for a bit and then gets lost. That's the beauty of it."

As they made their way upstream, deeper and deeper into the land-locked channel, green meadows stretched on either side of them, laced with spinneys of feathery trees. Small water birds bustled busily among the rushes at the water's edge, and called pipingly to each other. The sun shone hotly. ˙

"There they are," Rosemary said suddenly, and then, as loudly as she could bellow, *"Mary Jane ahoy!"* She stood up on deck and waved both her long arms above her head.

Mary Jane lay quietly at anchor on the port-hand side of the channel. At Rosemary's call, two supine figures on deck sat up and waved back. Alastair raised his beer mug significantly. This signal was evidently received and understood, for Colin and Anne were in their dinghy even before Rosemary had let go *Ariadne*'s anchor. The sails were lowered, the mainsail lashed neatly to the boom, and the helm

secured amidships. Colin and Anne clambered aboard, and
Rosemary brought up a fresh supply of beer.

"Did you know," Colin was saying, "that this place is
the original of Arthur Ransome's *Secret Water*?"

"Is it really?" Emmy was vastly intrigued. "I was
brought up on those books. I adored them." She looked
round her with a new, respectful interest. "Now that I've
actually been here in a boat, I'll have to go back and read
them all over again."

"Kid stuff," said Anne. She was wearing a swimsuit the
colour of a peeled grape, which displayed to full advantage
the tanned perfection of her small body. "If you're interested in sailing, read something useful, like Peter Heaton."
She sat up suddenly. "I'm going for a swim before lunch.
Anybody coming?"

Alastair jumped up. "Wait for me!" he shouted. He
plunged down into the cabin, and emerged a minute later in
his bathing trunks. As Alastair dived in, Anne sped away
downstream, doing a very efficient crawl. Alastair surfaced,
shook his wet hair out of his eyes, and set off in hot pur-
suit.

Rosemary watched them go without pleasure. Then she
said, in a strange, clipped voice, "Well, somebody's got to
get lunch. I suppose I'd better do it, as usual."

"Let me help you." Emmy quickly followed her below.

In the cockpit, Henry said to Colin, "Aren't you going
in?"

Colin shook his head. "I don't swim. Never learnt. No
proper sailor can swim. It only prolongs the agony if
you're wrecked."

"That sounds a gloomy philosophy," said Henry.

Ignoring this, Colin said, meditatively, "Anne's quite
right, you know. You ought to do some technical reading if
you're going to take up sailing at all seriously. Heaton,
certainly, and Illingworth and Voss. Not to mention *Reid's
Nautical Almanack*. They run good navigation courses in
London during the winter, too."

"My dear fellow," said Henry, "don't try to tell me that
you need celestial navigation to get a small boat from
Berrybridge to Walton."

"True," said Colin, "although it's well worth learning
just for the fun of it. All right, we'll let you off the navigation courses, but Voss you should read. You never know
when you'll get caught out in a blow and need to rig a
sea anchor. Besides, it's an immensely entertaining book,
full of the old boy's adventures. . . ." His voice trailed into
silence, and a sharp, speculative look came into his dark
eyes. "Yes," he said. "Yes, you'll find it very interesting
indeed. Then there's Illingworth's *Offshore:* that you
mustn't miss. I can lend it to you in London. And Ashley's
Book of Knots, to keep you happy through the long winter
evenings. Can you do a Turk's Head?"

"I doubt if I could do a reef," said Henry humbly. "It's
a long time since I was a Boy Scout."

"I get a lot of fun out of knots," said Colin. He picked
up a length of light rope. "Let me demonstrate the clove
hitch. One of the most useful knots of all. You make a loop
here . . ."

Henry watched with interest. He noticed that Colin had
not even once glanced downriver at Alastair and Anne.
When Henry had mastered the clove hitch and was strug-
gling with the intricacies of the running bowline, Colin
suddenly remarked, "Apropos of our conversation last
night, I wasn't joking you know. I'm convinced there was
something funny about Pete's death."

"Are you?"

"Yes. All sorts of loose ends don't tie up. I've got an
idea, too, but it needs some working out."

"I wonder," said Henry, "why it didn't occur to you
sooner that things weren't as straightforward as they
seemed."

Colin raised a face full of bland innocence, under which
a secret amusement pulsed, rather frighteningly.

"Oh, but it did," he said. "It occurred to all of us, except perhaps Alastair, who's a simple soul." He permitted
himself a brief look in the direction of the swimmers.
"Poor Alastair," he added, "he's very easily fooled, you
know."

In the cabin, Rosemary was tossing salad with hot, angry
tears in her eyes.

"Where's the butter?" Emmy asked.

"In the . . . the . . ." Rosemary's voice broke, and she turned her head away. "Oh, blast," she said. "I'm sorry."

"Rosemary," said Emmy, embarrassed, "I know it's none of my business, but——"

Rosemary buried her face in an inadequate handkerchief. "I'm so frightened," she said, in a voice muffled by tears and Irish linen. "So terribly frightened."

"What of?"

"Alastair and I . . . we've been married six years now . . . we've always been so happy . . ."

Emmy, who could think of no useful reply to this, tried to say nothing in a sympathetic way.

Rosemary blew her nose loudly, and then said, shakily but with some violence, "I believe she's a witch."

"I wouldn't worry too much," said Emmy. "Surely——"

"All of them," said Rosemary "Colin and Pete and . . . and David . . . and now Alastair. She sends them crazy. It's uncanny."

"Pete?" said Emmy. "I thought Pete jilted her."

"Pete was just as badly bitten as the rest of them," said Rosemary more calmly. "But he was older and more sensible and he saw the red light before it was too late. So he got out. That infuriated her. She's not used to that sort of treatment. If anybody killed him . . ." She tossed the salad with unnecessary force. "I'm sorry I made an exhibition of myself. It's just that with this business of Pete's death and . . . and everything . . ."

"I know it's hell," said Emmy, "but, seriously, don't worry. Alastair adores you."

"I wonder," said Rosemary. There was a long silence, and then she said, briskly, "The butter's in the starboard cupboard in a polythene bag."

After lunch, Colin announced his intention of going back to *Mary Jane* and getting his head down.

Alastair looked shocked. "And waste a perfect afternoon's sailing?" he demanded indignantly.

"Certainly," replied Colin, with some dignity. "I want to think."

"You're very welcome," said Alastair. "I personally intend to explore the upper reaches of Hamford Water. Coming, Anne?"

"No," said Anne. "I'm going ashore to pick buttercups. Coming, Henry?"

"I'd love to," said Henry promptly.

Emmy and Rosemary exchanged the briefest of glances, and Emmy was annoyed to feel a distinct and sickening pang of something very like jealousy. She shook it off angrily. She said quickly, "Have a lovely time. I'm staying with Rosemary and Alastair."

"Rendezvous here at four o'clock," said Alastair. He seemed none too pleased with the afternoon's arrangements. "No later. We've got a foul tide all the way back to the Berry and the wind's falling away light. That gives you just an hour."

So Colin rowed back to *Mary Jane*, and *Ariadne* got smoothly under way again, leaving Henry pulling for the green, reedy shore, with Anne perched like a water sprite on the transom of the dinghy. She had changed out of her wet bathing dress, and was now wearing minuscule shorts of blue denim and a blue and white striped cotton shirt. Her feet were still bare.

They beached the dinghy on the shingle shore, and set off across the dappled green meadow. For some time they walked in silence. Then Anne said, "I wish you didn't dislike me so much, Henry."

"Dislike you? Why on earth should you think that?" ("But it's true," muttered his conscience. "Why?")

"You don't trust me," Anne went on. "You think I'm wicked. . . . I suppose you think I'm marrying Colin for his money."

"It hadn't even occurred to me," said Henry untruthfully. "It's no business of mine."

"But I want to tell you," said Anne. "I like you so much, Henry."

"All right," said Henry. "Go ahead. What do you want to tell me?"

"Let's sit down," said Anne. She dropped onto the sweet-smelling grass and began to pull up long, feather-topped blades one by one. Henry sat beside her and waited. At length she said, "I don't pretend that I'm wildly in love with Colin. Not as I am—as I was—with . . . with Pete. That was something quite different. I don't suppose that'll ever happen to me again."

"My dear child," said Henry, "you're twenty-three and you're one of the most attractive creatures I've ever met. It'll happen again."

Anne turned to him gravely. "Do you really mean that?" she said.

"Of course I do. You've got your whole life ahead——"

"I didn't mean that," said Anne. "I mean—do you really think I'm attractive?"

"You must know you are," said Henry uncomfortably. He was aware of a growing mixture of embarrassment, irritation and excitement.

"You see," said Anne slowly, "you remind me so much of Pete."

"I'm interested in Pete." Thankfully, Henry grasped his opportunity of changing the subject. "You must have heard by now that I'm not at all satisfied that his death was—accidental."

"Oh, but it was." Anne appeared to be stating an incontrovertible fact.

"What makes you so sure?"

"I'm going to tell you a great secret, Henry. I went ashore to Steep Hill Sands in the fog that day."

"I know you did," said Henry.

"Oh," said Anne flatly. "So much for my big sensation. I suppose you've been talking to David. You don't waste much time, do you? What did he tell you?"

"Not much," said Henry. "I'd like to hear your version."

"I simply had to talk to him, you see," said Anne. There was no mistaking the simple sincerity in her voice. "I had to. I suppose I was a bit out of my mind just then. I made David row me ashore, and wait for me in the dinghy while I looked for Pete. I was on the end of a rope so as not to get lost."

She stopped, and looked sideways out of her green eyes at Henry, who was doing his best to preserve the traditional poker face of Scotland Yard.

Anne rolled over onto her face, as she did so touching Henry's leg with her own slim, brown one. "I suppose," she went on, "that David told you it was he who went ashore and left me in the dinghy. He has very old-fashioned ideas about chivalry."

Henry maintained a stubborn silence.

"Oh, very well," said Anne lightly. "Don't tell me. It makes no odds. I'm telling you the truth. It was I who went ashore, and I found Pete. That is, I found *Blue Gull*. Pete was below in the cabin. I tapped on the hull and called to him. He was very angry."

"He spoke to you?"

"Oh, yes. He came up into the cockpit. He was furious and he looked terrible. He told me I was a bloody fool and that I was to go back to *Pocahontas* at once. I said I must talk to him, and he said, 'I can't talk to anyone. I feel lousy. I've just cracked myself over the head with the boom.' Then I saw that he had a big bruise on the left side of his head."

Henry took a deep breath. "He said that? You're sure?"

"Of course I'm sure."

"Where was the boom? In the gallows or swinging free?"

For a moment, Anne hesitated. "I don't know," she said. "Swinging free, I think. I didn't really notice."

"What happened then?"

"I tried again to make him listen to me, and he got really livid. He said, 'Are you going back or do I have to take you?'—and he climbed out of the boat and on to the sand. I was scared then. I knew if he left *Blue Gull* he'd never find his way back. So I said, 'O.K., I'm going.' And then I went back. He was still standing there on the sand behind *Blue Gull* when I left him. He . . . he must have collapsed after I'd gone. A sort of delayed concussion, I suppose." Anne was speaking very quietly. "So you see, Henry, it was an accident. But if anybody killed him, I did. Because if it hadn't been for me, he'd never have got out of the boat. You can imagine how many kinds of hell I've been through since."

There was a long silence. "It's a pity you didn't tell the

coroner all this at the inquest," said Henry. "It certainly clears matters up."

"I didn't know anything about it. I went straight back to London with David, and the next day I went on holiday to the south of France. I didn't even know that Pete was dead until Colin wrote and told me. When I got home, it was all over. And anyway, they came to the right verdict, so what did it matter?"

Henry said, "You didn't see or hear anybody else on Steep Hill Sands?"

"No. Certainly not. Only Pete."

"Have you any idea what time you went ashore?"

"About ten, I should think. I don't know."

"And how long did you stay there?"

"Oh, hardly any time. Not more than ten minutes."

"You left Pete," Henry went on, "and followed the rope back to the dinghy. What did you tell David?"

Again there was a trace of hesitation before Anne spoke. Then she said, "I felt a bit of a fool and very angry by then. It was so humiliating that he wouldn't even speak to me. I told David I hadn't been able to find him."

"One more thing," said Henry. "How far away was *Blue Gull* from the dinghy? I mean, do you think David could have overheard your conversation with Pete?"

Anne considered. Evidently the idea was new to her. "It's terribly hard to say," she said, at length. "Fog does such odd things to sound. I don't know how far away we were. I suppose he might have heard."

"It's a very strange story."

Henry looked at Anne, and saw that her green eyes were full of tears. "You don't believe me," she said miserably. "I knew you wouldn't." She turned away, young and hurt and defenceless.

Without thinking, Henry laid his hand on hers. "I never said I didn't believe you, Anne. I only . . ."

Anne gripped his hand. "I'm so terribly unhappy, Henry," she said. And before he knew what was happening, she had thrown her arms around his neck and was crying on his shoulder like a child. Henry patted her comfortingly on the back, and felt her arms tighten. Then she stopped sobbing, and nuzzled her face into his neck. It was a distinctly pleasant sensation. It was at that moment that Henry saw Colin beaching his dinghy. He tried to push Anne away.

"Pull yourself together. Colin's coming."

Anne clung to him obstinately. Colin started to walk across the fields toward them. Henry said, "Be sensible, Anne, for God's sake."

Without moving, she whispered, "Say you believe me. Henry, darling, say you believe me."

In the grip of a nightmare, Henry said desperately, "All right, I believe you. Now behave yourself."

"You won't go on with this silly business of stirring up trouble, will you? Promise me you won't."

"I can't——"

"Promise!"

"Oh, very well."

She drew away from him then. "Thank you, darling Henry," she said. Her eyes were red, but she was smiling.

Colin came closer. It was inconceivable, Henry decided, that he had not seen what was going on, and equally inconceivable that he would not have put the worst possible construction on it. Feeling trapped and ridiculous, he scrambled to his feet.

"Don't get up," said Colin drily. "Forgive me if I join you. I got bored with my own company. I trust Anne has been entertaining you adequately."

Henry sat down again. Colin certainly did not appear either angry or upset, but in his embarrassment Henry felt sure he could detect an undercurrent of irony behind every word.

"Anne's rather upset," he said, and his own voice sounded hopelessly pompous in his ears. "My fault, I'm afraid. I started talking about"—it suddenly occurred to him that to mention Pete Rawnsley at this stage would be tactless in the extreme: he ended, wretchedly—"about death."

"Anne's a very emotional girl, aren't you, darling?" said Colin. He sat down beside her, gave her a sharp look, and added, "You've been crying."

"I'm all right now," said Anne. "I'm sorry I was so stupid. What have you been up to, darling?"

"Reading," said Colin. Again, his voice held the note of secret amusement that Henry had noticed the night before. *"The Venturesome Voyages of Captain Voss.* Hadn't looked at it for years. Most instructive. The fellow had some very ingenious ideas."

Only Colin appeared completely at ease. He turned to Henry and added, "I can't help feeling, Henry, that you'd have been more profitably employed reading a good book than playing at nymphs and shepherds with my feather-brained fiancée—especially as you succeeded in reducing her to tears. Some day you must tell me how you did it. I've never managed it."

This time there was no mistaking the malice in his voice, but Henry had the impression that it was directed at Anne. Colin, he reflected, must be quite used to situations of this sort, and even seemed to derive a perverse pleasure from them: but this mood of delicately cruel amusement contrasted sharply with the brooding anger which he had shown in the bar when Anne had referred to her affair with Pete Rawnsley. Was it that Colin knew that Pete had meant more to her than the casual flirtations into which she drifted so naturally? Or was it—?

"Of course," Colin was saying, "I could have told you that death—particularly sudden death—is Anne's least favourite topic of conversation. She's very sensitive about it just now. Aren't you, my sweet? Couldn't you find anything better to talk about in these idyllic circumstances?"

"Colin, you're being beastly again," said Anne lightly. "What time is it, Henry? Shouldn't you go back?"

Henry glanced at his watch. "Yes," he said, with some relief. "It's a quarter to four. I promised Alastair I wouldn't be late."

"Off you go, then," said Anne. "We'll stay a bit longer, shall we, Colin darling?"

Henry got to his feet. "Well," he said awkwardly, "I'll be seeing you. In The Berry Bush, I presume."

"You presume correctly," said Colin. "We won't disappoint you." He looked at Henry intently for a moment, with lively mockery and a hint of sympathy. Henry considered several remarks, rejected them all, and set off across the meadows to his dinghy.

Alastair was nothing if not punctual. *Ariadne* was already in sight, beating down Hamford Water towards the anchorage. Henry rowed out, Alastair put the nose of the boat into the wind to stop her, and helped him to clamber aboard.

At half past four, the wind had died away to the merest breath. At five o'clock, beating laboriously against the incoming tide, *Ariadne* was still well inside the narrow exit from the Backwaters.

Alastair said, "There's no sense in this. Come and take her, Rosemary, while I start the motor."

He removed several floor boards from the cockpit, to reveal a small, sturdy marine engine. It would be pleasant to be able to record that this miracle of modern science leapt into life at the first swing of the starting handle. It would also be untrue. However, it took little more than ten minutes of tinkering and profanity before Alastair emerged from the bowels of the boat, filthy but triumphant, to the accompaniment of an ear-splitting but reassuring roar. The sails were lowered, and *Ariadne* began to crawl confidently towards the open sea.

"Go and sit on deck, up fo'rard," Alastair yelled to Henry and Emmy. "Less noise and smell."

This proved to be quite true. Forward of the mast, there was nothing to be heard but a gentle purr, and conversation became possible.

Emmy said, "Did you have a nice walk?"

"Very enlightening," said Henry shortly.

"I was beginning to wonder," said Emmy, "whether Anne had designs on you."

To do him justice, Henry had fully intended to tell his wife the whole ludicrous story, to share the joke with her and implore her never to leave him alone with an unscrupulous minx again: but for some reason, when it came to the point, all he said was, "Good heavens, no. I only went with her because I wanted to talk to her about . . . you know what."

Emmy gazed out over the glassy sea, and said, "Did she have anything interesting to tell you?"

Henry told her Anne's account of her adventures on Steep Hill Sands. Emmy turned to him, her eyes shining. "Oh, darling, I'm so glad. That's the explanation. Now you can forget the whole thing, can't you?"

"Yes," said Henry, "I can."

"You fraud," muttered his conscience, nastily. *"Tell her what David said."*

"But I promised Anne . . ."

"Under duress," said Conscience, with a leer.

"I'm on holiday."

"That has nothing to do with it. I thought you cared about truth and justice."

"I care more about people," said Henry, crossly—and was horrified to realize that he had spoken the last words aloud.

Emmy, surprised, said, "More than what?"

"More than anything," said Henry.

"I don't understand."

Henry turned and looked at his wife. For the first time, he saw, consciously, that she had been putting on quite a bit of weight: he saw the crow's-feet of laughter at the corners of her eyes, and the occasional glint of grey in her black hair. A great wave of tenderness swept over him.

"I care about you," he said, and put his arm round her shoulders. "In fact, I love you very much. It seems a long time since I told you that."

Emmy relaxed against his arm, and shut her eyes. "I love you, too," she said. "I suppose we're just sentimental old fools. Do you know, I was actually worried about you and Anne."

"Idiot."

"I might have known you'd have more sense."

"I haven't got much sense," said Henry.

"Go on," said Conscience, approvingly. *"Tell her now."* But he didn't.

They reached the mouth of the Berry at eight o'clock. At ten past eight, *Mary Jane* passed them, gliding swiftly and beautifully through the still water to the gentle throb of her powerful motor. The chill of the evening had driven Henry and Emmy back to the cockpit, where they sat in enforced silence, since any attempt at speech was drowned under the harsh roar of *Ariadne*'s faithful but cacophonous engine. They were all glad to see the tall, angular chimney stacks and steep roof of The Berry Bush silhouetted against the sunset. Alastair took *Ariadne* upstream of her mooring, then swung her round into the tide, and switched off the motor, leaving the boat just enough way on her to carry her down to her buoy. As the engine coughed itself into silence, the full beauty of the evening became apparent for the first time: quietness streamed back over the river like cool rain on parched earth: the fading light turned the trees to black, amorphous shadows and the water to grey satin, shot with reflected pink and green and violet from the western sky.

By common consent, *Ariadne*'s crew had decided against going ashore, and it was without any great pleasure that, at a quarter to ten, they heard Colin's voice shouting, "*Ariadne* ahoy!"

"Oh, blast," said Alastair, "what does he want?" He got up slowly and went out into the cockpit.

Colin's dinghy was alongside. Anne sat in the stern.

"Aren't you people coming ashore for a beer?" Colin called.

"We weren't," said Alastair. "Too comfortable where we are. Besides, it's nearly closing time."

"Not till eleven, Alastair," said Anne. "Do come. We're only going to have one for the road."

"Wait a minute," said Alastair. "I'll sound out the feeling of the meeting."

He went below again, and put the proposition to the others.

"I'm certainly not going," said Rosemary. "In any case, I have to wash up."

"Count me out, too," said Emmy. "I'll help Rosemary, and then I'm ready for bed. I'm not used to all this fresh air."

"By all means, you go if you want to, darling," said Rosemary. Her voice sounded perfectly natural.

"I think perhaps I will, after all," said Alastair, with a trace of guilt. "What about you, Henry?"

Henry yawned. "Um," he said. "What a difficult decision. O.K., I'll come."

The bar of The Berry Bush on a Monday evening had an atmosphere which was entirely different from its weekend clamour. Herbert Hole sat in an inglenook, his greasy yachting cap still anchored firmly to his grey head, talking earnestly to Sam Riddle. Bill Hawkes was chatting to Bob at the bar. Hamish, looking unseamanlike in grey flannels and a sports jacket, was playing a desultory game of darts against Sir Simon. Old Ephraim sat by himself near the fireplace, puffing at an ancient and smelly pipe. Otherwise the bar was empty.

The four newcomers settled themselves at the big table in the window, where Sir Simon and Hamish joined them, thereby leaving the dart board free for a contest of deadly seriousness—Bill Hawkes and Bob against Herbert and Sam.

"Had a good day?" Hamish asked.

They told him, enthusiastically, about their trip to Walton Backwaters.

"Walton?" said Hamish. "Funny place to go today. Tide's all wrong."

"I wanted to go there," said Anne. "I love Hamford Water."

"Typical female reasoning," said Hamish, "completely devoid of even the most elementary logic. I suppose you had to motor all the way back?"

"So what? It was a heavenly sail down there."

"You're a fool," said Hamish indifferently.

"Yes," said Anne quietly. "I'm a fool. Colin, darling, I could use another beer."

Colin took the empty mugs to the bar.

The dart game was proceeding acrimoniously.

"We saw you out in *Priscilla*," said Henry to Sir Simon. "A wonderful day for a spin."

Sir Simon looked surprised. "Me?" he said. "No, I wasn't

out today, worse luck. Couldn't manage it. Had to take that bit of Wedgwood into Ipswich. They say they can mend it, but I doubt it."

"Your boat was out, at all events," said Alastair.

"Was she? Oh, very likely. Riddle went out for a spot of fishing, I dare say."

"That's right, Sir Simon," Bob put in. "Came up past the pub."

"He had somebody with him," said Henry.

"Old Ephraim, most like," said Bob. Lowering his voice, he added, "Knows where the fish are, 'e does. Proper old poacher."

"Yes, almost certainly. Ephraim." Sir Simon cleared his throat. "Well, who's for another drink?"

Colin looked at his watch. "Time we were away, thank you all the same. We've got a long drive ahead of us." He stood up. "See you all next weekend, I trust."

"Of course," said Alastair. "Saturday's the big night. The Civic Reception."

Colin was standing beside the table, putting on his duffel coat. He said, "By the way, Henry, this business of Pete. It may interest you to know that I'm a jump ahead of you."

A sudden silence fell on the bar. Sam said, "Your throw, Herbert," but nobody moved.

"I know," Colin went on, "at least I'm pretty sure I know, why. How, is quite easy. The only question is—who?"

"Don't be silly, Colin," said Anne sharply. "Henry wasn't serious. He's forgotten the whole thing, haven't you, Henry?"

She turned her green eyes to Henry. They held a challenge. Unhappily, Henry said, "Yes. I was only fooling. Everyone knows what happened. It was perfectly straightforward."

Colin looked briefly at Anne. "How very disappointing," he said. "I had such a nice theory worked out. Never mind. You presumably know best."

"Time," said Bob loudly. "Time, gentlemen, *if* you please."

EIGHT

Early the next morning, with a troubled conscience, Henry took the bus into Ipswich, leaving the others to go sailing without him. He had, he told himself firmly, every intention of keeping his promise to Anne. He wished heartily that he had held his enquiring mind in check from the beginning. However, he had set certain wheels in motion which could not be stopped immediately: and besides, Inspector Proudie was expecting him.

As the bus lurched along between hedges of wild rose and honeysuckle, Henry reflected that, after all, there was no reason why Anne's story should not be true. It accounted for everything, except the fact that Pete Rawnsley had apparently lifted the boom out of the gallows himself. Well, why not? He had probably had some good, seaman-like reason for doing so. The fact that David had lied to protect Anne from imagined danger was also perfectly feasible: he was only too clearly demented about the girl, and would have perjured his soul for her. But why had he gone out of his way to slander Hamish? Pure spite? Hardly likely. Certainly, there seemed to be no great amount of love lost between the two men, but that was not an adequate reason for an accusation of murder. But then, of course, David had not intended it to be an accusation of murder, merely a suggestion of accident. A hasty, not very well-thought-out explanation to cover the facts. The product of a vivid and disorderly imagination. Yes, that was logical.

There remained, of course, the matter of the Trigg-Willoughby robbery. Henry turned his thoughts to this with some relief. Here he was on the firm ground of routine crime, and there were no considerations of personal loyalty to confuse the issue. If his half-formed theories were correct, there might still be a chance of restoring to Priscilla at least part of her treasure. He began to look forward to the coming interview with more pleasure.

Inspector Proudie was a stout man with a round, guileless face. He greeted Henry with a nice mixture of friendliness, deference and defensiveness—defensiveness because, in spite of the Chief Constable's insistence that Henry's visit was motivated purely and simply by some interesting facts which he had stumbled upon while on holiday, Proudie could not quite rid his mind of the niggling implication that his own enquiries had been somehow inefficient.

He pushed a bulky file across the desk to Henry.

"It's all there, sir," he said. "I think you'll agree that we covered the ground pretty thoroughly, but you know as well as I do that putting your finger on a sneak thief is like trying to catch a trout in a bucket. At first it looked like a local, unprofessional job, and we reckoned we'd get the fellow as soon as he tried to market the stuff. Your people in London were on the lookout too, of course. But nothing traceable has come onto the market. So either the chap is in touch with a highly efficient disposal system, or he's hidden the loot and is prepared to lie low for years, if need be. Neither alternative sounds like an amateur."

"Unless," said Henry, "the local amateur is in touch with a professional fence."

Proudie sighed. "I know what you're thinking, sir. Bob Calloway."

"Exactly."

"We've watched him like hawks. But he's apparently leading a blameless life as a country publican. As I recollect, even in his Soho days nothing was ever proved against him."

"That's true," said Henry. He grinned, indicating that he had caught the innuendo that, as far as Calloway was concerned, London had had no more success than Ipswich. Proudie permitted himself a smile in return. The atmosphere warmed.

"In any case," Proudie went on, "don't forget that Bob didn't take over The Berry Bush until nearly a year after the robbery."

"He didn't?" Henry sat up. "That's very interesting. You mean, he's only been here a few months?"

"That's right. Eight months. Bought the pub outright from old Harry Potter when he retired. It's all there in the report. If you want my honest opinion, I think it's just one of those coincidences that make our work so confusing."

Henry opened the file, and took out the typewritten page on which the life history of Bob Calloway was summarized. He had apparently left the Duck and Doorknob three years previously, and had taken over a pub in Gloucestershire, where his behavior had been exemplary. As far as was known, none of his old cronies from the underworld of London had been in touch with him there, and his own trips to the capital had been infrequent. Eight months ago, he had sold the Gloucestershire pub and bought The Berry Bush. Since then, the only available information on his movements was that a constable on the beat had recognized him walking down Brewer Street one Friday evening in June—an activity that could hardly be classed as illegal or even suspicious. The official opinion was that he had long since retired from any sort of criminal practice, if, indeed, he had ever been engaged in it. Nothing had ever been proved against him, except that he kept bad company.

Henry looked up from his perusal of this document. "Bob was in London last weekend," he said.

Proudie made a gesture of helplessness. "What if he was? That's not an offence, is it? I can't have the man tailed everywhere he goes."

Henry put the paper to one side, and began reading the official reports of the police investigation into the Trigg-Willoughby robbery. He smiled to himself as he studied the orderly, official language of Priscilla's statement, and wondered how many patient hours had been required to condense her ramblings to this coherent form.

"I left Rooting Manor shortly after one o'clock A.M., accompanied by my brother. George Riddle drove us home. We arrived at Berry Hall at approximately one forty-five. I was at that time wearing the items of jewellery listed overleaf. I was extremely tired, and went to bed immediately. It was my normal practice to deposit my jewels in the safe every night, according to my dear father's wishes: but on that occasion my fatigue must have driven it out of my mind. I have no clear recollection of what I did with the jewellery. I imagine I must have left it on the table in my dressing room . . ."

A vivid picture came into Henry's mind of Priscilla in the Blue Drawing Room, giggling helplessly over the smashed Wedgwood urn. He could imagine only too clearly the painful scene at the Hunt Ball: the embarrassment as Priscilla was bundled out to the waiting car: the sniggers and the gossip: Sir Simon's mortification. He pictured the two men, Sir Simon and Riddle, guardians of a guilty secret that was a secret no longer, helping the pathetic, half-crazy woman into the dark house. . . .

He turned to Sir Simon's statement. It was typically crisp and to the point.

". . . certainly I did not accompany my sister to her room. There was no reason why I should. I had every confidence that she would lock the jewellery up in the safe, as usual. The evening's dancing had exhausted her considerably, but she was perfectly in control of herself. I locked the outer doors of the house and went to bed. I heard no sound of any sort during the night, but this is hardly surprising, as I sleep in the opposite wing . . ."

Every confidence. Yes, Henry thought, that was justified. Three-quarters of an hour in the car should have sobered Priscilla up considerably, and the habits of a lifetime are not easily broken. He himself could remember an occasion

—that terrible Old Boys' Dinner when he had mixed his drinks so disastrously: to this day he had no recollection of how he got home or to bed, but the next morning his suit was neatly on its hanger, his shoes in the right place on the rack. Drunken people tended to go through their regular routine, blindly. Unless, of course . . .

"I'm afraid, sir," said Proudie, "that the fact of the matter is that the lady was . . . em . . . intoxicated." He cleared his throat, and Henry saw that he had gone very red. "It's not a thing one likes to have to say, and we kept it as quiet as possible, of course . . . but the people who were at the dance——"

"They tell me the whole county was there," said Henry. "Not much hope of keeping it quiet."

"It's very understandable," Proudie went on staunchly. "A lady who isn't accustomed to strong drink . . ."

"Yes," said Henry absently. "Yes. How many of the local people would have known which was Miss Trigg-Willoughby's room?"

Proudie answered promptly. "Quite a few," he said. "Herbert Hole knows the house well—he's often helped Sir Simon out with odd jobs in the winter. He'd actually been repainting Miss Priscilla's room not long before. Then there's Sam Riddle—his son George is Sir Simon's man, you know—he does a bit of gardening up at the Hall every now and then. He'd been amusing the locals in The Berry Bush by telling them how Miss Trigg-Willoughby used to lean out of her window in the morning with her hair still in curling pins, and shout out instructions about where he was to plant the tulips. I believe Bill Hawkes has done carpentry jobs up there, too. And there's Tom Bates, the postman, and young Bill, who delivers the milk, and Alf, the grocery boy——"

"How would they know which was her room?" Henry asked, intrigued.

Proudie smiled. "Same way as Sam Riddle, sir. The lady's a little eccentric, as you'll realize if you've met her. Given to poking her head out of the window and calling out to people who come to the house. Her rooms are just over the front door, you see. Yes, I reckon most

people knew where to look for the stuff, all right. Trouble
is, none of them are cat burglars, that I know of."

"Yes," said Henry. "That's the trouble." He thumbed
through the file again, and found the statement which
had been signed, in the painstaking copperplate of village
scholarship, by George Riddle. Once again, character had
all but been obliterated by officialese, but the facts were
clear enough.

> "My name is George Jeremiah Riddle. I am employed
> as butler-handyman at Berry Hall by Sir Simon
> Trigg-Willoughby. I also act as chauffeur when re-
> quired. On January 16th last at approx. 7 P.M. I was
> summoned by Miss Priscilla to help her remove her
> jewellery from the safe, which is located in the cor-
> ridor outside her bedroom. The jewellery is normally
> kept in this safe in two steel boxes. I should explain
> that this safe, which is a large one, has an inner
> locked compartment for the jewel boxes. I have a key
> to the outer door, as it is part of my duties to clean
> the silver which is kept there. As far as I know, only
> Sir Simon and Miss Priscilla have keys to the inner
> compartment, and only Miss Priscilla has the keys to
> the jewel boxes themselves. She wears them [the keys]
> on a chain round her neck . . ."

Henry smiled to himself at the diligence with which
the local police had taken pains to ensure that nobody
should imagine Priscilla going round with two big steel
boxes slung round her plump throat. He said to Proudie,
"Is this accurate—Riddle's statement about the keys?"

Proudie nodded. "Yes," he said. "Well, almost. There's
actually a spare set of keys, but they're kept at the bank
in case of emergencies. I believe," he went on, comfortably
knowledgeable, "that Sir Simon has been worried for years
at the thought that Miss Priscilla was the only person with
keys to the boxes themselves. She's . . . well, she's an
unusual lady, sir, as you know, and quite naturally Sir
Simon felt he'd like to keep a bit of an eye on all that
valuable stuff. But the trouble was that the jewellery was

Miss Priscilla's personal property, and nothing nor nobody could make her part with those keys unless she wanted to."

"Surely," said Henry, "Sir Simon could have taken the spare keys out of the bank any time he wanted to check on the stuff."

Proudie chuckled. "That he couldn't, sir. Not Sir Simon nor anyone else. You see, Miss Priscilla had arranged with the bank that the keys could only be released on her signature. Old Charlie Piggott, the manager, he's a friend of mine. We go fishing together. That's how I come to know all this. He told me in confidence some years ago that Sir Simon had come to him several times and asked for those keys: but of course Charlie couldn't let him have them."

"So," Henry said, "Miss Priscilla herself was the only person who actually had access to the jewels."

"That's right," said Proudie. "And a very tight grip she kept on them, too. Loved showing them off, but wouldn't ever let anybody get too close, or touch them. It's funny, isn't it, sir," he added, with the air of one disclosing a great philosophical truth, "the effect jewellery seems to have on ladies? Still, of course, all this business of the keys has nothing to do with the case. We checked up, naturally, as a matter of routine, but it's perfectly clear that the boxes were left out on the dressing table. I saw them myself."

"Just where were they?" Henry asked.

"In Miss Priscilla's dressing room," Proudie answered. "It's a small room leading off her bedroom. The window was wide open, and the two boxes were lying on the table, unlocked and empty, except for a few worthless bits."

"Sir Simon told me," said Henry, "that the ladder had left marks in the flower beds under the window. Were there any footprints?"

Proudie grinned ruefully. "You bet there were," he said. "Beautiful, clear, easily identified footprints."

"There were?" Henry was extremely surprised. "Then why . . . ?"

"Because," said Proudie, "they were made by Sir

Simon's own sea boots—great big old rubber things.
They were in the shed with the ladder. Anybody could
have put them on over his ordinary shoes. We found them
with the ladder in the shrubbery."

"And no prints there?"

Proudie shook his head. "Not a hope. The ladder and
the boots had obviously been thrown into the bushes by
somebody standing on the gravel drive."

"What about the shed, where the ladder and boots came
from?" Henry persisted. "Did you look for prints there?"

Proudie looked hurt. "Of course we did, sir," he said.
"No hope of footprints—concrete path running from the
drive to the shed. And no fingerprints either."

Henry sighed. "Oh, well," he said. "You can't have
everything." He went back to Riddle's report.

> "At 8.45 P.M. I brought the car to the door in order
> to drive Sir Simon and Miss Priscilla to the Hunt
> Ball at Rooting Manor. Miss Priscilla was at that
> time wearing the tiara, the diamond and emerald three-
> strand necklace and pendant, with matching ear-
> rings, and two diamond bracelets, as well as the large
> solitaire diamond ring and several smaller ones . . ."

Crikey, thought Henry, as the monstrous vision of
Priscilla thus adorned took shape in his mind. It also
occurred to him that Riddle had been uncommonly ob-
servant.

> ". . . We arrived at Rooting Manor," *the statement
> continued,* "at about 9.30 P.M. I spent the evening in
> the servants' hall, where refreshments were avail-
> able for the chauffeurs and temporary staff. At 1.10
> A.M., I was called and told to bring the car round.
> Sir Simon and Miss Priscilla were waiting on the
> doorstep when I drove up, together with the two
> Mr. Rawnsleys. Miss Priscilla appeared to be un-
> well, and I helped her into the car. Sir Simon ex-
> plained that she had been overcome by the heat of the
> ballroom. We arrived home just before 2 A.M. Miss

Priscilla had slept in the car, and we had some difficulty in rousing her. Sir Simon and I helped her indoors and up the stairs. At the head of the staircase, she appeared to revive considerably. She said goodnight to us, and went down the passage to her room. I can positively state that she was wearing all her jewellery at that time. Sir Simon told me he had no further need of me, so I went to my room at the back of the house. I heard no sound during the remainder of the night.

"The following morning I stayed in bed until 8 A.M. My normal practise is to rise at 6 A.M., but in view of the fact that I had worked late, Sir Simon gave me permission to lie in. I had been instructed to prepare breakfast for 9.30, Mrs. Bradwell, the cook, being on holiday. Having cleaned the grates and stoked the boilers, I took breakfast into the dining room. Almost at once Sir Simon came in from the terrace and asked me if I had moved his sea boots, which he had left as usual in the potting shed. I replied that I had not, and he said, 'Maybe Sam has them, the old rascal. He appears to have pinched a ladder as well.' This I took to be a reference to my father, Samson Riddle, who was at that time working as an extra jobbing gardener at the Hall. It was then that we heard Miss Priscilla screaming." *A small shiver ran down Henry's spine. He read on.* "She came down the big staircase in her dressing gown, with her hair in curling pins, and screaming all the way. She was not wearing her dentures, which made it difficult to make out what she was saying, but she quite definitely said several times, 'I did it, I did it.' Sir Simon was very concerned. He said, 'Did what, Prissy?' Finally we understood that something had happened to the jewels. Sir Simon said to me, 'Quick, Riddle.' We both ran upstairs. The window of Miss Priscilla's dressing room was open and the jewel boxes were on the table, empty except for a few trinkets. Sir Simon told me to go and telephone for the police, but before I could leave the room,

Miss Priscilla came in. She was still crying and in an hysterical state. She came up to me, and she said, 'Don't ever trust anybody, Riddle. Not even yourself. Especially not yourself. What's the use of having keys if they weren't locked up?' She was twisting away at the chain that always hangs round her neck, and she pulled it so hard that the clasp broke and the two keys fell on the floor. 'So much for keys,' she said, half-screaming, as it were. Sir Simon said, 'Don't waste time listening to her, Riddle. Get the police.' I then proceeded downstairs . . ."

Henry read on doggedly to the end of this uninspiring and already yellowing document. When at last he had finished, he said to Proudie, "Well, Inspector, off the record and unofficially, what's your private opinion of this case?"

"Nothing private about it," said Proudie promptly. "Clear as mud. A very slick professional job, almost certainly the work of a lone operator. The way I see it, it went like this. Our man, whoever he was, turns up at the Hunt Ball in the guise of a hired chauffeur. He knows that a lot of valuable stuff is going to be flaunted around that night. He's already cased Berry Hall, of course, along with several other big houses in the neighbourhood. Well, Miss Priscilla and her jewels and her . . . em . . . overindulgence . . . are the talk of the evening in the servants' hall. We know that from Herbert and Sam and all the others who were there. The chap doesn't have to open his mouth. He just listens. He knows when the Trigg-Willoughbys go home. All he has to do is give them time to get to bed and to sleep and—there you are. Too easy."

"How would he know where to find the ladder and the boots?"

"He'd have marked them down when he cased the place. They were always kept there."

"That sounds reasonable," said Henry, "but who *was* this mysterious chap? Surely all the local chauffeurs know each other. They'd have noticed a stranger."

"I doubt it," said Proudie. "Quite a lot of the guests used chauffeur-driven cars from hire firms. The Mr.

Rawnsleys, for example. Mr. Pete and Mr. Hamish took a young lady to the dance, and Mr. Pete's M.G. wasn't big enough for the three of them. No, there were enough strange faces in the servants' hall that night. One more or less wouldn't have caused any comment."

"You don't happen to know," Henry asked, "which young lady Mr. Rawnsley took to the ball?"

"Not off-hand," said Proudie, "but I expect it's here somewhere. Let's have a look."

He flipped expertly through the file. "Here we are," he said. " '. . . *drove over with my nephew Hamish and Miss Anne Petrie* . . .' Does that mean anything to you?"

"Yes," said Henry. "Yes, it does."

There was a silence. Then Proudie shifted his large bulk in the straight-backed chair, and said, "Tragic affair that was, about the elder Mr. Rawnsley. I've got the reports on that, too, as you asked."

There was unmistakable curiosity in the inspector's voice, but Henry ignored it. He didn't even open the dossier containing the report of the inquest, which Proudie pushed across the table toward him. Instead, he lit a cigarette, and gave one to Proudie.

Proudie picked up a pencil, put it down again, and then said, "To be frank, sir, I had thought you might be coming to see me over something rather different. What I mean is—rumours get about pretty fast in the country, you know. One of my constables is from Berrybridge—Sam Riddle's nephew—and, well . . . not to mince matters . . . there's talk, sir. No denying it, there's talk."

"What about?" said Henry, as casually as he could. Mentally, he cursed Colin for his tactless remarks in The Berry Bush the previous evening.

Proudie hesitated. "Of course, there was talk at the time, too, sir. And then when you asked for the reports of the inquest . . ."

Suddenly, Henry grinned. "Inspector Proudie," he said, "could you arrange for a rumour to be circulated for me?"

"A rumour, sir?"

"A well-founded rumour," said Henry, "that Chief Inspector Tibbett has thoroughly investigated his suspicions about Mr. Pete Rawnsley's death, and come to the conclusion that the coroner's verdict was absolutely correct, and that the whole thing was an unfortunate accident."

A slow smile spread over the inspector's cherubic countenance. "That's easily arranged, sir."

"Thank you," said Henry.

NINE

Eleven A.M., Wednesday. High tide and a shining day, with a moderate easterly breeze.

"Let her go," called Alastair.

Emmy threw the red and white buoy overboard with a splash: Henry hardened in the jib sheet, then released it again as *Ariadne* turned downstream. Rosemary sat on the slightly tilting deck, munching an apple. The business of setting sails, of dropping and picking up moorings, had by now become a smoothly efficient routine, and Henry and Emmy felt justifiably proud of themselves. When Alastair shouted "Back the jib," or "Free the mainsheet," or "Oh, hell, the burgee halyard's snarled up again," they not only knew what he was talking about, but could even take appropriate action.

Since his interview with Proudie, Henry had resolutely cleared his mind of all thought of work, and had settled down to enjoy himself. Freed from Anne's conscious witchery, from Colin's dark irony and David's frenetic unease, the atmosphere on board *Ariadne* had become calm and idyllic. If Alastair was still obsessed by Dorinda and her blackguard boy, he managed not to show it. Rosemary was apparently her old, happy self again, singing tunelessly as she sat on the edge of the deck. Even the menace of Steep Hill Sands was obliterated, for the high tide had temporarily submerged the treacherous bank under a dazzle of blue water.

They passed Herbert, chugging in from seaward in his old grey launch, and they were overtaken by Sam Riddle's battered black fishing boat, which was rattling its noisy way out to the fishing grounds off Harwich, with old Ephraim steering, while Sam prepared the nets. Otherwise, the river, and, beyond it, the sea were theirs alone—clean and clear and empty.

They rounded Steep Hill Point and hardened in sheets as the nose of the boat swung to windward. *Ariadne* leant into the breeze and sped out to sea. A couple of miles out, they came about, freed sheets, and set a course on the starboard tack, headed north for the entrance to the River Deben.

So began a four-day cruise which included all the ordinary delights, hazards and small misfortunes which add up to the sport of boating. From the detection point of view, the four days were a dead loss. From every other standpoint, however, they were an unqualified success. Henry and Emmy got burnt brown with sun and salt water, soaked to the skin in the one heavy downpour, badly frightened in the one severe wind, and ridiculously elated at their own progress as mariners. They ate like lions and slept like logs, and Henry gave up shaving.

Ariadne's return to Berrybridge was planned for Saturday afternoon, in view of the mayoral celebrations taking place that day. It was not an easy sail, nor a particularly pleasant one. The sky was overcast, and a fresh nor'easterly breeze, running counter to the tide, had whipped the sea up into short, angry waves. It was a dead beat into the wind all the way, and *Ariadne*, wearing her smallest jib, butted and tossed and leant over at a tipsy angle, burying her nose in the lead-grey water and throwing back great fountains of icy spray. Every time they came about, the sails thrashed deafeningly, and the jib sheet developed a frightening habit of snarling itself round a cleat on the mast, which necessitated a hazardous journey forward over the steep, slippery deck before it could be freed.

Lunch was impossible, but Rosemary managed somehow to produce mugs of hot soup, which improved morale considerably. Although the boat was never in the slightest danger, it was nevertheless a cold, exhausting and exacting business: but, as is the way of life, these hardships brought their own rewards. The blessed, joyful moment when

Ariadne turned upriver, into the comparatively sheltered water inside Steep Hill Point: the serenity of the quiet Suffolk fields flanking the river: the final peace as *Ariadne* rode quietly at her own mooring at last: the immense solace of a huge, untimely meal of eggs and bacon and tea in the warm cabin.

Relaxing luxuriously against soft cushions, Henry suddenly remembered some lines he had heard somewhere, long ago.

> "Sleep after toil, port after stormy seas,
> Ease after war, death after life does greatly please. . . ."

Maybe he hadn't got the words quite right, but for the first time he knew what they meant. *Port after stormy seas . . . death after life . . .* Not death in battle, not murder . . . death crowning a serene old age . . . no, that wasn't right. The whole point was the abrupt contrast between storm and calm, like rounding Steep Hill. Suicide, then, perhaps. But that was taking a gloomy view: after all, stormy seas were stimulating and exhilarating and even pleasurable. It was just that one couldn't live at that pitch for ever. After the gale, the calm. After life, death . . . does greatly please. . . .

"I do believe he's asleep," said Emmy.

Henry opened his eyes with a jerk. "I'm not," he said. "I was thinking. Can I have some more tea?"

At half past six they went ashore. In honour of the occasion, they had all changed into their cleanest and most respectable clothes, and the men—after some debate—had actually shaved. As they pulled for the hard, speculation ran high as to the identity of the new mayor of Berrybridge. The polling booth was due to close at a quarter to seven, but they suspected that the result was already known, or at least that counting was by now taking place.

Rosemary came out strongly for Old Ephraim, but Alastair would have none of it. "It'll be new blood this time,"

he said. "You'll see. I wouldn't be at all surprised if Bill
Hawkes got in."

"Well, I'm for Herbert," Emmy said. "He'd be so
thrilled."

"Heaven forbid," said Alastair. "He'd be even more
impossible than ever."

"Of course, we mustn't forget Sam," Rosemary put in.
"Remember, he's got connections with the Hall. I think
we've been underestimating Sam."

The waterfront of Berrybridge Haven presented a bizarre aspect as they came ashore. Herbert's ramshackle,
black-tarred shed had virtually disappeared under a thicket
of posters. These were written in bold but shaky scarlet
letters on white paper: most of them read, simply, VOTE
FOR HOLE, but the writer had evidently tired of his repeti-
tive task, for occasionally he had substituted HOLE FOR
MAYOR, and in one case, in an excess of personal loyalty,
UP WITH HERBERT.

On the other side of The Berry Bush, Bill Hawkes's
smart, newly built boathouse had also been subjected to
electioneering zeal. He—as befitted the youngest and most
go-ahead candidate—had hit on the revolutionary and eye-
catching notion of writing his slogans in pale blue paint on
black paper. And the slogans themselves provided addi-
tional evidence that an imaginative mind had been at work.
WHO, demanded one poster, GOT THE NEW SLIP BUILT?:
WHO, echoed another, CLEANED UP THE FORESHORE?:
WHO, persisted a third, PAINTED THE NOTICES NEW?
To these superbly rhetorical questions, there was but one
answer. Along the front of the shed, a series of sheets of
black paper, each bearing a single letter in blue, spelt
out BILL HA KES. On the shore, a further sheet inscribed
with the letter "W" was being chewed systematically to
pulp by a fat, thoughtful-looking black spaniel.

The other two candidates had, Henry surmised, been
taken unawares by this high-powered campaigning, for their
attempts at retaliation bore all the marks of hasty im-
provisation. Also, Ephraim and Sam lacked the advantage
of the splendid display areas afforded by the professional
establishments of Messrs. Hawkes and Hole. However, to

do them justice, they had tried. A grimy piece of paper, tacked onto a tree, bore the scribbled retort EPHRAIM BUILT THE BRIDGE, DIDN'T HE?, while the black hull of Sam's boat, which was hauled well up onto the foreshore, was adorned with two sheets of newspaper, on which had been written, in enormous letters of black tar, HONEST RIDDLE.

The foreshore was deserted. If the shore was deserted, however, the pub was packed to suffocation, and an excited babble of voices drifted out into the yard. As *Ariadne*'s crew pushed their way into the bar, a sudden silence fell. Standing on tiptoe, Henry just managed to catch a glimpse of what was going on, over the shoulder of a very stout, grey-haired woman in a flowered rayon dress. A space had been cleared around the table in the window, at which Sir Simon and Bob Calloway were ensconced in official dignity. On the table stood five biscuit tins. Four of them were labelled, respectively, HERBERT, RIDDLE, HAWKES, and EPHRAIM, and each of these contained some small pieces of paper. The fifth was empty. Sir Simon, who had evidently just completed his count of the votes, was writing some figures on a piece of paper. Then he looked up, and rose to his feet. The crowded bar held its breath.

"Ladies and Gentlemen of Berrybridge Haven," began Sir Simon, pontifically, "I have much pleasure in announcing to you the name of your new mayor. After a secret ballot, held in the highest traditions of British democracy," Sir Simon went on, prolonging the agony, "I am delighted to be able to tell you that this borough has elected as its mayor for the coming year none other than that fine citizen and good friend to us all . . ." He paused for breath, looked at his paper again to make sure, and finally came out with it. "Our popular and esteemed Harbour Master, Mr. Herbert Hole."

Instantly, uproar broke loose. There were cheers and boos and stampings of feet and shouts of congratulation and defamation, and, above all, urgent pleas for beer. Herbert himself was persuaded to climb onto the table, whence he surveyed his constituents with—Henry was surprised to see—tears in his faded blue eyes. For once in his life, Herbert seemed to be at a loss for words.

He was given a chance to recover from his emotion, however, for Sir Simon—appealing for quiet in a stentorian bellow—was insisting on reading out the details of the voting. Through the cries of "Good old Herbert!", "Speech!" and "Pint o' mild, Bob!", he struggled to fulfill his duty to the electorate.

"Herbert Hole, sixteen votes," yelled Sir Simon. "Bill Hawkes—do you mind being quiet over there?—Bill Hawkes, fourteen votes. Ephraim Sykes—can you hear me at the back?—twelve votes. Sam Riddle, eight votes. Which means," he added, after a swift calculation, "that one hundred and six percent of the electorate registered their votes. Very creditable."

This got an enormous cheer, and there were renewed shouts of "Speech, Herbert!" By this time, Herbert had recovered his normal composure. He raised his hands in a strangely dignified gesture, and silence fell. Henry, glancing round, saw David, Colin and Anne standing together near the window. Hamish was beside the bar, behind which Henry was somewhat surprised to see, in addition to the barman, Miss Priscilla Trigg-Willoughby and George Riddle. He presumed, correctly, that Sir Simon had insisted on Priscilla being relegated to this comparatively calm vantage point, and that George was keeping some sort of discreet check on her consumption of alcohol.

Herbert began to speak. "Friends," he said. Everybody cheered again. "Citizens of Berrybridge, I thank you. On behalf of me and Mrs. 'Ole."

Amid acclamation, the large lady who had been obstructing Henry's view was propelled somehow through the mob, and a short delay occurred while several of Herbert's more ardent supporters tried to hoist her onto the table beside her husband. The Lady Mayoress herself, however, soon put a stop to this procedure.

"You take your 'ands off of me, Jim Sykes," she remarked tartly to an athletic-looking youth who had clasped

her round the knees as a preliminary to heaving her upwards to join Herbert. "And mind me pore feet, *if* you
please."

This rebuke went home. Jim Sykes retreated into the
crowd again, and Mrs. Hole favoured the company with a
brief simper and a murmured "Delighted, I'm sure," before
saying to her husband, in a fierce whisper, "Get on with it,
then."

Herbert got on with it. "Twenty year," he said, solemnly.
"Twenty year I bin 'Arbour Master of Berrybridge. Twenty
year 'Arbour Master and never Mayor, not till now. And if
I 'adn't 'ave got in this time, I'd 'ave known 'oo to blame."

This lapse into customary vindictiveness was not well
received by the electorate. There were several cries of
"Come orf it, Herbert," and "Wot you grumblin' at now?"

"Hay?" said Herbert loudly, clapping a hand to his ear.

"You 'eard," said a loud, rude voice, which was immediately followed by a thin, cracked one, which said, "Let 'im
be, Bill, lad."

Herbert cleared his throat. "I seen changes in Berry-
bridge," he went on, with a disapproving snort. "I seen
new folks come and I seen the sort of ways they bring with
them. I'm not talking about the old folk—Sir Simon and
Ephraim and Sam and the like," he added, unnecessarily.
"But there's others." His eye fell malevolently on Bill
Hawkes, then roved around until it came to rest on Bob
Calloway. "Some is generous and some isn't. Some play
fair and some don't. Some is gentlemen and some isn't."
Here his beady stare fixed itself on Hamish. "And some 'as
come and gone again, one way and another, and I say good
riddance."

Hamish put his tankard down on the counter with a
thump, and turned an angry red. Herbert was certainly
pulling no punches. Henry guessed that he had been looking forward to this moment for months.

"Then there's boats," said Herbert. "When I come here,
it were all working barges and fishermen, and not more'n a
couple of bloody yachts between 'ere and Woodbridge."

"Language, Herbert," said the Lady Mayoress loudly.
Herbert paid no attention.

"Look at it now." He gestured towards the window. " 'Ole bloody river full of 'em. Lunnon men, mostly, as we all know. Well, what I say is, it takes all sorts," he added, rather hastily. Even in his state of exaltation, he had not quite forgotten that the London men were his best clients.

"So," he went on, with splendid inconsequence, "what I say is jolly good luck to one and all, and a vote of thanks to Bob 'ere for the blow-out what we all know is waiting upstairs."

Thunderous applause greeted this graceful acknowledgement of the landlord's generosity. Herbert was about to climb down from the table, when Mrs. Hole plucked fiercely at his trouser leg and hissed something at him. Herbert straightened and added, cryptically, "And Mrs. 'Ole."

This enigmatic tribute seemed to satisfy the lady, for she simpered again, and accepted a small port from Sam Riddle. Herbert clambered unsteadily off the table and graciously allowed Alastair to buy him a large gin.

The big room on the first floor of The Berry Bush, which was the scene of every local wedding reception, christening party and funeral wake, had been laid out in style for the inauguration. Two long trestle tables, draped with spotless white cloths, were laden with dishes of cold meat, veal and ham pies, hunks of cheese and bowls of green salad. Two barrels of beer stood promisingly in the corner. At the head of one of the tables was a large armchair, covered somewhat haphazardly by an old red velvet curtain. This was the mayoral throne.

For the moment, there was no sign of Sir Simon, Herbert or Mrs. Hole, as these august personages had retired to collect the mayoral regalia, and incidentally to have a quick and privileged drink with Bob in his private sitting room. Meanwhile, the voters of Berrybridge, together with their guests from London, milled around the tables, remarking on the quality and quantity of the food as compared to last year, and expressing their satisfaction or otherwise with the result of the election.

The members of the Fleet greeted each other and sat down at the remotest end of the second table. Anne was in high spirits, and delighted by Herbert's success. Colin, too, seemed in a thoroughly good humour, and kept darting glances at Henry. He was obviously bursting to come out with some piece of information or other, but for some reason had decided to hug his secret to himself for the time being. David also seemed excited. He laughed a lot, particularly at Anne's witticisms: in fact, Henry thought, he seemed to regard the girl with a sort of stunned, bemused wonderment, as though unable to believe in her existence. Only with Hamish did he seem nervous and ill-at-ease, and this, Henry reflected, was hardly surprising: the more so since Hamish was in a thundering rage. He had, probably correctly, interpreted Herbert's remark about "good riddance" as expressing satisfaction over Pete's death, and he could not leave the subject alone.

"That bloody disgusting, dishonest old man," he growled, knocking back yet another beer. "I've never liked him, but this is the last straw. By God, I'd like to swipe that filthy grin off his ugly mug."

"I'm sure he didn't mean it like that, Hamish," said Rosemary soothingly.

"Of course he did, damn his eyes. He was looking straight at me when he said it."

"You shouldn't pay any attention to Herbert," said Anne, a little nervously. "He's just an old fool enjoying himself. Do forget it, Hamish."

Henry noticed, not for the first time, that Hamish was the only member of the Fleet whom Anne did not address as "darling." In fact, she seemed to have a certain respect for him, which was conspicuously lacking in her dealings with the others.

"Actually, of course," said Colin, "there'd be nothing easier than to demolish Herbert, if you really want to." Again, dark mischief bubbled in his voice.

"What do you mean?" said Hamish.

"Don't you know?" Colin's voice was full of mockery.

"If you mean that story of Pete's——"

"No, no. Nothing like that. Come over here and I'll tell you. I wouldn't even mind doing it myself. It would be rather fun."

"Oh, for heaven's sake," said David. "We've had enough trouble as it is."

"You mind your own business for a change," said Hamish rudely. He and Colin went into a corner by the beer barrels and began talking earnestly. Henry, who guessed what Colin was saying, felt distinctly apprehensive. When they came back to the table, Hamish seemed doubtful. But Colin said, "O.K., if you don't want to do it, I will. I feel just in the mood."

A few minutes later, the mayor's party arrived, to loud applause. First came Sir Simon, with Priscilla on his arm. Then Bob, carrying a dusty black garment trimmed with moth-eaten beige fur, a black cocked hat of ancient vintage and a long chain made of gilded tin. He was followed by Herbert (almost unrecognizable without his cap) and Mrs. Hole. George Riddle brought up the rear, bearing a large, rusty key on one of the metal bar trays.

This procession made its way to the head of the table with great solemnity. Then, while the rest of the company took their seats, Herbert stationed himself in front of the throne, with Mrs. Hole on his right. Bob and George stood behind the mayor's chair, each holding his precious burden.

Sir Simon, leaving Priscilla by the chair on Herbert's left, stepped up to the mayor-elect, cleared his throat, and said, "Herbert Henry Hole, inasmuch as you have been elected, by the free, fair and legal vote of the electors of the Borough of Berrybridge Haven to be their mayor for the term of one year, receive now the badges, insignia and privileges of your office."

George stepped forward. Sir Simon took the key from the tray, and solemnly handed it to Herbert.

"Do you receive the key of the borough?" enquired Sir Simon rhetorically.

"I receive the key of the borough," replied Herbert belligerently.

Bob stepped forward. Sir Simon took the dingy cloak from his arm.

"Do you receive the robe and hat of office?"

"I receive the robe and hat of office," said Herbert. This was not strictly accurate, however, for no sooner had Sir

Simon draped the robe round Herbert's bony shoulders
than it fell off again. Herbert made a grab at it, thereby
lowering his head at the exact moment when Sir Simon
was endeavouring to place the hat on it. The effect was
unfortunate. In the end, it was George Riddle who re-
trieved both robe and hat from under the table. Nobody
laughed. For all the idiocy of the proceedings, Berrybridge took its mayor seriously.

When at last Herbert was suitably robed and be-hatted,
Sir Simon cleared his throat again. The high spot of the
ceremony was clearly at hand. With a sinking heart,
Henry saw Colin and Hamish exchange glances. The latter nodded, almost imperceptibly.

"And finally," declaimed Sir Simon, with a parsonical
intonation, "finally, receive the chain, the badge and mark
of your——"

He got no further. There was a clatter at the far end
of the table as Colin stood up. In a ringing voice, he said,
"I object."

"Oh, God," muttered Rosemary.

"Bloody fool," said Alastair, under his breath.

In a stunned silence, Colin strode up to the head of
the table. Sir Simon, who had raised the chain in his hands,
preparatory to slipping it over Herbert's head, stood petri-
fied by sheer astonishment. On Herbert's face, incredulity
and fury struggled for supremacy. Colin turned to the assembled company and said, conversationally, "This inauguration is a fake. The election was rigged."

This was too much for the citizens of Berrybridge. Almost as bad as the implication that the election was fraudu-
lent was the fact that bets had already been paid out.
Angry voices broke out. Sir Simon put the chain down on
the table, and said, coldly, "That is a very serious accusation, Mr. Street. What do you mean by it?"

Colin was enjoying himself. He appealed for, and got,
silence. Then he said, "There are forty-seven registered
electors in Berrybridge. Herbert got sixteen votes, Bill got
fourteen, Ephraim twelve and Sam eight. That makes fifty.
Which means either that three unauthorized people voted,
or that three people voted twice, or that somebody managed

to slip three extra voting papers into the box. Herbert's majority is only two. If—and I emphasize the 'if'—the illegal votes were for Herbert, it brings his total down to thirteen, and Bill wins by one vote."

"Hear, hear," said Hamish, loudly.

Herbert had gone pale. "Prove it!" he shouted. "Allegations of dishonesty! Blackenin' my good name!"

"Disgusting!" said Mrs. Hole, loudly. Her large face had gone very red.

"There's a very easy way of putting matters right, however," Colin went on pleasantly. "All forty-seven electors are here. If they will indicate by raising their hands which candidate they voted for today, we shall know the truth at once."

For a moment there was silence. Then everybody started to talk at once.

Sir Simon said: "Most irregular. Can't have that."

Mrs. Hole said: "It's a disgrace, that's what it is."

Ephraim said: "I'm for it. Only proper, like the gentleman says."

Priscilla said: "This cold beef looks delicious. May we start soon?"

Herbert said: "I'm callin' the perlice, that's what I'm doing."

Bill Hawkes said: "Oh, what the hell. Let's get on with the grub."

The general tone of the meeting, however, was against this liberal sentiment. Colin's lucid explanation and its implications had penetrated the consciousness of the good people of Berrybridge, and, slowly, they became angry. Even Herbert's supporters, anxious to prove the validity of their winning bets, were disposed to clear the matter up. Eventually, Sir Simon took a vote: the result was forty-one in favour of a show of hands, and six against.

The visitors remained in an unhappy huddle at the end of the room, and cursed Colin quietly. Even Hamish, the instigator of the whole thing, now seemed to share their embarrassment. The villagers, however, had apparently forgotten that it was an outsider who had stirred up the trouble. Their only concern now was to reach the truth of the matter. In an atmosphere of almost unbearable tension, Sir Simon called for the show of hands.

"All those who voted for Sam Riddle," he said nervously, "please raise your hands."

Promptly, eight hands went up.

"Those who voted for Ephraim?"

Twelve hands were raised.

"Bill Hawkes?"

There was dead silence as Sir Simon counted the hands. There was no mistake. Fourteen.

"Leaving," said Sir Simon grimly, "thirteen votes for Mr. Hole."

At that pandemonium broke loose. Herbert, his cocked hat awry, turned on Colin in a fury.

"I'll get you for this!" he yelled, beside himself with rage. "I'll get you! Twenty year I've waited and you cheat me out of it! Bloody busybody! Bloody fine Lunnon gentleman, I don't think! Pity you didn't go the way of the other flamin' nosey-parker!"

The situation showed every sign of turning nasty. Only Priscilla, who had quietly started on the cold beef, remained quite unperturbed. For the rest, the general sentiment was, to put it mildly, anti-Herbert. Cries of "Cheat!" "Swindler!" and worse flew about the room, and several private fights showed signs of breaking out.

In the end, it was Sir Simon who, by sheer force of personality, restored order. He climbed onto a chair and stamped on the table with his foot until some semblance of quiet reigned. Then he said, "Now, my friends. Let us consider the situation quietly. Obviously, there has been a mistake. Obviously, illegal votes were cast, and the new Mayor of Berrybridge is, in fact, Bill Hawkes. But that's no reason for jumping to the conclusion that my friend Mr. Hole had anything to do with it. On the contrary, he deserves our sympathy in his disappointment. Whatever happened, you can depend on it that it was either a genuine mistake, or else a childish prank played by some irresponsible person. In any case, there's nothing to be gained now by throwing mud. Let us be sensible, and write the whole thing off as one of those mishaps that

may occur in any election. The thing to do now is to
inaugurate Mr. Bill Hawkes as mayor, and get on with
our food."

A rumble of discontent went round the room, but it
was plain that the force of the argument had come across.
Somebody said, "It's true, lads. We don't know as it was
Herbert done it."

"In fact," Sir Simon went on, gallantly throwing himself to the wolves, "in fact, the person most likely to have
made a mistake is myself. After all, I counted the votes.
As many of you know, arithmetic has never been my
strong point, even at the dart board."

This, blessedly, raised a laugh. At that moment, Priscilla looked up from her plate, and remarked loudly,
"This beef is really excellent, Simon. Do have some."

The tension was effectively broken. Everyone laughed,
and murmurs of "Poor old Herbert" began to replace the
ugly epithets. Sir Simon took advantage of the situation
to add, "And we should all be grateful to Mr. Street for
having brought the matter to light. Now that we are agreed
that no blame can be attached to anybody but myself,
let us get on with the business of the evening."

It was very well done. Miraculously, good humour was
restored all round. George Riddle, at a gesture from Sir
Simon, quickly divested Herbert of his hat and cloak,
leaving the Harbour Master standing, pathetically denuded
of his finery, his sparse grey hair sticking up like a halo
round his head.

"And now," said Sir Simon, "I suggest that we give
three cheers for Mr. Hole, and wish him luck in next
year's election. Hip, hip . . . hooray! Hip, hip . . ."

The cheers came, warmly. But Herbert was not to be
consoled.

"I'm goin' 'ome," he announced darkly, before the last
hurrah had died away. "I'm not stayin' to be insulted.
Me and Mrs. 'Ole, we're goin' 'ome." He rounded on
Colin. "And as for you and your bloody boat, you can
take it to Bill Hawkes and welcome. If you're still 'ere,
which I doubt."

With which parting shot, he and Mrs. Hole walked out

of the room. There was a movement to go after them and persuade them back, but Old Ephraim said, "Let 'im be. 'E's 'ad a shock, poor lad. Let 'im be."

It was only when Bill Hawkes had been duly and ceremoniously robed and chained that Priscilla, losing interest in her food for a moment, looked up and said in a bewildered voice, "Where's Herbert gone?"

"Home, dear," said Sir Simon hastily. "Don't you worry."

"But . . ." Priscilla's voice trembled. "But Herbert's the new mayor, Simon. He can't have gone home."

Sir Simon gave his sister a sharp look. Then he said heartily, "And home's the place for you, too, eh Prissy? You know you never like to stay out late. Riddle . . ."

George was at Priscilla's side in an instant. Unprotesting, she allowed him to help her to her feet and lead her out of the room, to a respectful chorus of "Good night, Miss Priscilla."

The door closed behind them. Sir Simon said loudly, "Well, after all that, I think we need a drink."

The evening proceeded with traditional merriment, only slightly dimmed by these unfortunate events. Everybody ate and drank heartily. Bill Hawkes made a somewhat unsteady speech, assuring the residents of the borough that their future was in good hands. Sir Simon paid a short tribute to the sportsmanlike qualities of British democracy, and told a couple of not-very-funny stories, at which everyone laughed politely. Ephraim, as the retiring mayor, rambled on at some length about handing over to young blood, and eventually sat down, befuddled, in the middle of a sentence. Then they all sang the Berrybridge anthem, the words of which had been written many years ago by Ephraim, and which fitted more or less to the Londonderry Air.

> "Oh, Berrybridge,
> Sweet haven on the Riverber—RY,
> Oh, Berrybridge,
> The home we long to see.
> Oh, Berrybridge . . ."

And so on, through an interminable number of verses. At
the conclusion of the anthem, as was the custom, the ladies
of the village went home. Rosemary and Emmy felt that,
as a matter of etiquette, they should do likewise, but Anne
was determined to stay to the end. Finally, they all stayed,
and apparently nobody minded. London people were expected to behave oddly.

Soon after this, George Riddle came back. He spoke
briefly to Sir Simon, and then settled down to the consumption of a modest half pint. Everybody else, however,
drank deeply. The party began to split up into smallish
groups. Sir Simon came down the table and joined the
Fleet, while on the opposite side of the table Sam and
George Riddle, with Ephraim and Bob, formed the sober-
est of the village groups, discussing fishing with some
passion.

It was shortly before Bob called "Time!" that Colin
dropped his second bombshell of the evening. He and
Anne had been fighting quietly, but with venom, ever
since the Herbert Hole episode. Anne remarked, acidly,
that she had found it neither clever nor funny to humiliate
Herbert in such a sadistic way. Colin retorted that he had
merely been upholding the principles of his profession by
seeking out the truth. Anne made a short, sharp remark
about his profession which prompted Colin, who had had
rather too many drinks, to reply briskly that at least it
wasn't as old as hers. At this, Anne grew really angry,
and declared roundly that if that was all he thought of
her, there didn't seem much point in being engaged.
David at once leapt hotly to Anne's defence. Hamish
remained silent. The Bensons and the Tibbetts, by common consent, tried to ignore the bickering: but Rosemary
whispered to Emmy, "I suppose this means that we'll have
Anne sleeping on board again, blast her."

Matters appeared to have reached an uneasy deadlock,
when Colin suddenly leant across to Henry and said, "My
charming fiancée may not think much of my mental ability, but I'll tell you one thing. I know all about Pete.
I'm right and you're wrong."

"Colin—" Anne began, but Colin was not to be stopped.

"Oh, yes," he said. "Pete was murdered. I know. And I intend to prove it." He was more than half tipsy, and his eyes blazed with excitement. "I've always wanted to beat the police at their own game, and now I'm going to do it, by God."

Henry said, uncomfortably, "You're making a big mistake, Colin. Leave it alone."

"Oh, no you don't," said Colin. "You don't get anything out of me. But you wait. No good this weekend. Tide's all wrong. Next weekend."

"Oh, well," said Henry, much more lightly than he felt, "that at least gives me a week to prove that you're talking nonsense."

"The best thing you can do this week," said Colin, slurring his words slightly, "is to relax an' read a good book. Don't tire out that precious brain of yours. May need it sometime."

"Rosemary," said Anne, very clearly, "may I sleep on board *Ariadne* tonight?"

"Of course," said Alastair.

"If you like," said Rosemary, with less enthusiasm.

Then Bob called "Time!" and they all clattered downstairs and out into the yard.

TEN

By ten past eleven, all the revellers were out of the pub, with the exception of George Riddle, who had stayed behind to give Bob a hand with the dirty glasses. The locals swayed happily homewards, and Sir Simon walked across to his ancient Daimler.

"Goodnight to you all," he called. "I'll just get the old girl warmed up while I wait for Riddle."

He climbed into the car as the others made their way down the hard, glad of the assistance of Alastair's powerful torch in the moonless blackness. The atmosphere was uncomfortably stormy. The Bensons and the Tibbetts walked together, and tried to keep up a semblance of light-hearted chatter. Behind them came David and Anne, arm in arm. Hamish followed, moodily. Colin, somewhat unsteady on his feet, brought up the rear. At the water's edge, Colin said loudly, "Anne, my beautiful, there's a complication that may have escaped you. Alastair's dinghy only takes four people."

Anne received this remark in a dangerous silence.

"By all means refuse to talk to me if it amuses you," Colin went on. "I am merely making a chivalrous gesture. I am prepared to row you to *Mary Jane,* pick up your sleeping bag, and return you and it to *Ariadne.* In the process, you may speak to me or not, as you wish. Personally, I find silence very restful."

"You're drunk," said Anne, clearly and bitterly. "I wouldn't be seen dead in your dinghy."

"Oh, for heaven's sake, go with Colin," said Rosemary irritably. "We can't possibly take five."

"I'm sorry," said Anne, obstinately.

Eventually, as always, David came to the rescue, and suggested that he should do the ferrying: demanding as his reward that Anne should take a nightcap with him on *Pocahontas,* before returning to *Mary Jane* to get the sleeping bag. He would then, he said, deposit Anne on board *Ariadne* for the night. This seemed an excellent idea to everybody except Colin, who was rapidly reaching a stage of morbid self-pity. When Anne and David had disappeared into the darkness, and Hamish had said "Goodnight" and made off to his cottage, Colin sat down firmly on the damp hard, and announced his intention of staying there all night. It was with some difficulty that Rosemary and Alastair at last persuaded him to get into his dinghy, and he had still not cast off the painter when *Ariadne*'s crew were ready to leave.

"I hope to God Colin's all right," said Rosemary anxiously, as Alastair pulled away from the hard.

"Oh, for God's sake," said her husband crossly, "leave him alone. He can look after himself. . . . That was a bloody awful evening. I'm sorry you people were let in for it."

"Oh, I don't know," said Emmy, gallantly, but without a great deal of conviction. "It had its moments."

"I don't know what's the matter with all of us," said Rosemary. "We never used to be like this. You must think we're a very odd lot."

"Don't be silly," said Emmy. But she shivered slightly.

When they reached the boat, Rosemary said to Henry and Emmy, "There's no need for you two to sit up for Anne. I'm going to turn in myself. If and when she comes, she's only got to put her sleeping bag on the floor between our bunks and climb into it. She's done it often enough before."

"I'll wait up for her," said Alastair.

"Please yourself," said Rosemary, with the faintest edge on her voice. "She probably won't come at all. She'll make it up with Colin and stay on *Mary Jane.*"

So Henry and Emmy climbed into the fo'c'sle, while Rosemary got into her bunk and instantly fell asleep. Alastair sat in the cockpit, smoking.

As they lay side by side in the darkness, Emmy said to Henry, "You've been very quiet all the evening, darling. What's up?"

"My nose," said Henry sombrely.

This was an expression with which all Henry's colleagues were familiar. By it, he meant that strange mixture of intuition and deduction which had led him to the solution of many difficult cases. Although he always maintained that he was the most unimaginative of men, Henry undoubtedly possessed a flair. Tiny inconsistencies of fact and, more important, of character, mounted up as an investigation proceeded until, taken together, they roused this constantly strengthening certainty of the direction in which truth lay hidden, which Henry had dubbed his "nose." But this was not an investigation: ever since the previous weekend, Henry had known—not the whole truth, but the direction in which to look. No amount of closing his eyes to facts, no amount of drowning his instinct in the pure pleasure of sailing, had been able to quieten the nagging insistence of the truth: and the events of the evening had clinched the matter. He knew now that, promises or no promises, he could not let it drop.

After a pause, Emmy whispered, "Oh dear. Is it that bad?"

"It's all *wrong*," said Henry. "I don't pretend to know everything that's going on, and I don't know what Colin's up to: but I do know that there's something very wrong, and if I'm not mistaken, it's going to blow up soon."

"Not tonight, I hope," said Emmy sleepily.

"I hope not," said Henry.

Some unidentifiable time later, they were both dragged back to the brink of consciousness by the bumping of a dinghy alongside. David's voice called "Goodnight," and peace descended on the river again, hardly broken by the murmuring voices of Anne and Alastair.

Henry drifted back into sleep. In a strangely vivid dream, he found himself in *Priscilla,* roaring downstream with Colin at the wheel.

"It'll be rather fun," Colin was shouting, and, in his dream, Henry knew that Colin was mad.

"Don't do it!" he heard himself repeating urgently, although he had no idea of what Colin was proposing to do.

"Hole for Mayor!" replied Colin, spinning the wheel. "Who painted the notices new?"

Another boat loomed up ahead of them. It became desperately important that Henry should read the name of it, but Colin would not keep the wheel still. All that Henry could see was that Anne was at the helm of the other boat, and that *Priscilla* was going to ram her. Anne waved gaily, and shouted, "Darling Henry!"

"Stop the motor!" Henry yelled. "There's going to be a collision!"

But the figure at the wheel had unaccountably turned into Hamish, who merely remarked, "A man has a right to do what he likes with his own money."

For some reason, Sir Simon suddenly appeared in the cockpit beside Henry. "Unfortunately," he said pompously, "I was in Ipswich at the time."

Henry threw himself at Hamish, and tried to wrench the wheel from his hands, but *Priscilla* kept relentlessly on course. As the two boats collided, there was a deafening crash. And another . . . and another . . . Henry opened his eyes, and identified the sound. It was Rosemary, banging a mug of tea on the floor boards beside his face.

"Eight o'clock," she said. "Time to get up."

It was a glorious morning, sunny and windless. They breakfasted in the cockpit. Ahead of *Ariadne,* a vacant mooring buoy bobbed in the water.

"Good lord," said Alastair. "David's out already." He looked sharply at Anne, but she turned her head away and gazed astern to where, some way downriver, *Mary Jane* rode quietly at her mooring.

Suddenly Anne said, "What's that?"

"What's what?" asked Alastair lazily.

Anne stood up and looked upriver. "It's a stray dinghy," she said. "Capsized."

They all stood up to look. Sure enough, a tiny shell of a boat was drifting slowly toward them on the tide, upside down.

"It looks——" Anne began, and then stopped.

Alastair dived down into the cabin, and came up with a pair of binoculars. He focused them on the little boat for a moment, and then said, "I'm going to have a look."

"I'll come with you," said Anne.

"No," said Alastair, with unexpected firmness. "Finish your breakfast."

He climbed into *Ariadne*'s dinghy, and they all watched as he pulled strongly upriver. Soon he had the dinghy in tow, and it was not many minutes before he was once again alongside *Ariadne*. His face was very grave and troubled.

"Is it . . .?" said Anne, quietly.

"Yes," said Alastair. "It's *Mary Jane*'s dinghy."

"Oh God," said Anne. "I thought it was."

"I'm going down to see if Colin's all right," said Alastair.

"May I come with you?" Henry asked.

"Of course."

Neither of them questioned the fact that Anne, too, got into the dinghy. Still towing the deadweight of the capsized boat behind them, they rowed downriver to *Mary Jane*, and pulled alongside.

"Colin!" shouted Alastair.

There was no reply.

"Colin, wake up!" Anne cried, a little desperately. There was no answer.

They all clambered on board. The hatchway leading to the cabin was swinging open. *Mary Jane* was in apple-pie order. Everything was neatly stowed, and the bunks made up in their daytime covers. There was nobody aboard.

In fact, it was Herbert Hole in his old grey launch who, two hours later, found Colin floating face downwards in the mud at the edge of the river, slightly upstream from *Ariadne*. He was quite dead, and there was no doubt at all that the cause of death was drowning.

The rest of the morning was spent in a nightmare of formalities. There would, of course, have to be an inquest. Alastair drove Henry into Ipswich, where the latter spent an hour talking to Inspector Proudie: Rosemary gallantly undertook to telephone Colin's parents and break the news to them. Anne, who had maintained a dry-eyed calm during the anxious hours of searching, collapsed in a dead faint when Colin's body was discovered. Hamish carried her up to his cottage, telephoned the doctor, and opened a bottle of whisky. In The Berry Bush, Herbert recounted the grim story of his find with much relish.

At midday, Henry and Alastair arrived back from Ipswich, bringing Inspector Proudie with them. Alastair parked the car outside The Berry Bush and walked across to Hamish's whitewashed cottage, which stood at the water's edge some hundred yards upriver. He came back with the news that Hamish was perfectly agreeable to lending his drawing room to Henry and Proudie for their interviews.

"Berry View" was a charming little house. Three years before, it had been nothing more than a pair of derelict cottages, once occupied by fishermen. Hamish had converted them without in any way destroying the charm and simplicity of the original. No wrought-iron whimsies or refurbished carriage lamps marred its clean, well-proportioned exterior, no lattice-work discouraged the sunlight from penetrating its neat, rectangular windows: instead of a phony and insanitary thatch, Hamish had re-roofed the house with large grey slates of pleasing irregularity. The solid front door of unvarnished oak opened directly into the main living room, which, with the kitchen and bathroom, occupied the entire ground floor. Here, black and white handwoven mats made a cool contrast to the warm glow of the ancient red tiles which still paved the floor. The furniture was sparse, good-looking and comfortable. At one end of the long room, a huge sofa and two armchairs, upholstered in dark blue whipcord, faced a simple, square fireplace: at the other end stood a plain oak dining table and four ladder-back chairs. On either side of the front door, the whitewashed wall was almost entirely covered with well-filled bookcases. A small oak coffee table, several early Picasso and Lautrec lithographs, two brass oil lamps and an assortment of ashtrays completed the furniture. Henry's first impression, as he stepped inside and looked around him, was of uncompromising masculinity.

Hamish was sitting in one of the armchairs, staring

moodily at the empty fireplace, with a glass in his hand and
a decanter on the table at his elbow. He looked somewhat
taken aback to see Proudie, but greeted him civilly enough,
reminding the inspector that they had met before during
the investigations into the Trigg-Willoughby robbery: he
then proffered the decanter all round. Proudie looked
shocked, and everybody declined politely, if with some
regret.

"Now," said Henry, "where is everyone and how is
Anne?"

"She's upstairs asleep," said Hamish. "Rosemary's with
her. The doctor came and gave her some sort of dope. He
says she's suffering from shock. David's still out in his boat.
Nobody's seen him all day. Since it's after twelve, I imagine
that Herbert and Sam and the rest of the locals are in the
pub. I haven't seen Emmy."

"That's all right," said Henry. "She's over at Berry Hall.
Well, I suppose we'd better make a start. Would you like to
come first and get it over with, Hamish? It's just a question
of getting some facts for the coroner. Inspector Proudie is
in charge of the investigations, of course, but since I was
involved, the Chief Constable agreed——"

"Of course," said Hamish, sourly and somewhat enigmat-
ically.

So Alastair wandered out onto the flagged terrace that
overlooked the muddy, reedy bank where Colin had been
found. He watched a fleet of sailing dinghies drifting idly,
their white racing burgees flapping sadly in the windless
air, and reflected bitterly on the general bloodiness of life:
in the drawing room, the police shorthand writer who had
been brought from Ipswich settled himself at the dining
table: Henry sat morosely in an armchair, while Inspector
Proudie took Hamish quickly and accurately through the
events of the preceding evening.

Emmy had been surprised and not a little dismayed
when, immediately after the discovery of the body, Henry
had told her to call for Berrybridge's only taxi, and drive
over to Berry Hall to break the news to Sir Simon.

"Why not telephone him?" she demanded. "Then he can
drive over here."

"Two reasons," said Henry. "One, I want you to observe very carefully the effect of the news on the various members of the Berry Hall menage. And secondly, I think you may find that there's something wrong with Sir Simon's car."

"Whatever do you mean?"

"I heard him trying to start her when we were walking down the hard last night," said Henry. "He didn't seem to be succeeding. I thought nothing of it then, but now it occurs to me that a man without a car is immobilized and therefore can't be in places where he shouldn't be or see things that he shouldn't see."

Emmy looked more and more mystified. "You think somebody deliberately put the car out of action?"

"I don't know," said Henry, "but somebody might have found it useful. In any case, I want you to bring Sir Simon and George Riddle back here, either in Sir Simon's own car or in the taxi, by about half past twelve."

In view of this conversation, Emmy was considerably impressed when, as she clambered into the venerable Lanchester which served as a taxi, the driver—a grizzled character referred to in the pub as Old George—remarked acidly, "Berry 'All. Berry 'All. Nothin' but Berry Bloody 'All."

"Why do you say that?" Emmy asked.

"Larst night," said Old George, "arter the binge. Drove Sir Simon 'ome. Ar parst eleven. Didn't get back till midnight."

"What happened to his own car, then?"

"Broke," said Old George succinctly. "Left Young George tinkerin' with 'er insides. No good. Garage towed 'er away first thing this morning."

"When you say Young George, you mean George Riddle?"

"That's right," admitted Old George grudgingly.

"So he didn't go back to Berry Hall last night?"

"No. Kipped at 'is Dad's place, I reckon."

"I see," said Emmy, in a small, thoughtful voice. She spent the rest of the drive trying to avoid discussing the subject of Colin's death with Old George, and finally left him in the drive of Berry Hall, sitting on the step of the Lanchester smoking a small, noisome cigar, with instructions to wait for her.

With some trepidation, Emmy walked up to the imposing, pedimented front door. Before she had mustered enough courage to pull the graceful iron doorbell, however, she was startled to hear the sharp rattle of a window sash being thrown up, and a shrill voice above her head cried, "Who is it? What do you want?"

Emmy took a step backwards and looked up. A first-floor window to the left of the front door was open, and from it, like a snail emerging from its shell, protruded the stout torso of Miss Priscilla Trigg-Willoughby. Her head bristled with chromium hair curlers, which glinted like a helmet in the sunshine.

"Who is it?" Priscilla demanded again, and added, "Why don't you ring the bell?"

"I was just going to," said Emmy, hastily.

"What's that? Speak up!"

"I was just going to," Emmy shouted. "It's Mrs. Tibbett. I wanted to——"

Priscilla's attention had suddenly focused itself on the Lanchester. "George!" she remarked, majestically. Old George jumped guiltily to his feet and stamped out his cigar. "Why are you still here, George? You were engaged to drive my brother home. That gives you no right to prowl around the house all night and smoke your horrible cigars in my garden. Go home at once!"

"I think I can explain, Miss Trigg-Willoughby," Emmy yelled hastily. "George hasn't been here all night. He's just driven me over from Berrybridge."

Priscilla's domineering mood crumbled suddenly into pathos. "Thank you, Mrs. Hibbert," she said humbly, with a trace of tears. "You explain things so clearly. Nobody else explains things to me. That's why I imagine things, you see. It's very difficult when nobody will explain."

Emmy felt a sudden surge of excitement—an instinctive feeling that she was about to learn something important, if only she played her cards right. Cursing the fact that this most delicate conversation had to take place at the top of her voice, she shouted, "What won't they explain to you? Perhaps I could help?"

Priscilla leant dangerously far out of the window, and spoke in a travesty of a stage whisper. "Mrs. Tappitt," she said, "I'm going to tell you something. You see, I happen to know that——"

"Good morning, madam," said a fruity, P. G. Wodehouse voice loudly. "Was there something?"

Furious, Emmy dropped her gaze to the front door. It was open, and George Riddle stood there, looking like a dentist in his starched white jacket. When she glanced up again, Priscilla's window was empty.

Biting back her anger, Emmy said, "I want to see Sir Simon, please, It's very urgent."

Riddle stood back to allow Emmy to enter the famous, marble-paved circular hall, with its spiral staircase leading to the circular gallery on the first floor. Then he opened the door of the Blue Drawing Room.

"If you will wait in here, madam," he said, in his carefully cultivated butler's accent, "I will inform Sir Simon."

On an impulse, Emmy said, "I'm sorry to hear about Sir Simon's car. I hope it's nothing serious."

Riddle looked far from pleased. "I really cannot say, madam. It is in the hands of the garridge."

"But you worked on it last night, didn't you?" Emmy persisted. "What was wrong with it?"

"I was not able to locate the trouble, madam," said Riddle angrily.

Oh, very well, thought Emmy. You'll have to tell Henry later on. Aloud she said, "You must have made an early start to get back here from Berrybridge this morning. There's not a bus, is there?"

There was a perceptible pause, and then Riddle said, in his normal voice and very fast, "I come on me Dad's bike." Then, quickly recollecting himself, he added, "I will inform Sir Simon of your arrival, madam," and withdrew.

Emmy gazed out of the window, over the vista of lawns, trees and water, and wondered miserably how she should handle the coming interview. Henry had given her so little to go on. He had told her to watch people's reactions to the news of Colin's death. Perhaps she ought to have sprung it on Priscilla and Riddle, instead of trying unsuccessfully to follow her own hunch that they might divulge certain information more readily before they heard the news. She felt that she was making a hash of things, and hoped that Henry was not counting too much on the results of her expedition.

At the back of her mind, with nagging insistence, a tiny conversation she had had that morning with Henry repeated itself like a worn gramophone record.

"Henry," she had said, "was Colin murdered?"

And Henry had replied, "I think so."

Emmy was jerked out of her reverie by the sight of Sir Simon. He was dressed in old tweeds and Wellington boots, and he was walking up towards the house from the path that led to the boathouse. Wiping his hands on his dirty trousers, he disappeared round the corner of the house towards the front door. A minute or two later, Emmy heard voices in the hall, and Sir Simon came in.

"My dear Mrs. Tibbett," he began, "forgive me—can't shake hands—covered with oil from *Priscilla's* engine— didn't even stop to wash. Felt I had to see you straight away when I heard the news. Tragic business."

Emmy's morale sank beneath the load of failure. "You mean—?" she began.

"Young Street, of course. Found drowned. Old George told me just now, in the drive. I suppose that's why you're here. Expect your husband sent you."

Emmy could have cried. "Yes," she said, inadequately and miserably.

"Lucky you got old George to wait," Sir Simon went on. "We can get him to drive us both back. Expect you may have heard about my old bus. Most mysterious. Running perfectly earlier in the evening, and then when I came to go home—just wouldn't start. Plenty in the battery, too. Riddle couldn't find what was wrong. And to crown it all, *Priscilla's* out of action, too. Oil in her plugs, I'm afraid. So we're well and truly marooned out here. My goodness, I

can hardly believe it. Young Street. Such a brilliant boy.
Tragic." Sir Simon paused for breath. "Well, if you'll excuse me, Mrs. Tibbett, I'll get some of this grease off my
paws and change my trousers, and we'll be off."

With that, he bustled out, leaving Emmy to her bitter
thoughts, and to the contemplation of the river. A few
minutes later he was back, spruce and clean in a faded pair
of grey flannels and a hacking jacket. He demurred somewhat when Emmy insisted that they should take George
Riddle back to Berrybridge with them.

"Don't like leaving my sister alone," he explained uneasily. "Since Mrs. Bradwell left, there's nobody else in the
house. Cooks are hard to come by, these days, and my
sister . . . nervous, you understand . . ."

It was then that Emmy had her inspiration. "I'm afraid
my husband was quite definite about wanting to see both
you and Riddle," she said, "but why shouldn't I stay here
with Miss Trigg-Willoughby? Whoever drives you back
here can pick me up."

Sir Simon looked uncomfortable. "It's very kind of
you, Mrs. Tibbett," he began, "but I wouldn't want to put
you to the trouble of——"

"It's no trouble at all," said Emmy firmly. "I can have
another look at your beautiful house, and I'm longing to
see the garden. It was pouring with rain last time I was
here, if you remember. I needn't bother your sister at all,
if she's resting. But I expect you'll feel happier, just knowing there's someone in the house."

"Well . . ." Sir Simon could not hide the relief in his
voice. "It *would* be most kind of you. I'll just tell Priscilla."

Emmy stood at the front door and waved goodbye to
the hearselike black Lanchester, as it rolled its stately way
down the broad drive. When it was out of sight, she turned
and went indoors. Her footsteps echoed across the marble
circle of the hall. At the foot of the stairs she paused in a
shaft of sunlight, and listened. The beautiful, pale house
was enveloped in a veil of bright silence, as though crystal-
lized in ice. Slowly, Emmy began to climb the spiral staircase.

* * *

The sunshine splashed onto the red-tiled floor of Hamish's drawing room in golden pools, and Inspector Proudie mopped his brow with a very white handkerchief. Hamish and Rosemary had given their accounts of the events of the evening before, and now Alastair was sitting, unhappily, on the edge of one of the big armchairs, trying to recall at what time Anne and David had arrived at *Ariadne* the previous night.

"It must have been after half past one," he said, at length. "I had given up waiting and gone to bed soon after midnight. I was dozing off when I heard David's dinghy alongside. I got up and helped Anne on board. She hadn't been back to *Mary Jane* for her sleeping bag after all—thought it was too late—so I gave her mine and made my bunk up with blankets. We tried to make as little noise as possible, and I don't think any of the others woke up—did you?"

"Not really," said Henry. "I just heard David's voice and then I went off to sleep again."

"I was pretty tired, too," said Alastair. "I didn't need any rocking to sleep. I remember hearing David rowing away again, and the next thing I knew, it was morning."

Henry leant forward. "David?" he said.

"Well, I presume so," said Alastair. "Nobody else would have been out at that hour. I heard a dinghy, anyway. It was an absolutely still night, and you know how sound carries over the water. I heard the splash of oars and that slight creaking you get from the rowlocks."

"David delivered Anne to *Ariadne,*" said Henry. "You and she discussed the matter of the sleeping bag, you remade your bunk, and you both went to bed. How long did all that take?"

"About a quarter of an hour, I suppose. I noticed it was ten to two by the cabin clock when I blew out the lamps."

"And then," said Henry, "you heard a dinghy. Meaning either that David had been rowing round in circles for nearly twenty minutes, or that somebody else *was* out last night."

"I never thought of that," said Alastair slowly. "Not that it matters. Poor old Colin must have been dead already by then."

"By the way," said Henry, "it's true, isn't it, that Colin couldn't swim?"

"Yes," said Alastair. "I often told him he ought to learn. It's not safe messing about in boats, unless you can at least keep yourself afloat in an emergency." He passed a hand over his brow. "It's hell," he said. "I ought to have gone after him last night and made sure he was all right. If only I——"

"Now don't worry about that, sir," said Proudie soothingly. "You couldn't possibly know what was going to happen."

"You see"—Alastair was talking to Henry—"I've seen old Colin a bit pickled many times, but he always managed the dinghy without any trouble. That's why I——"

"Nobody could possibly blame you, Mr. Benson," said Proudie, more firmly. Alastair gave him a glance in which gratitude and anguish were equally mixed. "And now," Proudie went on, "I think that's all for the moment. We needn't keep you any longer, Mr. Benson."

In the doorway, Alastair narrowly missed colliding with Sir Simon Trigg-Willoughby, who came striding in, bristling with anger. Before either Henry or Proudie could say a word, he barked out, "I have a complaint to make to the police. My car has been tampered with!"

Proudie looked taken aback; Henry, unsurprised, said, "I'm sorry to hear that, Sir Simon. What happened?"

"Last night." Sir Simon sat down heavily. "Last night, when I wanted to go home. Thing wouldn't start. Nothing unusual in that, of course, but damned annoying. I took Old George's taxi home, and left Riddle working on the car. He couldn't find the trouble—hardly surprising, really. Pitch dark and only a torch to work with. So very sensibly he left it and went home to his father's place. Early this morning he phoned the local garage to come and tow the car away. I've just been in to see them." Sir Simon paused, and snorted. "Rotary arm," he went on, outraged. "Delib-

erately removed. Nothing wrong with the car at all. And
what's more, we found it."

With that, he produced a small piece of bakelite trium-
phantly from his pocket and threw it down on the table.

"Where did you find this?" Henry asked, intrigued.

"Riddle found it, to be accurate," said Sir Simon. "Under
a bush in the pub yard, close to where the car was parked.
Disgraceful. Silly childish trick. Don't see why these
damned youngsters should get away with it."

"What makes you think a youngster did it?" said Henry.

Sir Simon did not answer this directly, but merely remarked with venom on the bad manners and misguided
sense of the humour of the younger generation in general,
and in particular of . . . at which point, he went ever
redder than usual, and stopped.

"You mean you think Colin Street did this?" Henry
asked.

"I'm making no accusations," said Sir Simon quickly.
"But he had a macabre sense of fun, poor boy, for all his
brilliance. Practical jokes. You know the kind of thing I
mean. Not funny, in my opinion."

Henry picked up the distributor head. "May I keep
this?" he asked.

"Must you?"

"It might be important," said Henry. "The garage has
surely supplied a new one."

Sir Simon grunted his assent. Henry wrapped the small
object carefully in his handkerchief, and then said, "By the
way, Sir Simon, were you planning to take the car out again
last night, or early this morning?"

"I wanted it for this morning," said Sir Simon. *"Priscilla's* motor is out of action, and I wanted to go to Woodbridge for some spares. The whole matter is extremely
irritating."

"Well, you can be sure that Inspector Proudie will investigate your complaint very thoroughly," said Henry.
Proudie looked none too pleased, and suggested a little
acidly that they might now get down to the business in
hand, asking Sir Simon to run through his recollections of
Colin's last hours: but apart from a positive and caustic

assertion that the latter had been drunk and incapable when he left The Berry Bush, Sir Simon had nothing to add to what Henry and Proudie already knew. He gave his answers brusquely and briefly, and seemed glad to escape into the sunshine.

By contrast, George Riddle was inclined to be garrulous.

"Terrible business, sir," he said earnestly. "Criminal offence, if you ask me."

"What's a criminal offense?" Proudie asked sharply.

"Falsifying the vote," said George Riddle, unctuously. "Disgrace to the borough. Just what you'd expect from Herbert Hole."

"We're not talking about that," said Proudie impatiently. "We're talking about Mr. Street."

"Not that he was much better," said George, with a self-righteous sniff. "Wrecking people's cars."

"What makes you so sure that Mr. Street took the distributor head out of the Daimler?" Henry asked.

"Just like him," said George.

"You didn't think of looking at the rotor arm last night?"

" 'Course I didn't. I thought it was the petrol pump—she's given trouble before, see."

"Why," Henry persisted, "didn't you go back to Berry Hall with Sir Simon in the taxi?"

"I could have," admitted George a trifle uneasily, "but I felt sure I could fix her, and Sir Simon didn't want to wait —doesn't like leaving Miss Priscilla alone in the house. And I knew he wanted the car first thing in the morning."

"Tell us," said Proudie, "what you saw and heard while you were working on the car."

"Me?" George looked surprised. "Nothing much. The ladies and gents from the boats all went off down the hard. Then Sir Simon went inside the pub with Bob Calloway, and they called Old George. He came round straight away, and took Sir Simon off. After that, Bob locked up The Berry Bush and put the lights out. It was all quiet and dark then."

"How long did you work?"

"About an hour, I reckon—maybe a bit less. Then I

got fed up and packed it in and went/to my dad's cottage."

"Where's that?" Henry asked.

George jerked a thumb. "Bit upriver from this one," he said. "Couple of hundred yards. I did notice the lights were still on in here. Fact, I saw Mr. Rawnsley through the window."

"What was he doing?"

"Nothing much. Sitting at that table, with a lot of papers and things laid out on it. Didn't stop to look."

When George had gone, Henry said to Proudie, "I'm bothered about the place where Colin's body was found. Why was it so much upstream from the hard?"

"That's easy," said Proudie. "Question of tides."

"How do you mean?"

"High water, four twenty-seven this morning," said Proudie. "That means, before half past four, Mr. Street's body—and the capsized dinghy—would have floated upstream. Half past four, dead water. Then, about five, they'd start drifting down again. That's what the dinghy was doing when Mr. Benson spotted it."

"So," said Henry, "we can be absolutely certain that Colin was drowned before half past four."

"Good lord, yes." Proudie frowned. "I'd say about two o'clock would be the latest time, judging by where the body was found. But of course you never know for certain. In any case, I'm afraid it's only too clear what happened." He glanced through the notes he had taken. "Mr. Street had had too much to drink. Nobody disputes that. Mrs. Benson was worried about leaving him to row back on his own, but her husband was annoyed—and very naturally, if I may say so—at Mr. Street's behaviour earlier in the evening, and took the attitude of letting him stew in his own juice. I hope Mr. Benson won't go on reproaching himself. Anyhow, it's perfectly clear that, in his drunken state, Mr. Street capsized his dinghy. We know that he couldn't swim, and it's well-known that bathing with too much alcohol in the system often causes cramp. He must have been too fuddled even to cry out. Just sank like a stone. A very nasty accident."

Proudie drew a firm line across his notebook. "Q.E.D." he seemed to be saying.

"I don't believe it," said Henry, stubbornly.

"Now, look, sir," said Proudie, trying not to sound exasperated. "You yourself were on board *Mary Jane* this morning. You saw for yourself that Mr. Street never reached her last night. His bunk wasn't made up. Nothing had been touched since he and Miss Petrie left the boat before dinner. You yourself saw Mr. Street just about to set off in his dinghy, at eleven thirty. So it's clear that he must have met his death while rowing out to his boat—say between eleven thirty and eleven forty-five. Where was everybody then? You and Mrs. Tibbett were on board *Ariadne* with Mr. and Mrs. Benson. Miss Petrie and Mr. Crowther were together on *Pocahontas*. Sir Simon was on his way back to Berry Hall in Old George's taxi. Bob Calloway was clearing up the pub with the barman."

"George Riddle," said Henry, "was allegedly tinkering with Sir Simon's car in the yard of the inn. And Hamish Rawnsley was allegedly here in his cottage, going to bed, although he was still up an hour later, according to George. Neither of them has any proof that he's telling the truth."

"I know that," said Proudie, "but what does it prove? Here's a perfectly straightforward accident, and you want everybody who knew the dead man to have an unshakeable alibi. It would be unnatural if they did."

"I suppose so," said Henry.

It was at that moment that the telephone rang. Proudie picked it up.

"Yes," he said. "Yes, speaking. . . . Yes. . . . Yes. . . ." There was a long silence. Proudie's face clouded with worry. "What's that? Say that again. . . . You're sure? No mistake at all? . . . I see. . . . Yes, it does change things. . . . Yes, I'll tell him."

He put down the receiver and looked sombrely at Henry. "Looks as though your hunch may have been right after all, sir," he said slowly. "That was the police doctor. He's just finished the post mortem."

"Well?" said Henry.

"Death due to drowning," said Proudie. "Body had been in the water between five and eight hours, as near as he could say."

"That's what we thought."

"But," said Proudie, "there's something else. The skull was cracked by a heavy blow before death. Mr. Street wasn't just drunk when he fell in the river. He was unconscious, and he might have died anyhow."

"Could it——" Henry began.

"He was already sitting in his dinghy when you left him." Proudie, who knew Berrybridge Haven as well as any man in Suffolk, was visualizing the scene. "He was still tied up to the hard. There's no obstructions other than moored boats between *Mary Jane* and the jetty, and if he'd bumped into anything, the dinghy could have taken the force of the collision. It's just not feasible that he could have dealt himself a blow with one of his own oars, even if he'd been trying. The doctor says it was a powerful crack delivered from directly in front of him, and above. No," said Proudie heavily, "I'm afraid we've got to face it, sir. This is a murder case. And it does strike me that—well, we've had another similar sort of accident in these parts lately. Chap hit on the head and then drowned. I mean Mr. Pete Rawnsley."

"Inspector Proudie," said Henry, "I don't know what you propose to do next, but personally I'm going straight out to have another look at *Mary Jane*."

"Mr. Street's boat? What d'you expect to find there?"

"First and foremost," said Henry, "a book. Secondly, if I'm lucky, fingerprints. Can you get your man out here and send him after me to take prints? I'm going to find Mr. Benson and borrow his dinghy."

Henry got up and hurried out of the cottage and down to the hard. It did not even occur to him to wonder where Emmy was.

"Please," said Emmy. "Please try to remember."

Priscilla looked at her stupidly, and pulled the orange silk kimono more tightly across her flabby bosom. A half-empty bottle of gin stood bleakly on the dressing table.

"We're all alone in the house," said Priscilla suddenly, with a little giggle.

"I know," said Emmy. "That's why I thought it would be a good opportunity to have a little chat."

"You have to be careful," said Priscilla owlishly. "People listen."

"Not today," said Emmy firmly. "We're all alone. Tell me about the night you lost your jewels. You locked them up, didn't you?"

"Hamish used to come and talk to me," said Priscilla inconsequentially. "Such a charming young man. Of course, he wanted money. They all do. Everybody wants money. I suppose it's only natural. How much do you want?"

"I don't want any money. I——"

"Of course, I can't give you any," added Priscilla, with genuine regret. "I'm so sorry. All gone now. Nothing left."

Emmy seized this lead. "Where has it all gone?" she demanded.

Priscilla waved a plump hand. "Bills," she said. "We have bills, just like other people. Simon deals with the money. He's very clever, you know. Very clever indeed."

"Where?" said Emmy, loudly and clearly, "does your gin come from?"

Priscilla looked startled. Then she lowered her voice, and whispered solemnly, "The wardrobe." She pointed an unsteady finger.

"Who puts it there?"

"Papa."

"Miss Priscilla," said Emmy briskly, "your father has been dead for years. Who brings you your gin?"

"It comes from Papa." Priscilla's voice trembled. "Dear Papa. Always so thoughtful. That's what he says."

"Who says that?"

"Why, everybody. Everybody loved Papa." Priscilla lost interest in the subject abruptly, and began to take the curlers out of her hair, unrolling each one with elaborate care.

"This morning," said Emmy, "you said people wouldn't

explain things to you, and you told me you knew something. What was it?"

"I think," said Priscilla, "that I will take a little drink now. It's good for me, you know. It stops me from worrying."

In silence, she poured a generous measure of gin into a toothmug. Downstairs, a clock struck once with a silvery chime. Emmy tried again.

"You remember Colin Street?"

"The ill-mannered young man," said Priscilla promptly. "Simon likes him. Simon says he's clever. I think he's just rude." She giggled slightly. "What about Colin Street?"

"He's dead," said Emmy, very distinctly.

"Dead, Mrs. Babbitt? How sad." Priscilla's voice expressed no more than a travesty of polite concern. "But then, of course, so many people are dead, aren't they?"

"He may have died," said Emmy, "because he found out what it is that you know."

"No, no, that's not possible," said Priscilla in a calm, earnest voice. "Nobody knows what I know. I haven't told anybody."

"You were going to tell me, this morning."

"Was I? Oh, I think you must be mistaken, Mrs. Humbert. I mustn't tell anybody, or Papa will be cross. I promised." She lifted the toothmug and sipped the neat gin. "In any case," she added, "it couldn't be important. That's what nobody will explain. Why it's important."

"You must tell me," said Emmy desperately. She had so little time.

"We are lucky to have this house," said Priscilla socially. "Of course, it is an expense, but Simon insists that everything should be of the best. It's what Papa would have wished."

"Miss Priscilla, I——"

"And the views are so fine," Priscilla went on relentlessly. "From my windows here, I can see everything—the front door, the drive, everything. It's most interesting. And then, from the Blue Drawing Room, one can see Steep Hill Sands—on a clear day."

Emmy's mood of despair turned abruptly to intense excitement. She sat quite still, hardly daring to breathe, lest the stream of chatter should dry up.

"So much coming and going," Priscilla went on with a little laugh. "Boats and cars and people. Day and night. You'd be surprised the people I've seen. Herbert and Sam and Hamish, and that nice Mr. Benson and his wife . . . there's a pretty girl who comes sometimes, too, and a tall, fair young man. And then the boats. *Priscilla* and *Mary Jane* and *Ariadne* . . . *Pocahontas* and *Tideway* and *Blue Gull*. . . . No, not any more. That was when it started. No, not then. Earlier. Much earlier, it started."

There was a silence. Then, suddenly, Priscilla turned to Emmy. Her eyes were bright, and she clasped her stubby hands together, like a delighted child.

"Mrs. Tibbett," she said, "I have made up my mind. I like you. I trust you. I am going to tell you." Emmy waited, breathless. Priscilla leant forward. "You see," she said, "it was before eleven."

"What was?"

"Why——"

A light footstep sounded outside in the white marble gallery, and a door opened quietly. Neither Emmy nor Priscilla heard it.

ELEVEN

Mary Jane was as trim and tidy as ever when Henry and Proudie climbed aboard her. Henry went straight to the bookshelf, ran his finger along the row of volumes, and said, "I thought so. It's not here."

"What isn't?"

"The Venturesome Voyages of Captain Voss. I," he added, "am a bloody fool."

"Oh, I wouldn't say that, sir."

"Colin as good as told me twice that that book was the key to the whole thing," said Henry moodily. "Voss on Sea Anchors."

"Sea anchors?" Proudie repeated, bewildered: and added, apologetically, "I'm afraid I don't follow you, sir. I'm a fishing man myself. What have sea anchors got to do with it?"

"I haven't the faintest idea," said Henry helpfully. "Thank goodness, Alastair has a copy aboard *Ariadne.* Would you like to row over and get it, Inspector, while I have a look around here?"

"Anything you say, sir," said Proudie, in the tone of one who has given up trying to make sense of the situation. He clambered laboriously out into the cockpit, as Henry turned his attention to Colin's bunk.

When Proudie got back to *Mary Jane,* with the little book tucked firmly into his pocket, he found Henry in a state of some excitement.

"I'm prepared to take a bet with you, Inspector Proudie," he said, "that Colin Street did come back to his boat last night."

"How do you work that out?"

"Little things," said Henry, with satisfaction. "We'll be able to check them with Miss Petrie later on—but for once, this is classic, story-book detection. Exhibit one: an unwashed mug in the galley, which has clearly contained Alka-Seltzer. Colin was pretty drunk, and he'd almost certainly have taken something for it."

"He might have taken it earlier on," objected Proudie.

"No," said Henry. "I've been on a boat long enough to know that one doesn't leave loose, unwashed crockery about. Everything is washed and stowed away as soon as it's been used. Then there's exhibit two—Colin's bunk. You see that mattress isn't rectangular; it tapers slightly towards the bows to fit the shape of the bunk, and the daytime cover is tailored to the same shape. Well, it's been put on the wrong way round. That's a thing Anne would never do. Then there's another thing. Anne's sleeping bag is stowed up in the forepeak, with the sails, while Colin's is under his bunk. We'll check with Miss Petrie, but it seems likely to me that they were both normally stowed in the forepeak. It's drier there. My guess is that Colin came back here, took an Alka-Seltzer, removed his bunk cover, laid out his sleeping bag, and probably climbed into it fully clothed, except for his shoes. In the state he was in, he must have gone out like a light, and almost certainly he wouldn't have woken up if anyone came aboard—especially as he was expecting Anne to come and get her sleeping bag, so that the sound of a dinghy alongside wouldn't have worried him. His murderer got aboard, knocked Colin out, probably with the dinghy oar, and heaved him into the water. Then he—or even possibly she—cast off *Mary Jane*'s dinghy, capsized it, and left it to drift upriver on the tide, meanwhile hastily tidying the cabin to make it look as though Colin had never been back aboard. It was obviously somebody who doesn't know the boat too well, or they wouldn't have made those mistakes about the bunk cover and the sleeping bag: but that doesn't get us far, because I don't suppose anybody here except Anne has actually slept aboard."

Henry paused for breath, and ran a hand through his sandy hair, so that it stood spikily on end. "Let's see that book," he went on. "And by the way, can you read Tide Tables?"

"I can, sir," said Proudie. "Most people can, in these parts."

"Then look up the tides for next weekend," said Henry, "while I wade through this."

For a few minutes there was silence in the small cabin. Proudie ruffled the pages of the *Nautical Almanack,* muttering to himself about Summer Time and variations on High Water Dover. Henry immersed himself in the chronicles of Captain Voss. Then Proudie said, "Next Saturday, high water Berrybridge eight four A.M. and eight sixteen P.M. Any use?"

"Not at the moment, but it will be," said Henry. "Write those times down, like a good chap."

He went on reading, flipping through the pages, devouring paragraphs whole. Proudie sat on the opposite bunk in silence. Suddenly Henry gave a shout. "We're getting hot," he said. "What about this for a chapter heading? 'History of the Great Treasure—Where is it hidden?—Prospecting and its Difficulties.' This is all about how Voss and a friend went hunting hidden treasure in the Cocos Islands."

"Blimey," said Proudie, but without emphasis. He was beyond surprise. "Did they find it?"

"I don't know. I haven't got that far." Henry read on, absorbed. Voss's simple, graphic prose had caught his imagination, and he felt the liberating exhilaration of following the great nineteenth-century seaman, with all his paradoxical romanticism and tough expertise, on the quest of pirate gold. He turned the page: read a paragraph: reread it with mounting excitement: then said quietly, "Inspector, I'm an even bloodier fool than I thought. It's so obvious. Listen to this.

"The island was then searched high and low by the crew of the cutter, but nothing was found. Not even traces in the vegetation.

"That no traces could be discovered in the vegetation so soon after the crew of the 'Mary Dyer' had left the island is almost impossible to believe. . . .

After looking carefully over the foot of the hills and
sand spit I came to the conclusion that if I had been
the captain of the 'Mary Dyer' I should certainly have
buried the treasure in the sand spit, for the following
reason. The spit is solid sand, and at low water is dry.
At high tide, it is submerged to a depth of three feet,
and it would have been very little trouble to take a
boat-load of the treasure over the spit at high water,
dump it overboard and bury it when the tide was out.
Then, in about six hours time, when the first tide
washed over the spit, the traces would have been
entirely obliterated. . . ."

Henry shut the book slowly, and he and Proudie looked
at each other in silence for a moment. Then Proudie said,
"So that's where the Trigg-Willoughby jewels are. Buried
in Steep Hill Sands."

"It certainly looks like it," said Henry. "That was the
conclusion Colin came to, anyway, and somebody was
sufficiently perturbed about it to kill him before he could
investigate. Now, what did you say? High water at eight
o'clock next Saturday? That means low water six hours
later. Two o'clock in the morning. And a half-moon. Perfect conditions for making a clandestine expedition to Steep
Hill. This weekend, high water's at two, and low water at
eight, which means that anybody trying to dig on the sandspit would have to do it in daylight."

"Mr. Street said," Proudie remarked, reflectively, "that
he knew the how and the why, but not the who. The how
is easy enough. Someone knocked Mr. Rawnsley out, and
left him to drown. The why—that's what we've just discovered—the buried jewels. Mr. Rawnsley must have dis-
turbed somebody digging up the loot." He reached for the
Almanack again. "Let's see what the tides were doing that
day. May twenty-ninth, it was. Here we are. High water,
six fifty-eight A.M."

"That's right," Henry put in. "Alastair said they'd left
at seven to catch the ebb tide. So low water was at one."

"Broad daylight," said Proudie. "Lunchtime."

"Now wait a minute," said Henry. "Don't let's go too

fast. Remember that this is only Colin's theory, and even if he was right about the jewels, Pete Rawnsley could have been killed for some quite different reason. Or maybe because of a complicated web of reasons. That's the first thing to remember. The second thing is the fog. That's a fact that cuts two ways. You see what I mean?"

"No," said Proudie. Henry explained.

"Which still leaves us," said Proudie, "with the question of who?"

Henry took a pen and a notebook out of his pocket and began to write. "There's a fairly short list of possibles," he said. "Look at it like this. The person we want has to have certain qualifications. Opportunity to steal the jewels in the first place. Let's put down both Rawnsleys, Anne Petrie, George Riddle, Herbert Hole, Sam Riddle. I wonder if David Crowther was at that Hunt Ball. Make a note to find out. Then, there's the question of opportunity to bury them—Herbert, Sam, George and any of the sailing people who had the chance of going out alone. Unless, of course, we're dealing with a conspiracy."

"The other day, in my office," said Proudie, "you came up with a theory about the robbery——"

"I'm afraid I was wrong," said Henry. "At least, it looks like it. I can check it to a certain extent by one or two questions to a couple of people." He paused, and considered his notebook. "It would be interesting to find out just what George Riddle was doing that morning," he went on. "And Herbert turned up unexpectedly in his launch. That's something that needs investigation."

"It occurs to me," said Proudie slowly, "that there's another way of tackling this. From the other end, as you might say. If somebody has been digging up those jewels, it's because they got short of cash and wanted to sell some of them. Since none of them has come onto the market in recognisable form, I'm inclined to think that our thief is using a highly skilled professional fence. Which leads us——"

"To Bob Calloway, who's been making frequent trips to London recently," supplied Henry. "I know. I'm prepared to swear that Bob knows a lot more about all this than he's prepared to say: but now that there's been a second, rather clumsy murder, he'll be scared stiff and we won't get a word out of him. I know Bob of old, Inspector. He just sits tight and refuses to talk—and there's not a damned thing one can do about it."

Henry closed his notebook with a snap, and stood up. "Let's get back," he said. "There's work to be done. I've wasted a hell of a lot of time already, trying to convince myself that Rawnsley's death was accidental. Now it's pretty clear that we've got a double murder to investigate. Two trails, one fresh and one stale. And somewhere in the two of them we're going to find a point of contact, a similarity——"

"Plenty of similarity," said Proudie, a trifle sourly. "Both victims hit on the head and left to drown. Both interested in Steep Hill Sands. Why don't we go and dig for the stuff, as a start, sir?"

"No," said Henry. "I daren't risk letting the criminal know that we've tumbled to the hiding place. Come on, let's get ashore. This afternoon I want to interview everybody again—in the light of a murder investigation this time. We've let things go far enough as it is."

As they rowed ashore, Proudie spoke only once, to ask, "Do we let on we know it's murder, sir?"

"Yes, I think so," said Henry. "But be sure not to give anybody the idea that we're interested in the sandspit."

"O.K. by me, sir," said Proudie. Several minutes later, he added gruffly, "Lovely day."

It was a lovely day. The tide was full, and the river was a sheet of frosted blue glass, ruffled by tiny wavelets. Once again, Henry experienced a sense of wonder at the subtle intensity of colour. But what had seemed to Henry a week ago to be the essence of calm, uncomplicated beauty, now created an atmosphere at once unspeakably sinister and sad, like the painted face of a corpse in an American mortuary parlour. He was briefly surprised at himself for conceiving such an analogy: he had never been to America, let alone into a mortician's den. Perhaps they weren't like that at all, in spite of all one read.

"Yes," said Henry, and Proudie was surprised at the grimness in his voice. "A lovely day for a sail."

Berrybridge was deserted. Henry found Rosemary and Alastair drinking a sombre pint of beer in The Berry Bush. From them, he learnt that Anne had recovered sufficiently to go off with Hamish for a drive in his car: that David had not yet returned from his lone expedition in *Pocahontas:* that George Riddle had driven Sir Simon's Daimler back to Berry Hall, followed by Sir Simon himself in Old George's taxi, which was to bring Emmy back to Berrybridge. There was no sign of Bob Calloway, and the garage which housed the red Aston Martin was empty. More surprising still, neither Herbert nor Sam Riddle was in The Berry Bush. The only other occupants of the bar were Bill Hawkes and Old Ephraim, who sat facing each other in one of the inglenooks, consuming mild ale in oppressive silence.

Henry took a long drink of beer, and then said quietly, "I'm afraid things are really serious now, and I feel it's my fault."

"Oh God," said Rosemary. She had been crying, and her blue eyes were rimmed with red. "Surely things couldn't be any worse?"

"Colin was murdered," said Henry. His voice sounded very weary. "And it's my fault because I started a hare and didn't follow it up."

"Murdered." Alastair repeated the word in a dull, unwondering way. "Yes, I thought as much."

"You didn't!" Rosemary was passionate. "You didn't, Alastair!"

"I'm not quite such a fool as I look, Henry," said Alastair, with a small, twisted smile. "It's obvious, isn't it? You put the idea into his head that Pete's death might not have been accidental—and he carried on from there and discovered something important. Then he got drunk last night and blurted out in front of everybody that he'd solved the mystery. So he had to be killed. Isn't that so?"

"Yes," said Henry. "I'm afraid that's how it was."

Rosemary was looking at the two men with mounting horror. "But what?" she said, and her voice was shaking. "Oh, it's not your fault, Henry. This would have happened sooner or later anyway. But what could Colin have discovered?"

"I know that now," said Henry. "I'll tell you later. Colin was quicker than I was: and I could have saved his life if I'd gone ahead and beaten him to it."

"It wasn't your fault," Rosemary said again, with curious emphasis. "It was all our faults. Especially mine."

"Yours?" said Alastair sharply.

"Of course," said Rosemary. "I begged Henry to drop the whole thing. I did everything I could to divert him——"

"Because you were afraid," said Henry.

"Yes." It was no more than a whisper.

"Because you knew that——"

"He told me."

Alastair was looking from one to the other in bewilderment. "What on earth is all this about?" he demanded.

"It's none of your business," said Rosemary tersely. She had gone very white.

"It certainly is my business," Alastair retorted angrily. "You're my wife, and——"

"That," said Rosemary, "is a fact which you only seem to remember when it's convenient." She stood up. "Excuse me please Henry. I don't feel very well. I'm going back on board."

"And how am I expected to get back to the boat?" said Alastair. "Don't be a fool, Rosemary."

"It's rather too late to say that now," said Rosemary. She walked out of the bar and into the sunshine. Alastair half-rose, then sat down again.

"Women," he said, bitterly. "As if things weren't bad enough already. I suppose I should go after her, but——"

"How long," said Henry, "did you say you two had been married?"

"Six years. Sometimes it feels like a hundred."

"When Emmy and I had been married six years, and there were still no children," said Henry, in deep embarrassment, "I started to think I was in love with—well, it doesn't matter who. A nice girl. Emmy guessed it, and retaliated, as any person of spirit would. Things had got pretty desperate before we both realized what fools we were making of ourselves."

Alastair was concentrating on the inside of his beer mug. "It's possible to go on being a fool for years," he said.

"You're telling me," said Henry, guiltily. "But there's no need to be a damn fool. The ordinary foolishness of the human animal, who is naturally polygamous, is—thank God—generally weaker than his capacity for common-sense. But damn foolishness gets you nowhere—except out in the cold, with a bad conscience. I came to my senses just in time. Some people don't."

There was a long and uneasy pause. Then Henry said, "I'm sorry. I didn't intend to tell you the story of my life."

"It's not a very original story," said Alastair.

"I know," said Henry. "It's commonplace and boring. Let's talk about something else. Like lunch, for instance."

"I don't feel like eating today," said Alastair.

"Nor do I. But Emmy and I always . . . by the way, where is Emmy?"

"Emmy? Haven't seen her since early this morning."

Henry felt a tiny pang of apprehension. "Surely Old George must be back by now," he said. "What time did Sir Simon leave?"

"About half past one, I suppose." Alastair looked up at the big, white-faced clock over the bar. "It's half past two now. Still, I wouldn't worry. She's probably stayed to have lunch with Sir Simon."

Henry stood up. "I think I'll just go and see . . ." he said, vaguely, and walked out into the yard.

With an increasing sense of uneasiness, Henry walked up the lane towards Old George's cottage. When he saw the black Lanchester standing like a monument in the open-doored garage, it was no more than he had expected. He quickened his pace, pushed between tall hollyhocks to the back door, and knocked. Old George opened the door.

Trying to keep his voice light and matter-of-fact, Henry said, "I'm sorry to disturb you. I was looking for my wife."

"Wife?" Old George glanced behind him, as though half-expecting Emmy to materialize in the kitchen.

"The lady you drove out to Berry Hall this morning," said Henry patiently. "You brought her back again, didn't you?"

"That I didn't," said Old George. "Left, she had."

"What do you mean?"

"What I say," said Old George, a shade truculently. "Waste of a journey. Sir Simon had me drive him back special to pick up the lady. Some people don't have no consideration."

"And she'd already left when you got there?" It sounded to Henry as though his own voice were coming from a long way away. "How very strange. Can you tell me just what happened?"

Old George shot him a suspicious look. "Nothing happened," he said. "I parks in the drive behind the Daimler, and Sir Simon goes into the house. He says for me to wait. A minute or so after, he comes out and says as how the lady's left, and I'm to go back. Anything wrong in that?"

"No, no," said Henry. "Nothing at all. Thank you."

He almost ran back to The Berry Bush, only to find that Alastair had left. Hurrying down the hard, Henry was just in time to see him clambering aboard *Ariadne* from Hamish's dinghy, which now bobbed astern side by side with the Bensons' own. Henry shouted and waved. Alastair waved back cheerfully. It wasn't until Henry had nearly dislocated his shoulder making exaggerated movements of beckoning that Alastair understood that his presence was required ashore. He nodded encouragingly, and disappeared below for what felt to Henry like an hour, but was in fact about three minutes. When he emerged into the cockpit again, Rosemary was with him. They took a dinghy apiece and pulled for the hard again.

Alastair was first ashore. "What's up, Henry?" he asked.

"It's Emmy," said Henry. "She's disappeared."

"Disappeared?"

"Old George says she'd already left Berry Hall when Sir Simon got back. That's impossible. She had no form of transport."

"She might have walked," put in Rosemary, who had pulled in alongside and was tying up her painter.

"If she'd walked," said Henry, "Old George would have met her on the way, or else she'd be back by now. Anyhow, she wouldn't have walked. I don't know what's happened to her and, frankly, I'm frightened."

"Oh, really, Henry," said Rosemary. "She probably decided to cut across the fields, or—well, after all, Emmy's not a child. She can cope."

"I'm sorry to sound melodramatic," said Henry, abashed, "but I don't think you quite understand. I feel like a man in a fog. We're dealing with somebody desperate and not entirely sane. I've got to be terribly careful."

There was a pause, and then Alastair said, "What do you want us to do?"

"I don't really know," said Henry. "Let's get into the car and drive slowly up the lane, while I think."

In the car, Rosemary said, "She might be anywhere."

"No," said Henry abstractedly. "Not far away. No time." Even as he said it, he remembered that the Aston Martin was not in its garage, but he put the thought firmly to one side. "Berry Hall is the obvious place to start. We'll go there."

"Perhaps if we were to ask Sir Simon——" Alastair began.

"No," said Henry. "Nobody. Not even him. Don't talk to anybody about it. It's too dangerous."

Alastair looked sceptical, but all he said was, "What shall we do then?"

"Is it possible," Henry asked, suddenly, "to drive a car right down to the Berry Hall boathouse?"

"Yes," said Alastair. "There's a drive that goes round the back of the house and down to the river. But we can't very well just take the car down there without a word of——"

"I don't want you to take the car down," said Henry. "I want you to drop me off just before we get to Berry Hall, and go on up to the house yourselves. Pretend it's an ordinary social call——"

"At three o'clock on a sunny afternoon?" said Rosemary. "Sir Simon will think we're——"

"Say you've come to collect Emmy. That you didn't know about the arrangement with Old George. Don't be perturbed when you hear she left earlier. Just say she's probably gone for a walk. Try to keep an eye on Riddle, and keep everybody away from the window of the Blue Drawing Room if you can."

"And what will you——"

"I'm going to investigate the boathouse. And anywhere else that might make a hiding place. I'll meet you at the same spot where you dropped me off. Wait for me."

"I suppose you know what you're doing, Henry." Alastair's voice sounded disapproving.

"I wish to God," said Henry bitterly, "that I did. On second thoughts, if I don't turn up by half past four, go to the nearest public telephone and get on to Inspector Proudie. Tell him to come to Berry Hall with a squad of strong men and a search warrant."

"Good heavens," said Rosemary. "I can't think what Sir Simon will——"

"I can't help that," said Henry. "Emmy was alone there this morning, apart from Priscilla, who doesn't count. Anybody could have gone in and——"

"This," said Alastair, "is just like a rather improbable thriller. I don't believe a word of it."

"I daresay Pete Rawnsley and Colin found it pretty unlikely, too," said Henry. "Right. I'll get off here. Good luck, and thanks a lot."

He watched the station wagon as it drove off down the lane and into the gates of Berry Hall. Then he pushed his way uncomfortably through a prickly hedge and headed towards the river.

TWELVE

When Emmy opened her eyes, she was lying on her back in darkness, aware only of the sound of lapping water and a splitting pain in her head. For a moment, she imagined that she must be in the fo'c'sle of *Ariadne*: then, as consciousness returned and she tried to move, she realized with a pang of horror that she was efficiently gagged with some soft material, and that her wrists and ankles were bound. Memory came flooding back. She had been at Berry Hall . . . and Priscilla . . . had just been going to say something important. And then, without warning, there had been a sickening, thudding crash: she recalled a glimpse of Priscilla's vacuous face expressing a mild surprise, and, after that, darkness.

Now, with returning lucidity, Emmy strained her eyes in the gloom to take in her surroundings. She had not been so far mistaken in her first impression. She was indeed in the fo'c'sle of a boat, and the uncomfortably lumpy surface on which she was lying was a coil of rope. She wriggled desperately, but found that she could not move more than a few, painful inches. As her eyes grew slowly more accustomed to the gloom, she turned her head agonizingly from side to side in an effort to locate anything sharp-edged against which she might be able to chafe the rope round her wrists. The only possible object seemed to be a muddy CQR anchor on her right, but its flukes looked depressingly blunt.

Still, thought Emmy, fighting back panic, it's better than nothing. She began to edge her way towards it. The situation had a ridiculous, nightmare quality. One came sailing with friends to Berrybridge Haven. One met charming people and grew to love a quiet, secluded corner of England. And then . . . Colin. Suddenly she remembered Colin. Colin was dead. Nice, intelligent Colin with his dangerous sense of humour—Colin had been murdered. Pete Rawnsley had been murdered. And she was in the process of being murdered, too. Hysteria rose from her throat and threatened to suffocate her. Somebody had knocked her out and tied her up and thrown her into the bows of a boat. Soon somebody would be back to finish the job. Soon . . .

Simultaneously, came noise and movement. The boat rocked violently, and there was the unmistakeable sound of a footfall on deck. Somebody had come aboard. Emmy froze into immobility. She heard the noise, immeasurably magnified by the echo chamber of the fo'c'sle, as somebody moved about the boat. There was the dull ring of metal on metal. And then she heard a voice, and tears of relief and joy came into her eyes. For it was Henry's voice, and it said, in a diffident and embarrassed tone, "Oh, hello . . ."

"Good heavens, Tibbett," said Sir Simon. "What on earth are you doing here?"

Henry had reached the boathouse by a devious route through bushes and undergrowth, and was considerably disheveled. Gingerly, and with a nervous glance in the direction of the house, he emerged from the shelter of shrubbery and made a run for it across the few yards of open field that separated him from the black wooden walls of the shed. A moment later, he was in the cool darkness of the boathouse, and looking straight into the startled blue eyes of Sir Simon Trigg-Willoughby, who stood in *Priscilla*'s open cockpit, a bag of tools in his hand. The two men regarded each other in silence for a moment. Then Henry, feeling exceptionally foolish, said, "Oh, hello . . ."

"Good heavens, Tibbett." Sir Simon put his tool bag down. "What on earth are you doing here?"

"I was . . . that is, I came over with the Bensons," said Henry.

"My dear fellow," said Sir Simon. He climbed out of the boat and on to the concrete landing stage. "You must come up to the house. I was just tinkering with *Priscilla*'s engine. Something wrong, as I told you this morning. Most annoying."

Even Sir Simon's well-bred politeness could not quite disguise the strong undercurrent of curiosity in his voice. Henry felt compelled to give some sort of explanation, and he decided that the least complicated one would be the truth.

"I'll be frank with you, Sir Simon. I came down here to look for my wife."

"Your wife? But she left some time ago."

"That's just what's worrying me," said Henry. "She hasn't arrived back in Berrybridge, and it's extremely unlike Emmy to go off on her own without leaving any message for me. I didn't want to trouble you, but I felt I must look for her. I don't suppose," he added, "that she could be anywhere in here?"

"In here?" Sir Simon was clearly taken aback. "Heavens, no. I've been working on *Priscilla* most of the time since I got back. There's certainly nobody here." He climbed out of the boat, and wiped his hands on a filthy rag. "This is very disturbing, Tibbett," he went on. "I got back about two o'clock, I suppose, and there was no sign of her. Thought it was strange, myself. Still, I'm sure there's a reasonable explanation. Come on up to the house. I've got the car down here—just been into Woodbridge to buy some tools I needed. I'll run you up, and we'll soon find out what's happened."

"It's very kind of you," said Henry. "I'm sorry if I appear to be panicking unnecessarily, but I may as well tell you that we now have definite proof that Colin Street was murdered. Inspector Proudie is back in Berrybridge, carrying out his investigations. It means that there's a very unpleasant character loose in the neighbourhood, and——"

"Murdered? My dear chap——" Sir Simon was momentarily speechless. "In that case, the sooner we locate your wife, the better. Come with me. I suggest we start by telephoning . . ."

The voices faded into silence. In the dark fo'c'sle, Emmy wept.

Rosemary and Alastair were sitting disconsolately side by side on the sunny terrace. They heard the Daimler draw up in the drive, and were more than a little surprised to see Henry getting out of it, in company with Sir Simon. Henry's passage through the undergrowth had not improved his appearance. His face and hands were scratched with brambles, and his sandy hair stood up like a halo round his thin, worried face. Sir Simon boomed an uneasy welcome.

"Ah, there you are. Henry told me. Council of war, eh?"

Rosemary and Alastair scrambled to their feet. "We just came over——" Alastair began.

"I know, I know. Mrs. Tibbett. Very worrying." Sir Simon turned to Henry. "Have you notified the police?"

"No," said Henry. "I am the police."

A depressed silence greeted this remark.

"All the same . . . search parties and so on . . . Inspector Proudie should surely be told." Sir Simon settled down happily into control of the situation. "Where's Riddle?"

"There doesn't seem to be anybody here," said Rosemary.

"What's today?" Sir Simon asked. "Ah, yes. Sunday. Of course. Riddle's afternoon off. And my sister's sleeping upstairs. In any case, she wouldn't be able to help. Mrs. Tibbett told me she didn't intend to go up and disturb her. Well, I suggest we ring The Berry Bush first, just to make sure that she hasn't got back, and then alert the good inspector and his men."

There was no doubt from his tone that Sir Simon reckoned the inspector and his men to be of considerably more practical value in a crisis than Henry. To Rosemary and Alastair, sanity seemed to be returning fast. Henry's melodramatic behaviour now appeared ridiculous. If Emmy really had disappeared, this was surely the sensible, businesslike way to deal with the emergency.

The telephone calls brought little comfort. Bob Calloway was still out, but the barman—having looked in
both bars and on the hard outside—confirmed that there
was no sign of Emmy. Inspector Proudie was taking a late
lunch at The Berry Bush. He listened respectfully to Sir
Simon, and then asked to speak to Henry. The latter
seemed to him distraught and unhelpful.

"No, she's not at Mr. Rawnsley's house. I've just come
from there. The best thing is to issue a description and
circulate it, sir. What was the lady wearing?"

"Blue jeans and a white shirt, with a navy blue sweater,"
said Henry. "It's very kind of you, Inspector. I expect
I'm worrying over nothing."

"Not at all, sir, not at all," said Proudie soothingly.
"After all, things are serious, as we know. But there, she'll
turn up all right. Anything special you'd like me to do?"

"No, no," said Henry. "I'm sorry to bother you. Everything is quite all right, really. It's just that one worries, you
understand. Just locate Mr. Rawnsley and Miss Petrie, if
you can. They went off at lunchtime in the black M.G.
In fact, round up everybody concerned, as far as you
can . . . see what they've been doing since noon. It may
be important. . . . I really don't know."

"Yes, sir," said Proudie. Privately, he thought, Funny
sort of Chief Inspector from the Yard. Lost his grip.
Happens sometimes. Aloud he said, "Well, if that's all,
sir . . ."

"That's all," said Henry. "I'll be in touch with you
soon." He rang off.

"Well, now," said Sir Simon soothingly, "it's late, and
I'm prepared to bet you people haven't had any lunch. If
you'd like to come into the kitchen, we'll see what Riddle has in the larder. Can't promise much, but there's sure
to be something. . . . This way . . ."

It seemed to Emmy that hours, days and weeks passed
in dark silence, broken only by the lapping of water. She
knew where she was, at least. In the fo'c'sle of *Priscilla*, in
Sir Simon's boathouse. Ever since the reassuring voices of
her husband and Sir Simon had faded into unintelligible

murmurs, and she had heard the car start up and drive
away, she had lain in a stupor of pain, misery and apprehension. She cursed the malignant workings of fate.
Henry had had the sense to look for her. Sir Simon had
mercifully come down to work on *Priscilla's* engine . . .
had, in fact, been in the boat earlier, while she lay unconscious. Either one of them, left to himself, would surely have found her. In silence, she would surely have been
able to make enough noise to draw attention to herself. As
it was, they had met, and their voices had drowned her
frantic efforts to create a noise. . . . She stirred herself
into some sort of life again. There couldn't be much time
left. Must try to get to. that anchor again. If only she
could get the gag off, or her hands free. . . . She began
the slow, dolorous process of movement again. Inch by
inch, she squirmed her way across the fo'c'sle floor. After
what seemed a year, she was touching the damp cold-
ness of the anchor. She rolled over, so that her bound
wrists could reach a fluke. If only she could free her
hands, she wouldn't be helpless . . .

It was at that moment that her ears, sharply attuned to
silence, caught the sound of oars. Somebody was rowing
into the boatshed from the seaward side.

Oh, God, thought Emmy. This is it. Well, he knows I'm
here. What does it matter if I make a noise? If I could
get my hands free . . .

The sound of oars grew louder. Then there was the
scraping of a dinghy alongside the concrete landing stage,
the clatter of oars being unshipped and laid in the boat.
Emmy made a tremendous effort. She rolled herself sideways, and, as she did so, knocked over a Primus stove. It
fell with an echoing crash. If only I'd been able to do
that before . . . she thought, in despair.

For a moment, there was dead silence. Then somebody
boarded *Priscilla.* The Primus was leaking, filling the con-
stricted space with the stench of paraffin. Emmy took another reckless lurch sideways. And the door of the fo'c'sle
opened.

Dim light poured in for a moment, and was immediately blocked again. Against the light, Emmy could just make

out the silhouette of a man's figure crouching in the hatchway. His hands groped blindly in the darkness, and then
brushed against Emmy's foot. For a moment, he did not
move, but she could hear his fast, nervous breathing. Then
the strong hands found her foot again. A moment later,
the man's arms grasped her legs, and Emmy was dragged
unceremoniously out into the cockpit.

Even in the shadows of the boathouse, there was no
doubt about who it was. Above the gag, Emmy's frightened brown eyes were staring up into David Crowther's
face. She could not make out his expression against the
light. For perhaps half a minute they looked at each other
in silence. Then David said, "Emmy . . ." in a strange,
apologetic sort of voice, and abruptly turned his back on
her and began rummaging in the after locker. When he
came back, he held an open knife in his hand.

Emmy closed her eyes, and tried not to faint. As he
rolled her over onto her face, she made a great effort to
pray—but all the time she was wondering, idiotically, how
he proposed to kill her, and if it would hurt very much,
and whether Henry would catch him in the end.

And then, suddenly, her hands were free, and the gag
fell away from her mouth, and David was saying, "Emmy,
what happened? Who did it? How did you get here?"

She managed to murmur, "David . . ." into a coil of
rope, and then everything went black, and she fainted
properly, and with great relief.

The party at Berry Hall had just finished a morose and
scrappy meal of cold beef and undressed lettuce in the
kitchen, when they heard David's voice calling from the
hall, "Anybody here?"

Henry jumped up and ran along the flagged corridor,
closely followed by the others. David was standing in the
centre of the white marble hall, with Emmy in his arms.
Sharply defined by the filtered sunlight, her dark head lay
limply against his white shirt, and her left arm swung
lifelessly, like the pendulum of a clock that is running
down.

David said, "It's Emmy. I f-found her."

Instinctively, Rosemary, Alastair and Sir Simon stopped dead, while Henry went forward. Sir Simon had gone as pale as his ruddy complexion would allow, and Rosemary grabbed Alastair's hand.

Hardly daring to trust his voice, Henry said, "Is she . . ." and when David said exhaustedly, "She's O.K. She's fainted," Henry just stood there. For a long moment, the sudden relaxation of unbearable anxiety robbed him of the power to move or speak. At last he stepped forward and took Emmy's limp hand in his.

Emmy opened her eyes. Momentarily, black terror returned. Then she saw Henry, and smiled tremulously. "I'm sorry, darling," she whispered. "Fool that I am . . . so much trouble . . ."

Henry said, "Give her to me," and gathered his wife awkwardly into his arms.

It was Sir Simon who broke the tension by saying, brusquely, "Where was she? Where did you find her?"

David told him. "Good God." Sir Simon was almost past surprise. "And to think that I was down there . . . and all the time . . ." He pulled himself together. "Well," he went on, briskly, "don't just stand there. We must get her into bed and call the doctor."

Henry was looking fixedly at David. "How did you come to be in the boathouse?" he asked.

David was trembling. "I . . . I r-rowed ashore and I heard . . ."

"It's about time you were back," said Henry, flatly. "I want to talk to you. Colin was murdered last night."

"M-murdered?" David's face went from white to grey, and he looked as though he, too, might faint. "W-what do you mean?"

"I mean that things are very serious indeed," said Henry. "I need to talk to you. Where's your boat?"

"Anchored out in the river. I . . . I j-just . . ."

"Then get aboard again and bring her up to Berrybridge as fast as you can. We'll see you there."

For a moment, David hesitated. He looked at Sir Simon with a sort of appealing indecision. His right hand was in his pocket, and Henry could see it clenching and unclenching nervously through the thin denim. Then he said, "Very well." He turned on his heel and almost ran out of the house.

"Now," said Sir Simon, "it's bed for you, young lady. Mrs. Denoon, if you'd heat some water, for——"

Henry could feel Emmy shivering in his arms. "Not here, Henry," she murmured. "Please not here . . . take me home. . . ."

So despite Sir Simon's vigorous protests, Henry carried Emmy out to the station wagon, and sat with her on the back seat, his arm tightly round her shoulders, while Alastair drove them back to Berrybridge.

The Berry Bush, fortunately, had a room free. Emmy, walking unsteadily, protested that she was now perfectly all right: but it did not take a great deal of persuasion on the part of the others to convince her that, for the rest of the day at least, bed was the best place. The doctor arrived, bustled about cheerfully and inquisitively for some minutes, and finally pronounced that the only trouble was slight concussion and shock. He prescribed rest, hot-water bottles and pills—whereupon Rosemary and Alastair immediately volunteered to drive with the prescription to the one chemist in the neighbourhood who functioned on Sundays.

At last, the bedroom door closed behind the last intrigued chambermaid, and Henry and Emmy were left alone. Henry sat down on the bed, took Emmy in his arms and buried his face between her breasts, and for some time neither of them said a word. Then Emmy said, "What a couple of old fools we are. Don't take it so hard, darling. It was all my own fault, and anyway I wasn't really in any danger."

Henry sat up and smiled at her, but his eyes were weary and worried. "You were," he said, "and you know it. Do you feel strong enough to talk about it? It's terribly important to know what happened."

Emmy raised her hands in a weak gesture of helplessness. "I know it is," she said, "and I can't tell you a thing. I was sitting there, and suddenly I heard a sort of noise behind me, but before I could turn round——"

"You've no idea who hit you?"

"None at all. Everything went black, with a tremendous crash, and the next thing I knew, I was in the boat." She shuddered. "The worst part of the whole thing was hearing you and Sir Simon talking, and not being able to attract your attention. I did try to make a noise, but I could hardly move with the ropes . . ." She rubbed her sore wrists.

"Don't think about that now," said Henry. "The important thing is—what happened before. Why should anybody have done this?"

Emmy wrinkled her brow. "I was talking to Priscilla," she began, and then suddenly she sat up and cried, "Henry! Priscilla!"

"You mean," said Henry, sharply, "that you were talking to Priscilla when——"

"Yes. Oh. Henry. Quick. I never thought——"

There was a knock on the door, and from the corridor the barman's voice said, "Inspector Tibbett? Telephone, sir."

"I'll be back in a moment," said Henry, and ran downstairs.

"Tibbett?" Sir Simon's voice crackled over the wire, urgent and strained. "Tibbett, a rather terrible thing has happened. I thought you ought to know——"

"Your sister——"

"Yes. How did you know? I told you she was asleep when I got in—I went up to take a look. Well, after you left, I went to see her again, and—well, frankly, I didn't like the look of her. Couldn't wake her. And then I saw the empty bottle. So I called the doctor." There was a pause.

"Well?" said Henry.

"Coma," said Sir Simon. There was a break in his voice. "Overdose, combined with . . . He . . . the doctor . . . he doesn't expect her to regain consciousness. . . ."

"What empty bottle did you see?" Henry demanded urgently.

"Sleeping pills. The doctor prescribed them after . . . after the robbery, you know. I don't suppose there's any connection between this and . . . well, the business of your wife. But with all that's been going on, I thought . . ."

Sir Simon's voice trailed off into a miserable silence.

"I'm most terribly sorry, Sir Simon," said Henry. "There's nothing adequate one can say or do in the way of sympathy." Sir Simon made an unidentifiable but moving noise of inarticulate grief. Henry went on. "But I can tell you that the two things *are* connected, and I'm afraid I'll have to send a policeman to sit by your sister's bed in case she does recover consciousness. I know that it seems like a brutal intrusion on your privacy, but——"

"I understand," said Sir Simon. "I understand. Thank you for being so . . ." Abruptly, he rang off.

Henry put through a quick call to Proudie, and then went upstairs again. Emmy was sitting propped up on her pillows, her dark eyes full of anxiety.

"What was it?" she asked. "Is Priscilla . . .?"

"Not so good," said Henry, sitting down on the bed again, "but she's alive. Now, darling, think. Think hard. What were you talking about?"

"I guessed," said Emmy slowly. "I guessed when I first got there and she put her head out of the window and starting talking. I knew that she had something important to tell me, if only I could get it out of her."

"So you stayed behind," Henry prompted.

The mists were clearing from Emmy's mind. "Sir Simon didn't want to leave her alone," she said, "so I offered to stay with her. Fat lot of good I did," she added, bitterly.

"And then you talked to her."

"I went upstairs," said Emmy. "It was very quiet and bright and eerie in the house. She was in her room, with her hair in curlers, drinking gin out of a toothmug. She talked about . . . oh, thousands of things. I couldn't get any sense out of her. She talked about her father and gin in the wardrobe and people wanting money. And then . . . yes, that's right . . . then she suddenly said she had such a wonderful view from her bedroom window, and all the people who came and went——"

"Who?"

"Well, that's all. She hadn't really started when it happened. That's the last thing I remember before I went out of the world, being furious because she hadn't had time to tell me after all."

"She must have said something," said Henry. "Think. She must have said something that somebody overheard, which made it imperative that she shouldn't say any more. What was it?"

Emmy closed her eyes and thought, desperately. At last she said, "There was something about a number."

"A number?"

"Eleven." Emmy opened her eyes, excited. "That was it. Eleven."

"What about eleven?"

"Before eleven."

"Ten, you mean?"

"No. That was what she said. Before eleven."

"What was?"

"That's what I asked her. And before she could answer——"

"Before eleven." Henry got up. "Something happened before eleven. And if only we knew what it was. . . . Well, there's only one thing to do now. Something I should have done long ago."

"Henry . . ."

"Yes, darling?"

"Henry, I know I'm a fool, but after this—well, honestly, I'm frightened. Whatever it is you have to do, can't you do it here?"

Henry grinned at her. "Yes, my sweet," he said. "I can. Right here in this room. I'm going to make a complete, detailed report of everything that's happened and everything we've been told about, properly tabulated. I'll need *Reid's Nautical Almanack*, Proudie's reports and mainly my tired old memory. I hope to God I can do it."

"And you think that'll give you the answer?"

"I'm pretty close to the answer already," said Henry. "I want proof. Something to go on, at any rate. And I hope to find out what happened before eleven, and why it's important."

"Poor Priscilla," said Emmy. "She's such a lonely person." She closed her eyes.

It was nine o'clock that night when Henry finished his report. The small, chintzy bedroom was littered with notebooks and files. Emmy dozed peacefully. Henry chain-smoked, wrote and studied what he had written. Occasionally he underlined certain words and put a big cross in the margin against them.

"What does that mean?" Emmy asked, sleepily.

"An inconsistency," said Henry. "A lie."

Twice, he called Alastair up from the bar, checked on a point, and nodded, gravely and sadly. At five past nine, Henry was called to the phone again. It was Proudie.

"Well, sir," said the latter heavily, "I'm afraid we'll never get any evidence from Miss Priscilla now."

"She's dead?"

"Ten minutes ago. My man Trouncer just phoned from Berry Hall."

"Poor old girl," said Henry. And then, "How's Sir Simon taking it?"

"Hard, sir. Very hard. Trouncer says the poor gentleman is quite distraught. Of course, it's understandable. There were just the two of them."

"I know," said Henry. "And how have you been getting on?"

"I've got statements from everybody about their movements this afternoon," said Proudie gloomily. "And a more unpromising lot you've never seen. Seems everybody remotely connected with the case was hanging round Berry Hall sometime this afternoon. I'll bring the transcripts up for you to see. And, incidentally, I've got everybody here in Berrybridge in case you want to see them. As far as I can make out," Proudie ended, "the only person we can put in the clear is Mr. Crowther."

"I suppose so."

"Well, he rescued Mrs. Tibbett, didn't he?" Proudie pointed out, somewhat aggrieved.

"Yes," said Henry, "he did. Thank God."

"But now that poor Miss Priscilla——"

"It's tragic," said Henry, "but from our point of view, her death isn't such a complete disaster. I'm pretty sure now that I know what her evidence would have been." As Proudie broke into an excited spate of questions, he added, "Give me another half hour or so, will you, and then come up? I can't talk over the phone."

Henry rang off, and walked down the dark passage. As he passed the brightly lit bar, he saw Bob Calloway busy serving beer. Hamish and Anne were sitting in an inglenook: David was talking to Rosemary and Alastair: Herbert and Sam Riddle were playing darts, while George Riddle chalked: Bill Hawkes and Old Ephraim were engaged in a discussion in a corner. It should have been a typical, jolly Sunday evening in an English country pub. But the voices were subdued, the faces strained. Berrybridge Haven was in the grip of a nightmare, faced with facts which it did not understand, and there was terror abroad. Henry, his heart filled with anger and compassion, made his way slowly upstairs.

THIRTEEN

Inspector Proudie walked, heavy-footed, into the bedroom, and greeted Henry and Emmy sadly, a load of distress weighing on his broad shoulders and clouding his normally merry face. In fact, the only ray of hope that he could see in the situation was that Chief Inspector Tibbett seemed to have recovered his usual brisk grasp of affairs, and Proudie charitably ascribed his earlier vagueness to acute anxiety over his wife. The latter's escape from the murderer's clutches was also gratifying, but somewhat outweighed by the tragic business of Priscilla's death.

Proudie sighed deeply, and, at Henry's invitation, sat down on the other side of Emmy's bed. "Well, sir," he said, ponderously, "I'm glad you've been getting on faster than I have. This is a nasty business, and I don't like it." He spoke with an air of personal affront, with which Henry sympathized. He realized that uppermost in the inspector's mind was the inescapable fact that here in Berrybridge, among his own friends and acquaintances, was a cold-blooded murderer who was by now so deeply committed as to be striking with lunatic ruthlessness against anyone and everyone who constituted a possible threat of betrayal.

"Before we compare notes," said Henry, "I'd like to hear how you got on. By the way, did your men have a look at Sir Simon's boat?"

"They did, sir. Nothing helpful. Mrs. Tibbett had been tied up with spare rope from the fo'c'sle, and gagged with an old white racing flag. No prints on the boat except Sir Simon's, Riddle's and Mr. Crowther's."

"So you've fingerprinted everyone already, have you, Inspector?" Emmy asked. "That's quick work."

"Voluntary, of course," said Proudie. "We needed the prints, and—well, I think myself it was a good move. There's nothing makes people take a case seriously like having their prints taken."

"I think," said Henry sombrely, "that everybody is taking this case pretty seriously by now. Well, let's get on."

Proudie pulled a thick notebook out of his pocket, and began thumbing through the pages.

"I saw everybody concerned," he said, "with the exception of Mr. Crowther, who only came ashore from his boat an hour or so ago. I took his prints, which seemed to upset him, and he said he wanted to talk to you. So I let him be for the moment. He's downstairs now."

"I'll see him later," said Henry. "Go on."

"Well," said Proudie, "after you rang, I started straight away by locating Mr. Rawnsley and Miss Petrie. That wasn't difficult. They were both back at Mr. Rawnsley's cottage. Just got in."

"Where had they been?"

Proudie shook his head in a sort of angry despair. "Berry Hall," he said.

Henry looked up sharply. "Berry Hall? When? What for?"

Proudie consulted his notes. "They left here about a quarter to two," he began. "Miss Petrie was feeling better and——"

Henry interrupted him. "Inspector," he said, "I'm sorry, but would you mind very much if I got these people to tell me their own stories? In any case, it might be interesting to see if they check with what they told you."

"Certainly, sir," said Proudie, without rancour.

"I'll go down and talk to them," said Henry. "Would you mind staying up here with my wife. She's had rather a shattering experience today, and she——"

"A pleasure." Proudie beamed. "So long as you explain it to *my* wife."

They all laughed with a polite pretence at roguishness, and Henry went downstairs and into the bar.

A sudden, uneasy silence greeted his entrance. David made as if to get up, but sat down again when he saw Henry making his way over to Hamish and Anne.

Henry said, "Would you two mind coming into the lounge and talking to me for a bit? This is official."

Anne stood up at once. She was solemn and very calm, like an overawed child. "Of course, we'll do anything we can to help," she said.

Hamish got up more slowly. He looked at Anne with some concern, and then said to Henry, "I don't think it's right that Anne should be worried by any more interviews. We've already had the inspector . . ."

"I'm really sorry," said Henry. "It must be done."

"I'm perfectly all right," said Anne, and walked composedly out of the bar.

The lounge was small and dingy, but unoccupied. The three of them sat at a small circular table, from which Henry removed a drooping green plant in a brass pot. Then he brought out his notebook and said, "Let's start with this afternoon. Inspector Proudie tells me you went to Berry Hall."

There was a tiny silence, and then Hamish said, "That's right."

"Why?"

"I——" began Anne, but Hamish stopped her.

"Let me tell this," he said. "There's nothing to it, anyway. I was feeling pretty bloody about what happened last night. Colin, I mean." He glanced surreptitiously at Anne, but she seemed quite unmoved. "I felt," Hamish went on, in a rush, "that it was all my fault. It was I who got angry with Herbert and provoked Colin into that ridiculous display, which got him overexcited, and when he's—when he was excited he always got drunk. I don't suppose all this sounds very logical, but I wanted to—to confess, as it were, and take the blame. There didn't seem to be anybody to apologize to, except Sir Simon. He's the person one tends to go to in these parts when there's any trouble. So I decided to go and see him and tell him it was my fault. I suppose I wanted an excuse to get out of Berrybridge, too. I'm afraid my motives aren't very clear, but——"

"All right," said Henry. "Never mind. Just go on. What happened?"

"I went upstairs to see Anne and tell her where I was going and why. We talked for a bit, and then she——"

"I insisted on going with him," Anne broke in. "I didn't want to be left alone, and I——"

"What time was this?"

Hamish frowned. "About a quarter to two, or a bit after, I suppose," he said. "Anyway, we set out in the car for Berry Hall."

"Did you," Henry asked, "meet anybody on the way? Think hard. It's very important."

Quickly, Hamish said, "We saw George Riddle."

"Where?"

"About a mile from the Hall. He was on a bicycle, riding towards Berrybridge, but as we came up to him he turned down the lane that leads to Woodbridge."

"That's very interesting," said Henry. "Anybody else?"

There was a pause. Then Anne said, "We saw Old George, too, in his taxi."

"Did we?" Hamish sounded genuinely astonished.

"I did," said Anne. "You were probably too busy driving. He was coming down the lane into Berrybridge as we went up it."

"Anybody else?"

"Not that I can remember," said Hamish. He looked interrogatively at Anne. She shook her head.

"No," she said. "I don't think we passed another car at all."

"And what happened then?"

"Nothing," said Hamish. "We drove up to Berry Hall, but it was completely deserted. We knocked and rang, but got no reply. So we came away again."

"You didn't go in?"

There was a silence.

"No," said Hamish.

"Neither of you?"

"Well . . ."

"I went in," said Anne. She turned to Hamish. "There's no sense in lying to Henry. I can't see that it's important, but I went in. Not for long. I just walked into the hall, and called, because the front door was open."

"And you saw nothing and nobody?"

"Not a thing." Anne was quite definite.

"You didn't go into the Blue Drawing Room and look out over the river?"

"No. I walked about a bit on the terrace outside. So did Hamish."

"I see." Henry made a note. "And then?"

"Then we came away," said Hamish.

"And you got to Berrybridge—when?"

Anne and Hamish exchanged the smallest of glances. Then Hamish said, "About half past four."

"What were you doing in the meantime?"

"Just driving."

"Where did you go?"

"I don't know. I just drove. Anywhere."

Henry looked at the two of them for a moment. They both seemed to be holding their breaths. Then he said, cheerfully, "Oh, well, that seems to cover the afternoon."

There was a perceptible relaxation. Henry went on, "Now I want to talk about something else. The day Pete Rawnsley was killed."

Instantly, the tension tightened again. Anne said, quickly, "Henry, I thought we'd——"

Henry said, "Everything has changed now, Anne. Colin's dead."

"Yes," said Anne. It was a whisper.

"First of all," said Henry to Hamish, "I'd like to know whether your uncle had made any night trips by himself in his boat shortly before he died."

Hamish looked very surprised indeed. "Why do you ask that?"

"That's my business," said Henry. "Had he?"

"No." Hamish was definite. "I'm certain he hadn't. I'd have known if he had."

"Right," said Henry. He made a note. Then turned to Anne. "Now," he went on, "I have two conflicting accounts of what happened after you and David rowed ashore that day. One from him and one from you. I want to know which is true."

Hamish looked at Henry with a sort of horror. "Anne wasn't on Steep Hill Sands that day."

"Oh, yes, I was," said Anne. A flush had come into her cheeks.

"It's not true."

"I was." Anne leant forward. "I told Henry. I went ashore and I spoke to Pete and he——"

"She's lying," said Hamish calmly. He squared his shoulders. "I suppose I'll have to make a clean breast of it. I was the only person who went ashore and spoke to Pete."

"No!" Anne cried. There was a suspicion of hysteria in her voice. "It's not true, Henry! It was me!"

Henry said to Hamish, "What time did you go ashore?"

"Ten o'clock," said Hamish. "I looked at the time before I went, because I wanted to be sure not to miss the weather forecast."

"You shared a house with your uncle," said Henry. "You could have spoken to him whenever you wanted to. Why couldn't you talk to him quietly in your own drawing room?"

"That's what I mean," Anne broke in. "It's so silly. Of course Hamish didn't go ashore. He's only——"

"Go on, Hamish," said Henry. "Why did you have to see him so urgently? It was about money, wasn't it?"

"Yes," said Hamish. There was a long pause. Then he went on, "I can't expect you to understand. You're not a sailing man."

"Tell me, anyway."

"Pete and I," said Hamish slowly, "inherited quite a bit of money two years ago. My parents are dead, you see, and Pete was like a father to me. A pretty heavy-handed father sometimes, too. This money was inherited jointly, but he had absolute control of it until his death, or until I reached the age of thirty-five, whichever was the sooner."

"And how old are you?"

"Twenty-five."

"That meant ten years to wait for your new boat, un-less Pete——"

"You're very quick," said Hamish ironically.

"Thank you," said Henry gravely. "Go on."

"I was sure I'd be able to talk him round," said Hamish. "So sure that I'd already had the designs made without telling him, and work had started on the boat. That morn-ing, I had a letter from the builders saying they must have their advance deposit, or . . . Well, Pete was off for a week's racing, and he'd already set sail when the letter arrived. I just had to talk to him."

"So when you saw him go aground, and the fog came down, you took the opportunity to——"

"Of course," said Hamish brusquely.

"And what did your uncle say?"

Before Hamish could answer, Anne cried, "Tell him the truth, Hamish. It's the only way. Tell him the truth."

"All right," said Hamish. "I was going to anyhow. Pete refused. We had a quarrel."

Henry said, "I'm glad you told me that."

"And so of course," Hamish went on, with rich sar-casm, "I killed him so that I could inherit. That's what you think, isn't it?"

"It's a tempting theory, you will agree," said Henry.

Anne, her green eyes shining with tears, said, "Oh, Henry . . . Henry, you must believe me. . . . Hamish——"

"I am not," said Henry, "quite as silly as you think."

Anne suddenly straightened her back. "What do you mean by that?"

Henry sighed. "You've fooled all of us, Miss Anne Petrie," he said. "Me included. I hope you won't do it any more. It's a dangerous game. You run the risk of being disbelieved even when you're telling the truth."

Hamish stood up, his face dark with anger. "There's no need to be offensive to Anne," he said. "Say what you like to me. I've got broad shoulders." He looked like a young bull, standing there in the cramped little parlour.

"I'm sorry," said Henry. He suddenly realized that he

was very tired, and middle-aged. "Just one more question, Anne? Where did you stow the sleeping bags on
Mary Jane?"

"In the forepeak, of course," said Anne, at once. "What
has that got to do with it?"

"Nothing much," said Henry. "You can both go now.
Would you mind asking David to come and have a word
with me?"

David Crowther came quickly and nervously into the
room, lit a cigarette, and said, "How's Emmy?"

"All right," said Henry, "thanks to you. I'll never be
able to tell you how much——"

"It was nothing." David sat down. "Just t-terribly lucky
that I happened . . . that I was there."

"It seems the worst sort of ingratitude to start asking
you awkward questions just now," said Henry, with some
diffidence, "but I'm afraid I must. For instance—just
what were you doing in Sir Simon's boathouse this afternoon?"

David gave the ghost of a grin. "That's not an awkward
question," he said. "I've been waiting to tell you about
it."

"About what?"

Instead of answering, David put his hand into his
pocket, pulled out a small object and laid it on the table
in front of Henry. It was a drop earring made in diamonds
and emeralds. The two men looked at it in silence for a
moment. Finally Henry said, "So you found it."

"Yes," said David. "I found it."

"By accident?"

"Good God, no."

"Please," said Henry, "tell me all about it, from the
beginning."

"There's no beginning," said David, with a trace of
nervous irritation. "Not until yesterday evening. I don't
know what you mean, from the beginning."

"Very well," said Henry. "Tell me about it from yesterday evening."

David took a long pull at his cigarette. "Anne and I,"

he said, "went back to *Pocahontas* after that ghastly party.
We had a drink and talked. About . . . about C-Colin."

"Of course."

"I was intrigued. I haven't got Colin's brains, and I
never will have. J-just good old reliable David. But
Anne told me that Colin had been reading Voss, and had
made a cryptic remark to you about it when you were all
in Walton Backwaters. And of course, we all heard what
he said at dinner. So even my f-feeble intelligence began
to click. After I'd ferried Anne to *Ariadne,* I went back
and took a look at my own copy of the *Venturesome
Voyages,* and of course it became obvious. Do you know
what I mean?"

"Yes," said Henry. "But I was even slower than you
were, if it's any consolation. Now, to get back to last
night. You and Anne talked for a long time on *Pocahontas.*
What else did you talk about, besides Colin?"

David studied the tip of his cigarette. "I d-don't think
that's any of your business."

"I'm afraid it is. I may as well tell you at once that
it's perfectly obvious to everybody that you're in love
with Anne."

David flushed. "That's my affair," he said.

"Colin and Anne had just had a big row," Henry went
on relentlessly. "It must have been an ideal moment for
you to—to put your point of view."

David said nothing. "I presume," Henry added, "that
she turned you down yet again. She probably told you
that the only two men she'd ever cared about were Pete
Rawnsley and Colin Street. Pete was dead. Colin was still
alive."

Slowly, David said, "If you're implying what I think you
are, it's m-monstrous."

"Perhaps Anne drew some withering comparisons between Colin's mental ability and your own, so you determined to beat him at his own game."

"That's nonsense. I——"

"Last night," said Henry, "when you had delivered
Anne to *Ariadne,* did you go in your dinghy to *Mary
Jane?*"

"Of course I didn't. If I had, I'd have seen that Colin wasn't aboard, and——"

"Colin was aboard," said Henry quietly.

"What?" David was obviously stunned by this piece of news. "But Hamish said——"

"What did he say?"

"Well, I mean, we've all been talking about it," said David defensively. "Hamish told me how Colin's dinghy had capsized on the way back to the boat and . . . I never meant . . . I mean . . ."

"Why," asked Henry, "didn't you tell Sir Simon what you had found on Steep Hill Sands?"

There was a long pause. David passed his hand over his forehead. "Can I go back and tell it my own way?"

"Of course."

"Well . . . last night, as I told you, I read Voss and came to the same conclusion as poor Colin had done. If you like, I did want to beat him to it. There's no harm in that, is there? I wanted to prove that . . . well, it doesn't m-matter. Anyway, I decided to go out and look for the jewels at low water this morning. I set sail at six—it was low tide at eight—and I ran the boat aground deliberately at about half past seven. I thought that would look less suspicious than rowing to the sandbank. Actually, I don't think a soul saw me. Anyhow, the sands were dried out already, so I s-started searching."

"How did you set about it?" Henry asked.

"I could remember roughly where it was that Pete went aground," said David, "and it seemed likely that the stuff was s-somewhere near there. But it was much too big an area just to start digging in."

"That's what I thought," said Henry.

"I decided," said David, "that whoever had hidden the jewels must have marked the spot in some way." He was speaking strongly and confidently now, with only the merest trace of a stutter. "A cross bearing seemed the obvious thing. It would have to be one that could be checked at night, and the only lighted objects in the neighbourhood are the flashing buoys—one off the sands and the other off the point. I reckoned our man would probably take the easiest and simplest method of marking. I got the compass out, and found there was a spot where I got a reading of due north on one buoy and due east on the other. At that point, I found I was almost standing on one of those biggish grey stones that you get washed up onto the sands at low water. I tried to lift it, and I couldn't. Then I saw that it had a hole bored through the bottom of it, and a small chain attached which ran down into the sand."

"So that's how it was done," said Henry. "Very ingenious. Nobody's going to notice if one of those stones is always in the same position. Go on."

"Well," said David, "I dug. I didn't have to go far down. On the other end of the chain was a metal box in a waterproof bag. The box wasn't even locked. And inside——"

He gestured toward the earring that glittered serenely on the table.

"So," said Henry, "you took just one earring to prove your story. What did you do then?"

"I b-buried the box again, in the same spot," said David. His voice, which had been calm and strong while telling his story, now trembled again. "I th-thought the police would want to see the box *in s-situ*, as it were."

"Quite right," Henry commented. "What time was it by then?"

"It must have been about half past nine. The water was coming up fast, and *Pocahontas* was afloat again."

"And then?"

There was a pause, and David said, "I went for a sail."

Henry said, mildly, "That seems a slightly eccentric thing to do, in the circumstances."

"I know." David lit another cigarette, oblivious to the fact that a half-burnt one was still smouldering in the ashtray. "I knew you'd s-say that. I wanted to think."

"About Pete Rawnsley."

"Yes."

"You wondered, suddenly, if Pete might have run his boat aground on purpose, because he knew very well where the jewels were. Because he had put them there."

David raised his hands and let them fall again in a vague, helpless gesture. "I didn't know what to think."

"Were you at the famous Hunt Ball at Rooting Manor?"

"Y-yes. I went with Rosemary and Alastair."

"Did you?" said Henry. "That's very interesting. What time did you leave?"

David considered. "About three in the morning," he said. "I know I got back to town about six, feeling lousy."

"You drove back alone?"

"Yes. Rosemary and Alastair were staying the night at the Bush."

"Right," said Henry. "Now to get back to this morning. You had plenty to think about. You knew that Hamish had gone ashore and quarreled with his uncle the day he died."

David managed to grin. "So you believe that now, do you?"

"Yes," said Henry. "Do you want me to go on?"

David said nothing. Henry went on. "You'd had a suspicion all along that Hamish killed Pete, accidentally. Finding the jewels put a much worse complexion on everything. You began to suspect that Hamish and Pete together might have organized the robbery. Hamish's remarks about money that day on Steep Hill took on a new and sinister significance. What's more, you knew that Anne was with the two Rawnsleys at the Hunt Ball, and that she stayed the night in their cottage. You may, by then, have known something else about Anne which would have provided an even stronger motive for——"

"I'm not saying anything," said David stubbornly. "You're doing the talking, not me."

"All right, we'll leave it at that," said Henry. "You wanted to think. So you went for a sail. What conclusion did you come to?"

"I couldn't decide what to do. The only certain, ethical part of the whole business seemed to be that the jewellery belonged to Sir Simon—or rather, to Priscilla, but one can't take her seriously. So finally I made up my m-mind to go and see him before I told the police. I b-beat back up the river to Steep Hill, anchored the boat, and rowed

ashore. I got into the b-boathouse, and I was tying up
the dinghy when I heard a n-noise in *Priscilla*'s fo'c'sle.
I th-thought perhaps . . . I don't know what I thought.
Anyway I had a look, and I found Emmy."

"Yes," said Henry devoutly.

"I c-carried her up to the house. I was considerably
shaken, as you can imagine. And then you told me . . .
about Colin. I realized then that the whole thing was
much too serious to fool about with. I f-felt I couldn't
trust anybody. So I decided to say nothing until I could
tell you."

"Quite right," said Henry.

"And here I am," David ended rather lamely.

"You behaved very sensibly," said Henry. "I'm more
than grateful to you."

David said, awkwardly. "I'm glad. I mean, I want to
help all I——"

"Just one more thing," said Henry. "What time did you
come back and anchor off Steep Hill?"

David looked surprised. "I don't know exactly, but you
can work it out. It must have taken me about half-an-hour
to row ashore, find Emmy and bring her up to the Hall.
I got there at a quarter to f-four, didn't I? So say quarter
past three."

"You didn't by any chance come back and drop anchor
earlier? Say about half past twelve?"

"Of course not."

"You didn't row ashore then, and find the Hall deserted, except for——"

"No."

"You could have," said Henry thoughtfully.

"I could have," said David angrily, "but I didn't."

Henry picked up the earring. "You haven't told anybody about this?"

David shook his head.

"Not even Rosemary and Alastair?"

"Not a soul."

"Good," said Henry. "Don't. May I keep it?"

"Of course," said David, with a kind of disgust. "I don't
want the bloody thing."

"Right," said Henry. "That's all. And thank you again."

At the door, David hesitated. "I know I've got no right to ask," he said, "but . . . well . . . how long do you think all this will g-go on? It's pretty intolerable for . . . for all of us. Besides, we should all go back to L-London, and I gather that——"

"Don't worry," said Henry. "It'll be over soon. One way or another."

"Thank God," said David. He walked out into the dark passage, a tall, disconsolate figure.

When David had gone, Henry sent for George Riddle. The first and most obvious thing that struck him about Sir Simon's manservant was that he was in a bad state of fright. His thin, white face was twitching with nerves, and his voice, dropping all pretensions at gentility, was unnaturally high-pitched and loud. He started to speak as soon as he was inside the door.

"I didn't 'ave nothing to do with it," he said, in a rapid, high-pitched whine. "Honest, sir, I didn't. I don't know where she got it from. I left on me dad's bike as soon as I got the Daimler parked. Never even went inside. It's my day off, and I went to me sister Lil, what's married to Johnny Burrows up Woodbridge way. You can ask 'er. I was there all afternoon."

"You don't know where who got what?" Henry asked patiently.

"Miss Priscilla. I just 'eard she's ill . . ."

"She's dead," said Henry flatly. "Sit down."

"Dead?" repeated Riddle, stupidly. "Gawd." Sweat broke out on his pale face. He sat down heavily. "It couldn't 'ave killed 'er," he said. "It couldn't 'ave."

"What couldn't have?"

"What I . . . I mean, nothing. I don't know nothing."

"You got Miss Priscilla's gin for her, didn't you?" said Henry.

Riddle was silent.

"There's no use denying it," said Henry. "Bob Calloway has told us."

This was a shot in the dark, but Henry felt perfectly

secure that it would find its target. Sure enough, Riddle
gave in at once.

"I was under orders," he whimpered. "I couldn't do
otherwise. It wasn't none of my business."

"Whose orders?"

"I don't know."

"Pull yourself together, man," said Henry a trifle irritably. "If you were under orders, somebody gave them to
you."

"Honest, sir, I don't know. Miss Priscilla. Must have
been." Riddle was an unprepossessing picture of abject
misery. "Every so often, when I was in here, Bob used to
tip me the wink. 'Got another consignment for the 'All,
George,' 'e'd say. And I'd collect the case and take it up.
The first time, he explained what I 'ad to do. 'It goes
straight in the lady's wardrobe,' 'e says. 'Don't let anyone
else see, least of all Sir Simon. It's all paid for proper.
And remind the lady as 'ow it comes from 'er Dad, and
she's not to tell 'er brother about it. She might, see, bein'
forgetful.' "

"You didn't see anything wrong in what you did?" Henry
asked drily.

Riddle licked his lips. "It didn't seem right to me, at
first," he said uneasily, "but Bob said, 'The pore lady
wants it and why shouldn't she 'ave it? It's 'er only
pleasure.' Well, when 'e put it like that . . ."

"And I suppose you got a nice tip each time?"

"Only a bit for me trouble, sir, like anyone might.
All the same, I didn't like doin' it. I said at the time——"

"Skip that," said Henry briefly. "Let's go back a bit.
What happened before Bob got here? Miss Priscilla was
drinking pretty heavily even before then, wasn't she? At
the time of the robbery, for instance?"

"I don't know nothing about that," said Riddle desperately. "I swear I don't. I 'ave my suspicions, though," he
added, suddenly sly.

"What suspicions?"

"Well, the old man left a goodish cellar when 'e died, so
they say. I reckon Miss Priscilla went through that, or

most of it. Sir Simon, now, 'e 'ardly touches a drop, except for the odd pint in 'ere. 'E never went near the cellar, and the key was 'anging in the kitchen for anyone to take. Then one day—soon after Bob came, it was—Sir Simon goes down there for something, and 'e comes up all angry and worried-like, and 'e says to me, 'George,' 'e says, 'I'm keepin' this key meself from now on, and nobody's to be allowed down there but me. If you 'ave occasion to want something, you arsk me.' Well, I mean, it all adds up, don't it?" George sniggered unattractively.

"Maybe," said Henry. "Maybe not. That's all for the moment, but don't leave the pub."

Henry followed Riddle out into the bar. There was no sign of Bob Calloway, and the barman hazarded that he must be in his private quarters, and went to investigate. A few minutes later, he was back, with a puzzled expression.

"Not there, sir," he said. "That's funny. He was here—well, say half an hour ago, that I'm sure. Better see——"

"I'll go," said Henry, and ran out into the yard. The garage was empty. Bob Calloway and the red Aston Martin had both disappeared.

Cursing himself for an inefficient fool, Henry hurried to the telephone and rang the Ipswich police, telling them to stop and apprehend the car and its occupant at the earliest possible moment. Then he went into the bar and collared Herbert.

The Harbour Master was still smarting under his humiliation of the previous night. Not even the kudos which surrounded him as the discoverer of Colin's body could dissipate his rage and gloom.

Henry steered him into the lounge and into a chair, and said, "Now, Herbert, I've a few questions to ask you, and I want straight answers. This is a murder investigation."

"Hay?" said Herbert truculently.

"Murder," shouted Henry.

"Ar," said Herbert. "Deserved it," he added.

"Who did?"

"Both on 'em. Mr. Bloody Interferin' Rawnsley and Mr. Bloody Interferin' Street." Herbert sniffed.

"Why," Henry asked, "did you dislike Mr. Pete Rawnsley so much?"

Herbert cackled without humour. "Why?" he echoed. "Ingratitood, thats' why. Takin' his boat to——"

"That's not the real reason, and you know it," said Henry.

"Hay?"

"Do you want me to shout at the top of my voice so that the whole pub can hear?" Henry asked conversationally. He filled his lungs, and began in a stentorian bellow, "Mr. Pete Rawnsley found out that——"

" 'Ere." Herbert's voice was urgent and concerned. "No need to shout. I'm not deaf."

Henry suppressed a grin. "Good," he said. "Then we can proceed. Mr. Pete Rawnsley found out that you'd been dishonest over——"

Herbert was really worried now. "It was nothing," he muttered. "Nothing as could matter. Taking a few bob over the odds for a few mingy moorings. Threatenin' to do a man out of 'is livelihood, wot 'e's worked at, man and boy, for——"

"I see," said Henry, trying to sound more severe than he felt. "So Mr. Rawnsley found out that you were accepting bribes to allot people moorings which are the property of the Council, and should be given in strict rotation. Quite enough to lose your job. A fine Mayor of Berrybridge you'd have made."

Herbert, reduced at last to silence, sat twisting his rough hands unhappily, and darting furtive glances at Henry out of his rheumy blue eyes.

"However," said Henry, "we'll say no more about that if you'll tell me one thing. What were you doing near Steep Hill Sands in the fog the day Mr. Rawnsley died?"

Herbert's face cleared. He chuckled. "Poachin'," he said.

The frankness of this reply took Henry by surprise, so that he merely repeated, "Poaching?"

"Oysters," said Herbert richly, savouring the word. "Berrybridge Natives. Sir Simon's got a couple of nice beds in under the point. Didn't you know?"

"No," said Henry weakly.

"Fog," added Herbert succinctly. "I know this 'ere river like me own . . . well, lived 'ere sixty-five year, man and boy, since I was born, you might say. Nothin' like a bit of fog for poppin' out and gettin' a few——"

"It was out of season," said Henry indignantly.

Herbert grinned. "All the more reason," he said informatively. "Big prices they pay, Lunnon way, in May."

"London?" said Henry. "I suppose Bob disposed of them for you?"

"Arsk no questions," said Herbert, with a prodigious wink. He was rapidly recovering his customary bounce.

"So," said Henry, "you went out as soon as the fog came down. Where are the oyster beds? Which side of Steep Hill?"

"Beyond it. Under the point."

"You didn't hear any other boats coming or going?"

"Too far orf," said Herbert briefly.

"And you were on your way back, after the fog lifted, when you saw——"

"Didn't see nothin', only *Blue Gull* riding to 'er anchor, as sweet as you please. I went up Steep 'Ill Creek to see young George and get a cuppa in the kitchen. Cold and wet I was, with everything in the boat clammy from the fog, and a long run 'ome. 'Herbert,' I says to meself, 'Young George'll give you a cuppa at the 'All.' So I——"

"You actually took your boat into Sir Simon's shed with a load of his own oysters?" Henry asked incredulous. Herbert looked at him pityingly.

" 'Course not," he said. "Those I'd netted and buoyed to pick up arter dark. I can see," he added patronizingly, "as you've never done no poachin'."

"Supposing Sir Simon had been at home?" Henry asked.

Herbert sniffed. "Wouldn't 'ave mattered," he said defiantly. "Not that he was. Young George told me the night before as Sir Simon was going to be in Ipswich all morning. 'Ad an appointment at nine, 'e said. So I knew the coast 'ud be clear."

"Has it struck you," Henry said, "that poaching is an offence against the law?"

Herbert looked indignant. "I've told you the truth," he said virtuously, "because you asked. I thought you said this was murder."

"It is indeed," said Henry, "but——"

"Sir Simon's a friend of mine," said Herbert. "He doesn't grudge me a few oysters now and then. You ask him."

"I will," said Henry.

The barman of The Berry Bush was calling "Time" when Henry went upstairs again to Emmy's room. He found her engaged in a fierce game of demon patience with Proudie, who showed an exceptional quickness of mind and hand.

Henry sat down wearily and said, "Bob Calloway's hopped it."

"That's bad," said Proudie. "Should we . . . ?"

"I've done all I can," said Henry. "Now it's time to sort out all the threads and put the case in order. I know the answer, and I've got no proof."

Proudie looked profoundly worried. "If you know the answer," he said, "then we'd surely better arrest the fellow right away. We've had more than enough trouble already."

"I can't," said Henry. "I told you, I've got no proof— nothing that would stand up in a court of law. We've got to set a trap, and I'm damned if I know just how to bait it."

"Well, let's have it." Proudie swept up his patience cards. "Whodunit, as they say?"

Henry said, "It'll take some time to explain, and we'll need all these. . . ." He waved a hand at the pile of notebooks, almanacks and dossiers. "I hope I can convince you that I'm right."

"The main thing," said Proudie doggedly, "is this. Is

anyone else in danger of being killed? I'm not prepared to risk——"

"No," said Henry. "Not at the moment, in any case." Surprisingly, he added, "We're not dealing with a violent murderer."

"Not . . .?" Proudie was speechless.

"Basically a gentle person," said Henry sadly. "But violence breeds violence, and one stupid action leads to another, until . . . Oh, well, let's get on with it. This is what I think happened. . . ."

When Henry had finished, Proudie said, "It's a funny case, all right, but I believe you've got the truth of it."

"But no proof," said Henry. "And Bob Calloway has bolted."

"So the only thing to do——"

"This particular drama," said Henry, "will end, appropriately enough, where it began—on Steep Hill Sands." He thought for a while, and then said, "Is there a typewriter in Bob's office?"

"Yes," said Proudie.

"I'm going to borrow it," said Henry. "I'm going to write a note and hope for the best."

He was in the small, cluttered office, and the bar clock had ticked past midnight, when the phone rang shrilly, scattering the dark silence. It was the sergeant from Ipswich. The Aston Martin had been found, neatly parked in a municipal car park outside Colchester. Of Bob Calloway there was no sign whatsoever.

"Never mind," said Henry. "It's just as well."

"But——"

"Call off the search," said Henry. "And if anybody does spot him, tail him but don't arrest him. Let him have all the rope he wants."

Cutting short the sergeant's protests, he rang off and went back to the typewriter.

"You know who this is from," he spelt out, laboriously. *"Bring in the rest of the goods tomorrow evening. I'll be*

waiting. H.T. knows quite a bit, but he's nowhere near the truth. I fooled him nicely today. Good luck."

He put the note in an envelope, addressed it, and left it in a conspicuous position behind the bar. Then he went upstairs to bed.

FOURTEEN

The next day passed with interminable slowness. It was cloudy and overcast, with a sharp little breeze from the north which had a tang of autumn in it. Henry and Emmy stayed in bed until ten, and then, at Henry's suggestion, went for a walk along the foreshore. The church bell, monotonous and mournful, tolled unemotionally the passing of the lady of the manor. With anger and pity, Henry visualized the announcement in the *Times*. "*Suddenly, at Berry Hall, Suffolk, in her 61st year, Priscilla Trigg-Willoughby, beloved sister of . . .*" The curtains of polite behaviour and social usage pulled quickly together to hide that pathetic, raddled corpse.

Henry and Emmy walked in silence. He was in the grip of that most trying form of depression—the melancholy of enforced inaction.

At noon, they returned to The Berry Bush. The bar was already crowded, but the usual genial atmosphere was noticeably lacking, as was the familiar and integral figure of Sir Simon. The sole representative of Berry Hall was George Riddle, who sat with his father in one of the inglenooks, looking thinner and more lugubrious than ever.

The Fleet—Anne, Rosemary, Hamish, Alastair and David—occupied the large table in the window, where they sat gazing out over the grey river in depressed silence. Bill Hawkes stood stolidly at the bar, exchanging an occasional morose word with the barman. Only Herbert seemed in macabre high spirits, as he regaled two serious-faced young men in blue jeans with a preposterous story of how he had once salvaged a yacht single-handed in a Force 9 gale. From the conversation, it became clear that these two strangers were prospective buyers for one of the boats which Herbert had to sell, and the latter was evidently not going to let a small matter like murder come between him and his commission. He was, in fact, putting up a very good performance—only occasionally darting venemous glances at the other occupants of the bar, who, he clearly felt, were letting down the reputation of Berrybridge as a colourful and picturesque anchorage. For the first time, Henry realized just how much of the popularity of the place depended upon Herbert and his outrageous, quotable conversation.

As he and Emmy made their way over to the window table, Henry glanced briefly at the bar, and was gratified to see that his note had disappeared. So far, so good. He thought of it now, crumpled hastily into somebody's pocket, and permitted himself a small, grim smile.

The arrival of the Tibbetts lightened the atmosphere a little. Everybody enquired tenderly about Emmy's state of health, and professed pleasure at her recovery. Everybody remarked on the dismal weather. Nobody mentioned Colin.

At a quarter to one, Hamish said to Anne, "What about that joint we left in the oven? Shouldn't we be getting back?" To the others, he added, "Anne's a very fair cook, you know. She even baked an apple pie this morning."

Anne smiled wanly, and Emmy warmed to Hamish. It showed, she thought, understanding and consideration of a high degree to have appreciated that what Anne needed most at the moment was to be kept occupied at something she did well.

Hamish went on. "I'd have liked to have asked you all back to lunch, but I'm afraid the cottage is just too damned small. Anyhow, I reckoned that Rosemary would have something splendid laid on aboard *Ariadne,* knowing her. But you'll come, won't you, David? I know your bachelor meals on *Pocahontas*—half a tin of cold baked beans and a bun."

David, who had been gazing out of the window, turned his head and looked straight at Hamish. In the moment of silence which followed, many things were said. Then David gave a tired half-smile, and said, aloud, "Thanks, Hamish. By the way," he added, turning to Henry, "I really ought to get back to town. But I don't know if——"

"That's all right," said Henry. "Go back this afternoon if you want to."

The three of them went out together, Anne's tiny figure seeming to link the two men, as she walked between them as surely and beautifully as a small cat. Alastair watched them go with a curious expression on his face, half regret and half relief, as though he were seeing a part of his life disappear through the black-framed doorway. Then he turned to Rosemary, and said, with great gentleness, "Have you got something splendid waiting aboard *Ariadne*?"

Rosemary gave him a grave look from her blue eyes for a moment before she answered lightly, "Not all that splendid, darling. Hot baked beans—and a bun."

They all laughed, and the laughter shattered tensions. Alastair finished his beer, and said to Henry and Emmy, "All right then. Come and see how the poor eat."

Ariadne's cabin was warm and snug after the chilly trip in the dinghy. Alastair lit the paraffin stove, while Rosemary busied herself in the galley. The hot baked beans were accompanied by poached eggs, bacon and an excellent salad, and proved delicious. When they had all eaten, Alastair stretched his arms above his head, and said, "Well, I don't know about anybody else, but I don't propose to go sailing today. It's cold and miserable and there's not even enough wind to make it amusing."

"I'm sorry you feel like that," said Henry, "because I was going to ask you if we could go out this evening."

"This evening?" Rosemary's eyes widened in surprise. "Whatever for? Honestly, Henry——"

"Not you," said Henry. "Not you or Emmy. Alastair and I can manage the boat alone, can't we?"

Rosemary's jaw became stubborn. "I don't know what this is all about," she said, "but if Alastair's going, I'm going too."

"Rosemary——" Emmy began, but before she could get

any further, Rosemary went on. "And in any case, you can't possibly sail *Ariadne* without me. It's all very well for you to talk, Henry, tied up snug in harbour, but suppose a gale blew up? It might easily. The glass is dropping. I don't want to be offensive, but you just don't know enough about boats. Does he?" She appealed to Alastair, who was looking uncomfortable.

"I don't know what to think, Henry," he said. "There's something in what Rosemary says, you know. Couldn't we take David or Hamish?"

"I told David he could go back to London this afternoon," said Henry. "As for Hamish—well, to be frank, I'd rather keep this thing between ourselves, if you don't mind."

Emmy sat up very straight, and said, "Look here, Henry. If you're going to involve Alastair and Rosemary in something dangerous, it's surely only fair to tell them what it is."

Henry, who was feeling tired and not a little depressed, said, "Of course. I was going to do that anyway." He turned to Alastair. "I'm asking you to take *Ariadne* out to catch a murderer—the person who killed Pete Rawnsley and Colin Street."

"It'll be a pleasure," Alastair said grimly.

"It may not be such a pleasure when you realize who it is," Henry said sadly.

"Who is it, then?"

"I can't tell you, yet," said Henry, with genuine regret. "You see, I've no proof. I'm morally certain, and I've set a trap which I intend to spring this evening on Steep Hill Sands. If the murderer doesn't take the bait, I'll have to think of something else. This much, though, I can tell you . . ."

Rosemary distributed cups of coffee in silence, and then came and sat on her bunk, deeply absorbed, as Henry outlined the story of Colin's deduction and David's discovery of the jewels. He said nothing about the note he had written, but ended by remarking, ". . . and I have reason to believe that the murderer—who is, of course, the same person who stole the jewellery—will go out to Steep

Hill Sands again this evening to dig up the rest of the stuff. Our only hope is to be there, on the spot."

Alastair took his pipe out of his mouth, and said slowly, "That's a pretty tall order, Henry. Anybody on Steep Hill would see us coming and——"

"So far," said Henry, "the murderer doesn't suspect that we know where the jewels are hidden. We'll go for a perfectly ordinary sail—in fact, we'll spread it around the Bush early this evening that we're going out tonight. Where would it be reasonable for us to make for?"

"The Deben," said Alastair promptly. "We could catch the ebb downriver and turn north."

"Well, that's exactly what we'll do," said Henry. "Except that in fact we'll anchor just round the point, and you'll put me off in the dinghy——"

"Not alone," said Rosemary quickly.

"Of course not," said Alastair.

Henry looked at them gratefully. "Perhaps, after all," he said, "we'd better all go. You three can stay aboard, and——"

"No," said Alastair, with great firmness. "I'm coming with you."

"I don't think," said Henry carefully, "that the murderer will put up much resistance, once it's established that——"

"Don't talk rot," Alastair interrupted brusquely. "We'll leave the girls on board and you and I will put ashore."

Henry smiled. "I'm very grateful," he said. "So be it. I hate letting you in for this, but you understand that if I had Inspector Proudie roaring around in a police launch——"

"We can handle this ourselves," said Alastair.

"Right," said Henry. "Now, if you've a detailed chart of the river, we can lay our plans. . . ."

They went ashore promptly at six. As they walked up the hard to The Berry Bush, Henry noticed a black police car parked in the yard outside the pub. Sure enough, Proudie was there to meet them.

"I'd like a word with you, sir," said the inspector, adding somewhat aggrievedly, "Been looking all over the place for you."

"O.K.," said Henry. "Sorry, Inspector. You three go on in and order me a beer."

As the others disappeared into the bar, Proudie said, "We're on to Bob Calloway."

"Really?"

"Phone message from London. He's been spotted in Soho this evening."

"Very interesting," said Henry drily. "Who saw him?"

"One of your own chaps," Proudie replied. "Saw him walking down Old Compton Street as bold as brass. Since you'd given orders not to arrest him"—Proudie could not keep a slight note of resentment out of his voice—"the constable shadowed him as far as the Club Parisienne, where he went inside. They've got a tail on him now. I suggest we——"

"We'll do nothing, for the moment," said Henry. "Let London look after Bob Calloway. There are things to be done here."

He spoke quietly to Proudie for a few minutes, and then made his way into the bar.

Henry's idea of spreading the news of *Ariadne*'s projected trip seemed doomed, for Alastair, Rosemary and Emmy were The Berry Bush's only customers. A few minutes later, however, Old George came in with Herbert and Sam Riddle. Alastair took the opportunity of buying the Harbour Master a gin, furnished the others with pints of ale, and began at once to enlarge on the idea of a night sail to the Deben.

Herbert was gloomy. "Bad night," he said, sticking his long, thin nose sadly into his gin. "Glass fallin'. Wind gettin' up. Silly, if you arsk me."

"Ain't so bad nor that, Herbert," Old George protested.

"Them as knows what's good for 'em," said Herbert cryptically, "'ull stay put at their moorings tonight."

"Well, we've made up our minds," said Alastair firmly. "Mr. Tibbett here wants to try a bit of night sailing, and that's what we're going to do."

"What time you plannin' on leavin', then, Cap'n Benson?" Herbert enquired.

Alastair glanced at his watch. "Soon," he said. "Low

water is at a minute past nine. I'll need at least two hours of ebb to get me down the river and up the coast."

"You beware of Steep Hill Sands, sir." From his table, Sam Riddle spoke slowly, and with weight. " 'Tisn't a healthy place, not on a night like this."

The others nodded, sagely.

"Don't worry, we'll be O.K.," said Alastair cheerfully. "Well, Henry, I reckon we'd better be moving. There's quite a lot to do on board."

They drank their beer, and left. Henry suggested that they should drop in on Hamish on the way back, to tell him about the proposed trip.

The cottage was cheerful and warm. Hamish and Anne sat one on each side of the fireplace, where sweet-smelling cherrywood logs were blazing. For all the cosiness, however, Henry sensed an atmosphere of strain as they came in. Anne's mouth was set in mutinous lines, and she looked as though she had been crying. Hamish seemed larger, darker and more overpowering than ever, and there was no laughter in his eyes.

Both of them got slowly to their feet as the visitors came in. There was a curious air of defiance in their attitude, as if they had been expecting something other than a friendly call.

"So there you are," said Henry, with slightly forced brightness. "We missed you at the Bush and guessed you'd be here."

Hamish seemed to relax a little. "Come in and have a drink," he said.

When they were all comfortably seated and furnished with alcohol, Alastair said, "Well, there's one born every minute, Hamish. Henry wants to try his hand at night sailing, so we're going up to the Deben tonight."

Hamish, who had been in the act of raising his glass to his lips, stopped abruptly and sat very still for a moment. Then he took a long drink, and said, "Hardly seems an ideal evening for it."

"We all want to go," said Rosemary. "I just want to get away from Berrybridge, myself. I can't bear sitting here doing nothing, when . . ." She shivered slightly, although the room was warm.

"I thought we were all suspects, and not supposed to leave the place," said Anne, in her sweet, husky voice. "But of course, since you'll have the law itself on board with you, I suppose . . ."

"I haven't told anybody not to leave," said Henry. "Do you want to go back to London? Nobody's stopping you."

Hamish and Anne exchanged the briefest of glances. Then Anne said, "Oh, Henry. Don't take it personally. I'm quite happy where I am."

"Good," said Henry. "Well, wish us luck. It's going to be a cold, clammy trip, but I think it'll do us all good."

Suddenly, Hamish said, "Can I come with you?"

"Sorry, old man." Alastair spoke quickly and definitely. "There's really not room for more than four."

"Suppose it blows up into a gale," said Hamish. He was not asking a question, but stating a fact.

Alastair shrugged. "I don't think it will," he said.

"You never know. The wind's getting up steadily, and the glass is dropping." Hamish sounded worried.

"It's not all that far, after all," said Rosemary. "We should be in the Deben by ten."

"If we start now." Alastair downed his drink and stood up. "Come on then. All aboard that's going aboard." He turned to Anne, who was nursing her big tumbler thoughtfully. "Goodbye, Anne," he said.

Anne looked at him steadily for a moment. Then she said gravely, "Goodbye, Alastair."

Henry and Emmy were already on their feet.

"Shall we see you tomorrow?" Hamish asked.

For a moment, nobody answered. Tomorrow seemed a thousand years away, a new world, not to be reckoned with, not even to be dreamed about. It was Emmy who recovered first, and said, warmly and naturally, "I hope so, Hamish. I expect we'll be back."

Hamish came outside with them onto the terrace which overlooked the grey river. Outside, he said, tentatively, "About Colin. What's——"

"Don't worry," said Henry. "It's all under control."

Hamish gave him a short, unamused look. "I hope so," he said. "Well—goodnight. Good luck."

As they walked along the foreshore back to the dinghy, they could see Hamish's massive figure silhouetted against the light from the open doorway. They could not see his face.

The breeze from the north had freshened considerably by the time that *Ariadne* slipped her moorings and began to run downstream. Ashore, Henry could see lighted windows in the gathering dusk, and had the impression of being watched by secret eyes. As they came within sight of Steep Hill Sands, already gleaming whitely as the tide retreated, a single light—a single eye—glowed from the ghostly façade of Berry Hall. Henry had the curious impression of a composite sigh of relief going up from the unhappy landscape. A breathing space. He dismissed this as wishful thinking. Perhaps nothing would happen. Perhaps this whole cold, uncomfortable adventure would end in a dismal and fruitless vigil. Heaven knew, he had made enough mistakes already. If he had been cleverer, Colin might be alive now. Depression set in, with the first drops of chilling rain. Swiftly and silently, *Ariadne* ploughed her way downstream, her great white sails spread like swans' wings. Henry glanced miserably at Alastair, and was surprised to see that the latter was smiling.

"Lovely sail," said Alastair.

Rosemary came up from below with mugs of hot soup. "This is fun," she said. "I mean, the whole situation is awful, but it is fun all the same. Have some soup, Henry."

"Thank you," said Henry, from his heart. Everything suddenly seemed more reasonable and more exhilarating. He realized gratefully that the rain was failing to penetrate the thick black oilskin he was wearing, and the soup brought a reassuring glow.

"Whatever you do, don't get cold," Rosemary admonished him. "It's hellishly difficult to warm up again once you're chilled through. Put on an extra sweater before you think you need it."

She grinned, and retreated into the golden-lit haven of the cabin.

The dusk was deepening fast as *Ariadne* swung round Steep Hill Point. "Harden sheets," called Alastair. Henry pulled on the jib sheet as the boat swung broadside on to the wind. At once, she heeled over smartly, and tossed up a spurt of spray over her bows, which caught Henry neatly in the back of the neck.

Alastair was watching his course like a hawk. After some time, he said, "We're out of sight of everyone by now. O.K. to go in and anchor?"

"Fine," said Henry. The water had trickled down under his oilskin, making his shirt cling clammily to his back, but he was aware of a rising sense of excitement. "Any time you like."

"Harden in a bit more, then, and watch out down below."

As *Ariadne* put her nose to windward, she leant over with a vengeance. From the cabin, Rosemary swore as a badly stowed saucepan fell to the floor with a tinny crash. Lee rail under, *Ariadne* roared towards the shore. Great sheets of water broke over her bows, but she settled down happily enough on her new course, bucking and buffetting into the powerful breeze and riding the short seas with surprising ease.

"Come and take her, Rosemary," called Alastair above the scream of the wind. "I'll let go the anchor."

Rosemary climbed up from below.

"What shall I do?" yelled Henry, feeling useless.

"Get below and out of the way," Rosemary called back gaily. "O.K., darling. Got her."

Obediently, Henry went below. Emmy was doing her best to sit on one of the bunks, which now lurched at a frightening angle. She looked slightly green, but she said bravely, "Isn't this fun?"

Henry grunted noncommittally. It was, in his view, far from fun.

Then there was a yell from Alastair, a wild thrashing of sails, and the boat steadied herself onto an even keel. From outside, the Bensons' voices came indistinctly.

"Down main!" "Wait till I get the gallows up!" "Hurry up, blast you, woman!" "O.K. now. Let her go!" "Smother it, for God's sake. Where are the tyers?" "Right. Down jib!"

And then, suddenly, a blissful silence except for the singing of the wind in the shrouds. Rosemary and Alastair, drenched and dishevelled, came stumbling down the companionway and into the cabin.

"Well," said Alastair, "here we are. Safely anchored. But I don't want to stay here any longer than I must. It's an exposed position and the wind's freshening all the time."

"I'm sorry," said Henry apologetically.

Alastair grinned. "Not your fault," he said. He looked at his watch. "Half past eight. We'd better get ashore."

For the first time, Rosemary seemed worried. "For heaven's sake, be careful," she said. "I hate the idea of your going."

"I promise you, Rosemary, that——" Henry began, but Rosemary cut him short. "I'm not worried about your wretched murderer," she said. "I'm worried about taking the dinghy ashore in these seas."

Alastair put his arm round her shoulders. "I'll be careful, I promise, darling," he said. "This has to be done."

"Yes," said Rosemary. "Yes, I suppose it does."

Henry and Alastair climbed up on deck again and surveyed the scene. *Ariadne* was anchored, according to plan, as close inshore as she could safely go, under the line of dark, close-set trees that hid the eastern elevation of Berry Hall from the open sea. As they looked southwards, they could still just distinguish how the trees thinned out and eventually disappeared altogether at the point where Steep Hill Sands ran out into the river. That afternoon, at their planning conference, there had been some argument as to what to do with the dinghy. Clearly, the ideal solution was to beach it under the shelter of the trees and to walk out over the sands: but both Henry and Alastair were uncomfortably aware that if they had to wait any length of time, the tide would come in and leave them stranded on the sands, out of reach of their

boat. In the end, Henry had managed to convince Alastair
that the latter should stay with the dinghy, while he
himself walked ashore. At a given signal, Alastair would
row out and pick Henry up from Steep Hill. It was a
haphazard and unsatisfactory arrangement, but it would
have to do. Each man carried a shrill whistle, of the kind
used for fog signals, and a powerful electric torch.

Now, as they stood on *Ariadne*'s heaving deck, the
whole idea seemed much less attractive than it had in
the shelter of Berrybridge Haven. Between the boat and
the shore, angry white crests of foam broke incessantly, and
the rain drove steadily in their faces. *Ariadne* herself
bucked and tossed restlessly at her anchor, grinding the
chain against her bows with each convulsive movement.

"I can't row broadside on to these seas," said Alastair.
"Too dangerous. We'll have to run more or less with the
wind until we're in more sheltered water, and then turn
up."

Getting into the dinghy was a feat in itself. The cockle-
shell boat plunged from crest to trough of the waves
like a demented creature, as she lay tethered alongside
her parent vessel. Alastair climbed in first, with infinite
care, and was able to steady the little craft somewhat for
Henry.

"Whatever you do, step in the middle," he said. "Hold
on to my shoulders. O.K. Now!"

Somehow, Henry tumbled clumsily into the dinghy. It
rocked alarmingly, but remained the right way up.

"Now," said Alastair. "Sit in the middle and don't
move. Don't shift your weight an inch, or you'll have us
over. Right. We're away."

After the comparative stability of *Ariadne*, the dinghy
was a nightmare. Sitting so low on the water, Henry had
the impression that every wave was going to swamp them.
Grimly, he held on with both hands to the thwart, and
concentrated on not moving. After a seeming eternity of
travelling in the wrong direction, nearer and nearer to
the open sandspit—though edging always closer and closer
to the shore—the seas grew calmer, and Alastair said,
"Hang on to your hat. We're turning up-wind."

If Henry had imagined that the first part of the journey was hazardous, he had had, mercifully, no conception of what the second part was to be like. As the dinghy turned her nose against the wind, the curling, icy waves began to break over the bows in great arcs of spitting spray, drenching the two men. The boat itself was tossed like a shuttlecock in the foaming water. Alastair, grim-faced, rowed with careful, dogged determination. Inch by painful inch, they crept inshore and nearer to the sheltering shadow of the trees. At long last, after what seemed an eternity, there was a crunching sound and a sharp lurch.

"Here we are," said Alastair. "It means wading ashore, I'm afraid."

Henry was only too pleased to be free of the dinghy and to have his feet on firm ground again—even if it meant standing knee-deep in swirling, bitterly cold water. Together they dragged the boat up the beach until it was safely hidden in dark shadows.

"Well, this is where we part company," said Alastair, and added, after a pause, "Good luck. And for God's sake, don't let's have any heroics."

"Heroics?" Henry laughed, ruefully. "Do I look like a hero?"

He didn't. He looked like a small, chilled, forlorn figure in oilskins several sizes too large, shivering wretchedly as his bare feet sank into the clammy sand, and his wet jeans flapped about his thin legs.

"All the same," said Alastair, "I know you."

Henry put on his sopping plimsolls. "Well," he said, "goodbye for now. And thanks."

He left Alastair perched on the edge of the dinghy, and made his way cautiously in the direction of Steep Hill Sands, keeping always under the protective darkness of the trees. It was while he was still engulfed by their reassuring shade that he heard the unmistakeable chugging of a motorboat.

Henry stopped, stock still, and then edged his way cautiously forward. What with the rapidly falling darkness and the silver screen of the rain, visibility was very poor, and

he had only the vaguest idea of the direction from which
the engine noise was coming: but, beyond all doubt,
somebody was nearing Steep Hill Sands. A few more
steps, and Henry had reached the limit of the trees' protective cover. He strained his eyes to see ahead, but the
sands only glimmered faintly, dusky and unrevealing. The
sound of the motor grew louder. There was nothing for it
but to step out onto the exposed expanse of the sandbank.

Henry moved forward, silently as a cat. Suddenly he
froze again, as the engine of the motorboat cut out. Somewhere ahead of him, somebody had beached the boat. Now
only the thin screen of the wind and rain broke the silence.
Henry began to move forward again. One thing he realized
only too well: on that bleak stretch of sand, neither he
nor his adversary had any advantage of cover. They would
see each other at the same moment—unless, of course,
the other was too occupied in what he was doing to notice
Henry's approach.

The sound of a shovel, scraping delicately at the sand,
came as a shock. It was surprisingly close. Henry held
his breath, and could hear someone else breathing heavily.
Then he saw the faint outline of a motorboat. Beyond it,
somebody was digging for treasure, as Captain Voss had
dug in the Cocos Islands nearly a century ago.

Henry took a deep breath. Then he stepped out from
behind the beached boat, and shone the searching beam of
his torch directly onto the crouched figure. Abruptly, a
face turned towards the source of light—and in an endless moment of silence, the cruel torchlight played merci-
lessly on the haggard features of Sir Simon Trigg-Willoughby.

"It's Henry Tibbett, Sir Simon," said Henry. He was
not feeling heroic, nor was he enjoying himself.

"By God." Sir Simon scrambled to his feet. "What in
hell's name are you doing here?"

"I'm arresting you," said Henry, "for the wilful murder
of Pete Rawnsley. The cases of Colin Street, your sister
Priscilla and my wife, we can discuss later."

Sir Simon gave a short laugh in which there was more than a trace of hysteria. "Have you gone mad?" he demanded.

"No," said Henry, reasonably.

"I've never heard such appalling nonsense in all my——"

"For a start," said Henry, "we might get on with the job in hand. I see that I interrupted you in the process of unearthing a boxful of jewellery, the property of the Mutual and General Insurance Company of Lombard Street."

He directed the beam of the torch downwards. Already, the heavy metal box was half uncovered. There was a movement in the darkness and Henry swung his torch up again. Sir Simon had backed away a couple of paces, and was leaning heavily against the hull of *Priscilla*.

"Insurance company be damned," said Sir Simon. His voice was thick and somnambulic. "It's mine."

"It was never yours, even in the first place," said Henry. "It was your sister's."

There was a moment of silence, and then Sir Simon began to speak. The fact that he spoke in his usual, robust, bar-side voice merely enhanced the nightmare. "Have you ever considered, Tibbett," he said, "the toughness of a diamond? They're almost indestructible, you know. They don't perish or crumble or get dry rot or need to be repaired or restored. That's what was so monstrously unfair about it. Father's will, I mean. Prissy got the imperishables, and I got . . ." He stopped. Henry said nothing. Sir Simon went on. "I've never been married, Tibbett, but you have. Can you imagine what it would feel like to watch your wife slowly dying for want of medical treatment . . . to watch her growing old and crumbling away? That's as near as I can put it, in your terms. That's how I felt about the house. I loved it, you see. At the beginning, I couldn't see anything wrong in what I did. A man can't steal his own property, can he?"

"A narrow-minded person," said Henry, "might say that you robbed first Priscilla and then the insurance company."

"Narrow-minded," repeated Sir Simon, thoughtfully. "Yes, that just about sums it up. Priscilla was narrow-minded. I tried to reason with her. No good. All she wanted was gin. Well, I gave it to her. I thought a lot about it, Tibbett. I promise you that. I weighed my sister in the balance, and tried her worth against the house. And what did I find? On the one hand, a selfish and petty old woman. On the other, a thing of lasting grace and beauty. I made the right decision. I never regretted it."

"You spent the insurance money," said Henry, "and it wasn't enough. You needed more. So you started to raid the jewellery, and sell it, bit by bit. That was what you were doing when Pete Rawnsley——"

Sir Simon sighed, loudly. "Poor old Pete," he said sincerely. "One of the best. One of my only friends. I suppose that was when I began to go mad. How was I to know he'd be here? I told you I saw him go aground. I'm afraid that was a lie." Sir Simon sounded genuinely apologetic.

"I know it was," said Henry.

"You know now," said Sir Simon, with a touch of pique.

"I've known for some time," Henry answered gently. "That was what first gave me an inkling of the truth. And then when I realized that you'd got home from Ipswich before eleven——"

"Ah." In the torchlight, Sir Simon nodded, slowly and gravely. "She remembered, did she? I never dreamt you'd be clever enough to put two and two together. Ah, well." He paused. "I'm sorry about young Street, too," he added. "Really sorry. He had no right to play that cruel trick on Herbert, but he was brilliant. A great career cut tragically short. Sometimes I wonder if perhaps I'm not just a little mad. It's a great relief to talk about it."

"I suppose it was you who rigged the election?" said Henry. "And you let Herbert poach your oysters. How much did he know?"

"I don't know. He just hinted . . ."

"And Riddle. Was he in on all this?" Henry tried to

keep his voice light and conversational, above the moaning of the wind. He was acutely aware of the fact that he was very cold and wet indeed.

"Riddle knew nothing," said Sir Simon sharply. "You don't imagine I would discuss such a thing with a servant, do you?"

"It was a stroke of luck for you," said Henry, "finding Bob Calloway."

"You think so?" Sir Simon laughed dangerously. "On the contrary, it was the greatest possible mistake. I could have managed alone. I should have managed alone. I don't know if you're aware of it, Tibbett, but the man is a criminal."

"He deals in stolen goods," said Henry.

"Precisely. And he is untrustworthy into the bargain. He tried to swindle me," said Sir Simon, with profound indignation.

"Don't worry," said Henry. "He'll be dealt with."

"I'm extremely glad to hear it."

Henry was seized with a sense of wild unreality: and at the same time, with the conviction that this situation, this illogically logical conversation, was a repetition, in essentials, of another conversation that had taken place on this very spot, on a morning in May, under a veil of damp, clinging fog. That time, though, it had been Pete Rawnsley who had stood where he was standing now. And that time, it had ended in . . .

"Well, Tibbett," Sir Simon was saying, "mustn't take up any more of your time. The tide's rising fast, and——"

There was a quick, convulsive movement in the darkness, as Sir Simon ducked away from the beam of light. A clatter of metal on wood. Henry swung the torch, just in time to see the grotesque figure bearing down on him. In Sir Simon's hand was a huge, heavy spanner.

In one movement, Henry flung himself down on the sand and put out the torch. He was aware of a sharp, glancing pain as the spanner grazed the back of his head. With numbed fingers, he managed to get his whistle to his mouth, and blew for all he was worth, shattering the night.

Instantly, Sir Simon made for the source of the noise. Henry, hampered by his heavy oilskins, launched himself in a rugger tackle at the other's knees. They went down onto the sand together, rolling over and over, clenched in a stranglehold of desperation. For seeming hours they wrestled, grimly, in the darkness. Sir Simon, in his agony, was possessed of the legendary strength of a lunatic. Henry concentrated on maintaining his grasp on the deadly right wrist—the wrist of the hand that held the spanner: but he felt his strength ebbing. And as he rolled over yet again on the clammy sand, he became aware of another and even more sinister sensation. The sand was no longer just damp: it was wet. The tide was rising. By the millimetre, the water grew deeper, and Henry realized that his opponent had changed his tactics. No longer was Sir Simon trying to free his right hand to deal a stunning blow: rather, he was using manic force to get a grip on Henry's throat, to press his face downwards into the rising water.

Henry knew that he could not hold out much longer. Complete unreality took over. There was salt water and sand in his eyes, in his nostrils: there was no air, no breath. Only a choking sensation of darkness and despair. He made one last, superhuman effort at recovery, with the unimagined strength that comes to a man fighting for his life. Slowly, painfully, he pressed his body upwards against the tower of brute force that held him down: but he knew in his heart that it was impossible. The grip on his throat tightened. It was at the very moment when he lost consciousness that he was aware, as in a dream, of a sudden, blinding light. And then everything was dark.

Henry opened his eyes slowly, and with surprise. It even occurred to him to marvel that there was, after all, survival after death. Then he saw that he was in the cabin of *Ariadne*, and that Emmy and Rosemary were kneeling beside him. Both their faces were wet, though whether with tears or rain Henry never knew, nor did he ask. He tried to speak, but the words would not come from his bruised throat. Gently, Emmy held a cup of cool water to his lips.

Henry mustered all his strength to speak. In a croaking whisper, he managed, "Where are we?"

"On the way home," said Rosemary.

For the first time, Henry was aware of the throbbing of *Ariadne*'s faithful motor. Through the hatchway, he could just make out the dark mass which was Alastair, as he stood at the helm.

Once again, he made the effort of speech. "And . . . and what . . . did he . . . ?"

"He got away," said Emmy. "In his boat. When he saw Alastair coming, he panicked and ran for it. Alastair says he was heading out to sea."

Henry said, "Thank Alastair for me."

Emmy said, "I've already done that."

Henry smiled at her with difficulty. Then he murmured, "Poor Sir Simon. One can't help . . ."

And then he fell asleep.

FIFTEEN

It rated a small paragraph in most of the national dailies the next morning. *"Baronet lost at sea. Tragic mishap to motor yacht."* The local press did better, with large photographs of Sir Simon, of Berry Hall, and of the wreck of *Priscilla,* which had been washed ashore near the mouth of the Orwell. Current gossip maintained that Sir Simon, in an excess of grief at his sister's death, had deliberately set out in impossible weather conditions, thus virtually committing suicide. The sadness and sympathy of Berrybridge were sincere.

In Hamish's cottage, the members of the Fleet were solemnly assembled. Henry, recovered but still shaken, held the place of honour in a large armchair near the fire. Emmy sat at his feet, on the hearthrug. Hamish and Anne occupied the sofa, while Alastair shared the other armchair with Rosemary by the simple expedient of sitting her firmly on his knee.

"I suppose I behaved very foolishly," said Henry, rubbing the back of his neck with a freckled hand.

There was a chorus of dissent.

"Oh, but I did. It was lunacy, and I bloody nearly got killed, and serve me right, too. If it hadn't been for Alastair——"

"I only did what you asked me to do," said Alastair, "and pretty inefficiently at that. I didn't realize how long it would take me to get to you after I heard your whistle. Thank God I was in time. You were out cold, face downwards in the water. That's why I let him get away. I felt I had to——"

Henry nodded. "It was just as well," he said. "Heaven

knows if I could have proved anything against him, other than assault and battery against me."

"But Henry, when did you realize that it was Sir Simon who——" Anne began.

"I'd been growing more and more certain all last week," said Henry. "I should have tumbled to it sooner. But it was an accumulation of small things that led me to it—and I may say that I wasn't helped by the deliberately confusing attitude of some members of the Fleet."

Anne blushed. "Well may you blush, young woman," Henry went on, severely. He looked at Hamish. "I take it that you two are going to get married."

"Yes," said Hamish. He took Anne's hand is his huge one.

"I should have realized sooner," said Henry to Anne, "that it's a matter of common human nature that since every man in sight, bar one, was more or less in love with you, you would automatically fall for that one exception. You've been in love with Hamish all along, haven't you?"

Anne nodded mutely. Hamish looked at her with incredulity. "Is that true?" he demanded.

"Of course it is, you big fool," said Anne.

"So," Henry went on, "you behaved very badly. You flirted with every man in sight, in a desperate attempt to make Hamish jealous. In fact, I don't suppose he even noticed." Hamish grinned. "You even got yourself engaged to poor Colin, though I'm sure you never had the faintest intention of marrying him. As for Pete—you may have been momentarily infatuated with him, but that soon faded. You carried on your affair with him simply because it gave you an entrée to this house, so that you could be near——"

"Henry, can't you spare us this?" Hamish asked.

"Let him say it," said Anne quietly. "It's all true, darling. I'm so ashamed."

"You're a minx," said Henry, not unkindly. "You're not really ashamed at all. You enjoyed it. But you went through a bad time after Pete was killed. You had insisted on David rowing you ashore that day, because you thought you could use your influence with Pete to make him give Hamish the money for his boat. David went off to look for Pete, and came back and said he hadn't been able to find him. But he forgot that sound carries strangely in fog. While you were sitting there in the dinghy, you heard what David heard—Hamish and Pete quarrelling. Afterwards, you came to the same conclusion that David did—that Hamish had accidentally killed his uncle. That's why you lied to me and tried to vamp me and all the rest of it."

Emmy looked up sharply. She caught Rosemary's eye, and they both smiled.

"That night on *Pocahontas*," Henry continued, "the night Colin was killed, I think you finally confessed to David how you felt about Hamish. That's why David behaved even more oddly than usual after that. Why he went off sailing by himself and—well, never mind. I'm sorry for David, but I'm glad you told him the truth at last. So much for you.

"Then Rosemary was obstructive, too. David had told her that he was ashore the day of Pete's death. She knew that David hated Pete, and she was afraid he might have had something to do with his death. So, out of . . . loyalty . . . she tried to put me off the scent. As for Hamish, he knew how black things would look for him if anyone suspected foul play. You all knew perfectly well that there was something very strange about the way Pete died—but for one reason or another you all decided not to pry into the matter. All of you except Colin, that is."

"This still doesn't explain how you cotttoned onto Sir Simon," said Alastair. "The other night in the Bush, you asked me some questions, and I couldn't for the life of me see what——"

"I asked you," said Henry, "two things. I asked you if you were certain that the cushions in *Priscilla* were damp when you brought Pete's body into the Berry Hall boathouse. And I asked you if you were prepared to swear that Pete was flying his racing burgee that day."

"Yes, but——"

"That day I went out in Sir Simon's boat," said Henry, "it had been pouring with rain and everything was damp and clammy. But *Priscilla* had a waterproof cover, and the cushions were perfectly dry. Sir Simon swore that the boat hadn't been out on the day Pete died. But obviously, she had. That was the first thing that made me suspicious. The first lie. Mind you, at that stage I didn't suspect Sir Simon. He had allegedly been in Ipswich all day. I merely thought that somebody else had used the boat.

"But then a curious thing happened. Sir Simon had told me that he'd left home early that day, and had seen nothing of any of the Fleet boats—or at least, that was the impression he gave: but later on, in The Berry Bush, he went out of his way to remark that he had seen Pete go aground before the fog came down."

Anne wrinkled her forehead. "I don't see," she said. "Had he or hadn't he? What was the point of——?"

"He hadn't seen a thing," said Henry. "His appointment in Ipswich was at nine, so he would have left home before Pete went aground. But, after we'd been to Berry Hall, he was tipped off on the telephone by Bob Calloway that I was a policeman, and he thought he'd better protect himself by pretending that he had seen Pete on the sandbank. You see, he envisaged the possibility that I might find out how he had stolen his sister's jewels and where they were hidden. That would have been bad enough for him—and it provided him with a strong motive for murder, once we started considering the possibility that Pete might have stumbled on him digging up his hoard in the fog. But supposing he had seen Pete go aground on that very spot. Then nobody would ever believe that Sir Simon would have been fool enough to go out to Steep Hill and start digging so close to a grounded boat. It let him out of any suspicion of murder. Unfortunately for him, he overembroidered his story. He told me he had been able to pick out Pete's Royal Harwich burgee through his binoculars. But Pete was flying his white racing flag that day. It seemed such a strange and unnecessary lie that I didn't pay much attention to it at the time. But then there was Priscilla's cryptic remark to Emmy about something happening before eleven. It suddenly occurred to me that Sir

Simon might have come home before eleven that day. Then everything began to fall into place."

"Henry," said Rosemary, "I'm still dreadfully muddled. Can't you tell us exactly what *did* happen—over the robbery and everything?"

"Of course," said Henry. "It's a pathetic story really, of a smallish crime that snowballed into a series of more and more horrible ones. I don't suppose there's ever been a more reluctant murderer than Sir Simon Trigg-Willoughby. It all started with the division of property between Sir Simon and Priscilla after their father's death. The old man knew that Priscilla was mad about the family jewels, while Sir Simon had a positive obsession with the house. So—very sensibly, on the face of it—he left each of his children the thing that they loved most. What he didn't reckon with was that in these days of inflation and taxation, there would be nothing like enough money to maintain Berry Hall. As Sir Simon said, Priscilla got the imperishables, while he got a load of bills and responsibilities. The obvious solution, to him, was to sell the one to pay for the other. But Priscilla wasn't having any.

"So, in desperation, Sir Simon resorted to a course which he had convinced himself was justified. He took Priscilla to the Hunt Ball, and allowed her to get thoroughly drunk. He took her home, waited until she was in bed and asleep in an alcoholic stupor—very likely assisted by some sleeping pills. Then he stole the keys from the chain round her neck, unlocked the safe, and abstracted the jewellery, leaving the open boxes in Priscilla's dressing room, and replacing the keys. He put a ladder up to the window, making it look like a clumsy outside job. He left his own footprints, in his own sea boots, which confused everybody. Then he took the boat out and buried the loot in Steep Hill Sands. He's a boating man—or he was—and we can be sure he got the idea from Captain Voss."

"But I thought everyone agreed that Priscilla had left her jewels out that night?" said Rosemary.

"That was what made me suspect an inside rather than an outside job," said Henry. "I became convinced that

Priscilla was telling the truth when she said she had put the jewels in the safe. She was certainly drunk that night, but she was coherent enough to be able to put herself to bed, and even drunken people go through the routines of a lifetime automatically. When I heard that she had even put her hair in curling pins as usual, it was unthinkable that she shouldn't also have locked up her precious jewellery. Then there was another thing. Everybody knew which was Priscilla's bedroom window, because she had a habit of shouting to visitors out of it. A thief would surely conclude that the jewellery would be there. Why should he climb in through the window of the next room? How would he know either that it was her dressing room, or that she would leave the jewels in there? From Sir Simon's point of view, however, there was always the danger that his sister might wake. He preferred to work in the dressing room. The more I read the police reports, the more suspicious I grew. Then there was the question of the gin which was being bootlegged to her by Riddle. Somebody was paying for that—paying to keep the poor woman in a state of semistupor so that nobody would believe her rambling about having locked up her jewels. Besides . . ." Henry paused. "I once said that crimes were committed for love or money. In this case, who got the money? A mythical thief apparently got the jewellery, but was doing nothing about disposing of it. But Sir Simon got the insurance money."

"It was soon after the robbery that he had the East Wing completely restored," said Hamish thoughtfully.

"Exactly. He had the ready cash he needed to indulge his obsession, and for some months all went well. But then the inevitable happened! The insurance money ran out. The situation, for him, was maddening. He had the jewels, but he hadn't the faintest idea of how to turn them into cash. It was about this time that, by bad luck, Bob Calloway took over The Berry Bush."

"Bob Calloway?" echoed Alastair, surprised. "Is he . . . ?"

"He's under arrest," said Henry, "and this time I'm damned if he's going to get away with it. He's been under

suspicion as a fence for years, but we've never been able
to prove anything. We'll never know, I suppose, how Sir
Simon heard of his reputation, but I suspect that it may
have been through Herbert, who was indulging in some
faintly illegal deals with Calloway himself. Anyway, Bob
and Sir Simon got together. It had to be very discreetly
done. They would, I imagine, take trips in *Priscilla* to discuss their business. It must have been Bob we saw in the
boat with Sir Simon, the day he seemed so anxious to
avoid us, and denied having been out at all. Sir Simon
was wise enough not to let Bob into the secret of Steep
Hill. He merely brought the jewellery to the pub, piece
by piece, to be disposed of. But Bob was taking more
than his share of the profit, and the bills were mounting.
At the time of Pete's death, Sir Simon's financial situation was in a bad way. And the tides were running against
him."

"Henry, you're getting poetic in your old age," said
Emmy.

"No, I'm not," said Henry. "I mean that literally. Sir
Simon only dared to go out to his buried treasure on a
moonless night, when the tide was low in the small hours
of the morning. He knew that channel from the boathouse
like the back of his hand, and he could easily manage it
in the dark. But just then, low tide fell at seven o'clock
one day, eight the next, nine the next. Even the following
week, when low tide was at two or three in the morning,
the moon was full. I've looked it all up in Reid's," he added,
with a modest pride.

"So when the fog came down——" Hamish began.

"Sir Simon was in Ipswich with his solicitor at nine,"
said Henry. "He saw the fog come down, and he saw his
chance. Instead of hanging round in Ipswich, as he told us,
he came hurrying back—driving as fast as he dared, because visibility was worsening all the time. By about half
past ten, he was home: and Priscilla knew that. She saw
him arrive. He went straight down to the boathouse, and
after the three of you had been ashore and gone back on
board, he took *Priscilla* out and made for the sandbank."

"I think I heard his motor," said Alastair thoughtfully.

"Either his or Herbert's, or both," said Henry, with a smile. "Herbert was out on a dubious mission of his own, which doesn't concern us. Anyhow, Sir Simon beached his boat some way from where the jewels were buried, because the tide was very low by then. He made his way across the sands to the marking stone, and began to dig. Of course, he hadn't the faintest idea that Pete was there, within a few yards of him. I suppose it must have been the noise of the shovel that attracted Pete's attention. He walked a few paces from his own boat through the fog—and caught Sir Simon red-handed. And so the comparatively innocuous crime of robbery grew into murder. One can imagine that Pete was probably too puzzled by what he saw to realize his danger. He very likely expected that there was a reasonable explanation. It was foggy, and hard to see. Easy enough for Sir Simon to attack Pete—probably with the shovel—before he knew what was happening. Damn it, he nearly succeeded with me, and I was prepared for him."

Henry paused, and Emmy took his hand and held it tightly.

"We know what happened then," Henry went on. "Having knocked Pete out, Sir Simon dislodged *Blue Gull's* boom, and hit the unconscious man again with it. A pity for him that he didn't notice the racing burgee—but he had other things to think about."

"You could barely see the top of the mast in that fog anyway," Alastair remarked.

"Anyhow, he left Pete on the sands, with the tide coming up, and made his way back to the house. There, once again, he met Priscilla, and his mistake was to overimpress her not to tell anybody that he had been home before eleven. Priscilla loved secrets—but no woman keeps a secret indefinitely.

"Sir Simon then got into the car and drove at a snail's pace back to Ipswich. He didn't have to worry about the car being recognised in that fog. He then went to the cinema, just as he told us, arriving back at Berry Hall after you had got Pete ashore. He must have been very pleased with himself. The inquest went off perfectly. No awkward questions. His secret was safe—until I came along and started meddling, and until Colin decided to turn private detective." Henry paused. "Can I have a drink?" he asked. "I'm losing my voice."

Hamish brought him a whisky and soda. Henry sipped it gratefully, and then went on. "Now we come to the story of Colin. That, too, confirmed all my suspicions. It was clear from the beginning that it was Colin's ill-judged remarks at dinner about tides and books that warned Sir Simon that his secret hiding place was about to be discovered. There's no doubt that by this time he was slightly mad. It's just about impossible to murder one of one's best friends and remain sane. In any case, he had killed once. The second time is easier. He decided that Colin must die. He heard with great relief that Anne was not proposing to spend the night on *Mary Jane*. That meant his victim would be alone. As soon as I satisfied myself that Colin had, in fact, gone back to his boat and been attacked there, it became obvious that Sir Simon, Herbert, Ephraim or one of the Riddles must be the murderer."

"How did you work that out?" Hamish asked. "We all heard what Colin said."

"Yes," said Henry. "We all heard what Colin said, and what Anne said. But we—the Fleet—went down the hard together afterwards, and we all knew something that the others didn't. Namely, that Anne was proposing to go back with David to *Mary Jane* some unspecified time later to pick up her sleeping bag. I trust that, in view of that, none of us would have been such fools as to contemplate attacking Colin in his boat. It was the greatest good luck for Sir Simon that Anne didn't, after all, go back."

"Might it have—I mean, might Colin still be . . . ?" Anne began, tremulously.

"No," said Henry. "Don't reproach yourself. It's highly unlikely that you'd have caught him in the act. In fact, Sir Simon arrived after you were safely on *Ariadne*—Alastair heard him. But I'll come to that later. The only difference would have been that we'd have known right away that Colin did get back to *Mary Jane*—and we worked that out soon enough."

Anne nodded sadly.

"What finally made up my mind for me," said Henry, "was the matter of the car. Clearly, it had been put out of action deliberately. Why? So that somebody shouldn't be where he wasn't wanted that night. The only two people who had any motive or opportunity for tampering with it were Sir Simon and George Riddle, one of whom clearly wanted to be rid of the other for the night. With my suspicions piling up against Sir Simon, I was never in any doubt. He removed the rotor arm from the car when he went, ostensibly, to start her up. Then he left Riddle working on her, with instructions not to bother to come back to the Hall that night if he couldn't get her going. Sir Simon himself travelled back in Old George's taxi. Priscilla was already asleep, doubtless full of gin as usual. There was nobody to see the other *Priscilla* slipping quietly out into the river in the small hours. Sir Simon boarded *Mary Jane,* knocked Colin out—probably with a dinghy oar—and threw him into the river, at the same time freeing and capsizing *Mary Jane*'s dinghy."

"But surely we'd have heard *Priscilla*'s motor," Rosemary put in.

"We might have," said Henry. "That was why he anchored her downstream from the moored boats, and finished the trip rowing his old racing dinghy, which he had towed behind him. *Priscilla*'s anchor was still wet and muddy when Emmy made its acquaintance the next day, even though Sir Simon swore that the motor was out of action and that the boat hadn't been out. No, he rowed to *Mary Jane,* and Alastair heard him."

"If only I'd known——"

"Nobody knew," said Henry. "I might have guessed, but I didn't. So Colin died, and I was certain in my own mind who had killed him, without having a smattering of proof. So we come to the matter of Emmy." He smiled at her and took another drink of whisky.

"My wife," Henry went on, kindly, "is brighter than she looks. She's also a sympathetic character. When she found herself alone in Berry Hall with Priscilla, she realized it

was a chance to coax some secrets out of the old dear.
And she was right. But Priscilla had only just got around
to it when Sir Simon came back from Berrybridge. He
heard voices, and went up to Priscilla's room. There he
saw Emmy, who had her back to the door, talking to his
sister. And he heard Priscilla say the words, 'before
eleven.' That was enough. I don't know what he hit you
with, darling, but he grabbed whatever came to hand and
let you have it. As for Priscilla—who certainly must have
objected to such behaviour—he managed to subdue her
with gin and sleeping pills. I'd like to think that he didn't
mean to kill her, but I'm afraid he probably did. After
all, he couldn't rely on her to hold her tongue if she ever
regained consciousness.

"Meanwhile, he had to decide what to do with Emmy.
Clearly, she couldn't be killed in Berry Hall. She must
disappear, and be found drowned, like the others. It's
curious how conservative murderers are in their methods.
Fortunately, George Riddle had just departed on his bicycle. The coast was clear. Sir Simon carried Emmy downstairs and bundled her into the Daimler. Then he drove
down to the boatshed. That's why the car wasn't in the
drive when you two arrived," he added to Hamish and
Anne. "It should have been, of course. That confirmed my
suspicions. Sir Simon tied Emmy up and dumped her in
the fo'c'sle of *Priscilla*. It must have been then that he
saw your car turning into the drive. You saved Emmy's
life by that visit, and I'm eternally grateful."

"We did?" said Anne. "How?"

"Because," said Henry, "Sir Simon realized he must produce an explanation of why he wasn't there when you
called, and produce an alibi for himself. So, as soon as
you'd gone, he left Emmy and drove to Woodbridge,
where he bought some tools. By that time, I was getting
worried, and I had a good idea of where Emmy might
be."

"You had?" Emmy sat bolt upright in indignation.
"Then why the hell didn't you rescue me, instead of——"

Henry grinned at her. "My love," he said, "I'm sorry

you had to be uncomfortable for another half hour or so, but there was nothing I could do. I got to the boathouse in the nick of time, just as Sir Simon got back. So long as I could divert him and keep him under my eye, I knew you'd be all right. Unless, of course, you were already dead, in which case it didn't really matter."

"You monster," said Emmy, and kissed him.

"In any case," said Henry, "I knew you weren't dead, because I heard you wriggling about in the fo'c'sle. But what could I do? I was still hamstrung by having no proof. Once I'd really alarmed Sir Simon, I'd have no hope of catching him. So I'm afraid I left you where you were, and I had to act dumb with Inspector Proudie. I didn't, by then, want a hoard of policemen tramping round Berry Hall. All the same, I'm glad David found you when he did."

"So am I," said Emmy, fervently.

"Well, that's about all, except for my final effort. Bob Calloway found that things were getting too hot, and disappeared to dispose of the jewels he had on him as fast as he could. That suited me beautifully. I wrote a note to Sir Simon, purporting to come from Bob, and left it in the bar. George Riddle must have taken it up to the Hall. In it, I told Sir Simon to bring in the rest of the jewellery last night. This he was only too pleased to do. After the episode with Colin, and a few hints I'd dropped, he knew we were getting close to the hiding place. So he went out to collect the loot. Fortunately, Alastair and I were there to meet him."

"You were there," said Alastair.

"And a fat lot of good I'd have been without you," said Henry.

"He damn near killed you," said Alastair. "He didn't look a reluctant murderer to me."

"What I meant by that," said Henry, "was that the situation had a tragic irony about it. Sir Simon was in love with the house. And the house demanded from him, as victims, all the people he really cared about. Pete, his best friend: Colin, whose brain he admired: and finally, his own sister, his only surviving relative. In the end, it demanded his own life, too."

There was a long silence. Then Henry said, "Well, that's the story, and thank God it's over. Let's go down to the Bush."

EPILOGUE

The station wagon was loaded once again, and stood on the hard, trembling with the vibration of her pulsing motor. Beside her, the M.G. stood, black and sleek.

"We'll say goodbye now," said Alastair to Hamish. "You'll be in London before us."

"You'll come down to Lymington next weekend to see the new boat?"

"Of course. By the way, this trip of yours to the Canaries——"

"Is off," said Anne firmly. "But we will go to Holland, when Hamish can take a holiday."

There was a round of farewells. The Bensons and the Tibbetts piled into the station wagon. Anne jumped into the M.G. without opening the door, and kissed Hamish on the nose before the little black car roared up the hill. The station wagon followed more sedately.

As the hum of the mysteriously, the landscape sank the mud calmly out to the sea, white and beautiful and very quiet.

In The Berry Bush, Bill Hawkes said, "Game o' darts, then, Herbert?"

"Hay?"

"I said, game o' darts?"

Herbert looked quickly round. They were alone in the bar. He winked, and a slow grin spread across his wizened face.

"Don't mind if I do, Bill," he said.